SEBASTIAN'S PROPHECY

WAKING DARKNESS

ERIC SANTIAGO

outskirts press

Sebastian's Prophecy
Waking Darkness

v2.0

Outskirts Press, Inc.
http://www.outskirtspress.com

ISBN: 978-1-9772-4261-7

PRINTED IN THE UNITED STATES OF AMERICA

PROLOGUE

"My name is Nathan Tunnel. I once lived in a time when society was thriving. But those days are gone. All that is left after the apocalyptic fall of man is a feuding world. People seem to have become primal and controlled by a group of great influence. I know little of this group but a name that tends to show their agenda. They call themselves the Sovereign League."

I recall the days I worked as a simple lawyer in a law firm before the last war. I was preparing to go to court on a big case. While preparing the final comments of my opening speech to the jury on this important case as I was watching the news. When I was about to shut off the T.V. and walk out suddenly a frantic reporter came on to advise of a Late breaking news! It appears many of our nation's enemies have launched a massive missile strike. The government leaders have acted by all account in striking back. It pains me to state the world is at full war.

That was the day my life changed. I headed to the closest shelter just to realize it was really happening. The first of the onslaught came into view as I was barely able to enter the building. The few of us there knew we would never be the same again.

The corridors are empty as the two disciples of the order rushed to their master's chamber. They vehemently pound on his door to rouse him quickly. A soft acknowledgement form within the chamber confirms their success as the door slowly opens. Both rush in the attempt to advise their master of the news they have just heard from the T.V.

"Master!!" they shout with no restraint of the volume of their voices. Hearts pound in their ears like a thunderstorm without relent. Faces flushed of the very color of life that most men would normally have but the fear consumed them to the very depth of their souls.

"Yes, what is it that causes you to need me so late in the eve." Looking upon the two faces he can see they are in distress he has never seen them to be any time before. "Enter quickly and tell me the need you have of waking me my pupils. Has there been some type of nightmare or have you just heard some news of the darkness?"

"We have just received word that the world has gone into a state of war. Your prediction has come to pass. Our doubt has been wash away thinking it would not come true as soon as you have said." They grip their amulets and bow in request for forgiveness for the master in the cause of ever doubting him. The sweat dropping in rivulets upon the floor from the haste they made running across the courtyard and corridors in the long trek from the far point of the towers.

"What!!! Are you certain?" asked the old monk. His present concern expressed on his face which only showed the need to act upon the matter as quickly as possible. Setting himself to a point of self-control of his mind to a range of clarity for the action that now must be set into order.

"Yes, we must hurry, or all is lost! Our order is in jeopardy as is the rest of the world to this attack and the prophecy must be fulfilled. What are we to do master?" Each wait upon the precipice of a new dark age and the future is now in question with all that is happening. The order must do again what is has been born to do upon this time for what few humans now exists among them.

"So be it, Joshua go ring the bells of quickly and wake the

others." The two apprentices looked upon each other with confusion stirring in their minds as though his request was unbelievable.

"But master there is little time. We are at the verge of our own demise how can we wake so many brothers of the order." With faces flushed of color they look upon him for the answer they have momentarily lost to fear.

"NOW JOSHUA!!!! We must try and get everyone to the archives where it should be safe. If our order falls so does the hope of man." staring straight upon the two he bears a look of utter determination they have never seen within his eyes. Like of white fire that would burn any who came to close.

"Yes master. It shall be done as you have ordered. Come Damian let's get going." As if given the wings of angels the two fly down the corridor to complete the task laid before them one goes unto the north and the other to the south bell towers so they may ring the bells.

Author goes to the door across the hall and awakens his servant for another task that must be done at once. With great force he pounds upon the door of the chamber. The door opens quickly to show a young lad no more than 15 years of age which he looks upon as his own son. "Alexander, I need you to go and get as many people as you can to guide the rest unto the archives. The dark days I have taught you about are here. I will open the doors unto the archives chamber. You know the way. Now go."

Watching the young boy head to the paladin chambers where the youth of the order sleep he sees hope for them. Yet he has no time to revel in such thoughts and turns to need of the archive chamber doors which must be opened immediately. As he rushes a single prayer comes across his lips. "May God help us all!!!?"

CHAPTER 1

When we were past the worst of it we began to leave little by little against all warnings. The ones that left soon died almost instantly from exposure. It was weeks before I and another group left. I only wondered what would happen next as we emerged from the shelter. As we entered what was left of the world our eyes had to readjust to the light of day which seemed brighter than normal. Yet I did not realize the young lad who stood next to me.

"Sir, what do we do now?" I turned to see a young child with tears in her eyes that seemed to be confused on how life would be from now on. Yet first thing I thought of was "Where are your parents?"

"Are you all alone kid?" as he looked upon her, he noticed how young she was to be left all alone. With blondish-brown hair, with a dark complexion that seem to be unnatural for any normal person.

"Yes sir!" as they both stand there Nathan wonders what is next to come with this child. His mind a whirlwind of questions with no answer of what is to come next.

"What is your name and where your parents are?" he then that the die is cased and the world have changed without any idea if it was for the better or if it will get worse. So he turns his attention to the young little lady that seems to need his help.

"My name is Beatrice Mallow. For my parents I really don't know. I was brought here by my teacher when it all started. I hope they did not try to look for me at the school. My whole class was brought here, and they seem to have left without me. Do you think that my parents are at the school looking for me?" He thought flowed out like an innocent rain that has just begun to flow through time.

"I'll go with you and check." replied Tunnel.

"Thank you, sir, !!" As they bright smile seem to cross her face. Tunnel can see the sense of relief in her for the fact that she has someone to help her.

As we walked, we noticed many did not make it to the safe zones as they call them. So much senseless death and destruction. For what did all this have to happen? I could feel the kid squeezing my hand cause of the dreadful sites we passed. All I could say to her was "You'll be okay I am here kid." Hopefully that can ease some of her fear.

"Can you remember the days we walked these fields when we first got engaged Sam?!" As the lilies showed their splendor in full bloom.

"Yes Jen! This has always been my favorite get away spot. I just never been next to someone I like you here. I didn't even think you liked me when I first tried to talk to you at the news station." as a grin crossed his face in his own quirky way.

"Well I noticed you the first day you walked in the door. You seemed too focused as a reporter; I didn't believe you would ever want to be with someone like me."

"I guess everything turned out quite well. Let's just enjoy the day and leave that funny past where it belongs." While they both move into a closer embrace upon the blanket overlooking the city.

As dusk approached, they fell into a serene revelry that took the worries of the world to a faraway place in their souls. The only thing that mattered at that time was the love they shared for each other.

"Jen look a shooting star!" As they peered into the distance, he noticed the shimmering streak blaze its path across the sky.

"Where did you see it?" as she concentrated on finding what Sam was looking at in the darkening sky above.

"Right over there beyond the willow."

They continued to watch with mounting curiosity. Suddenly a rush of dread overwhelmed Jen when the object plummeted to the earth less than a mile from them into the heart of the city. Instantly light filled the night sky while a sudden rush of hot wind propelled the both into the dirt.

"Jen wake up!"

"Huh?" The sounds of great concerned echoed through her ears like the beat of a wild drum. "What happened?"

"I don't know! Seems as though an explosive or something went off close to where we are. All the windows on the upper floors are blown out and the power is out."

"Is everyone okay?" Her heart was for all the others who may have been hurt in the blast.

"Adam is checking as we speak. Yet it seems we have a lot of casualties."

"Oh!! My head is pounding."

"Look at me Jen!!! Do you remember where we are?" As her co-worker tries to access her level of injuries.

"Yeah, we are in the video room." Jen attempts to stand yet feels an overwhelming dizziness that causes her to be eased back against the wall to let her head clear a bit. The room a complete shamble after the mayhem caused by the explosion.

"GOD! What is going on? Do you remember?"

"Last I can recall Sam was making a report that the world went through missile attack. Oh God Sam!! What is going on?"

Seeing the reminiscence of what a busy street was once gone to hell from the attack. Looking at the buildings now with broken windows and vacant interior is unnerving. Now with this child I can even think on how I am going to help her find these parents of hers. Must I now become something that I was told when I was a young child on the reservation? Just as he was told as a young man, he is now to become something greater than he once was.

I remember those days when I and the others would be taught the ancient stories of the ancestors. Yet I can remember when I and Malcolm would speak with grandfather. He would invoke the old ways to tell us what our lives would be when we got older.

Grandfather once said to me "Nathan Tunnelwalker you will one day lead many from the shadows to the new light." When he talked of my best friend Malcolm grandfather said "A vision will be given by the ancestors to walk the path of shamans. Be that man which the spirits speak." Just thinking of that day makes me wonder is tis the time he spoke of. God I am just so confused on all these events.

Long gone are the days when this chamber brought me fears of the powers chosen here. Looking now at the banners of each house banging against the walls of granite. The faces of all the men who sat at these chairs guiding the dark fate of the mankind. Now I am one of those men like my father before me.

"Gentlemen it is now time to give this world a sense of hope in this dark day. Even though it is for our gain they shall flock to us like sheep to the dark shepherd. The years of planning are now finally in our grasp." Soba you old foul speaking as always in his pompous manner. I will be overjoyed the day he dies. I only wonder who will do the honors of killing him. For he deserves the darkest type of death I could only imagine.

Just sitting here as I listen to the counsel speaks of their own personal plans makes me despise them to the very pit of my dark heart. Yet I just set here admiring the central hall in which we confine our meetings. The great tapestries in which the emblem of each house stands upon brazen posts. The great marble columns engraved with the ancient histories and names of past leaders. I can recall the days my father lead the group though he enjoyed staying in the shadows with few to ever truly see his face and that bitch that would be at his side every waking moment of his day.

"Brother Darius can you consider the need to supply the necessary provisions to sway the survivors to our control. We must survey the warehouses in which our stock piles we have been accumulating for this time." With a great disdain for them all he answers the call with a proclamation of authority that none can challenge.

"Soba I am well aware of those warehouses inventory and there are other supply lines in which to provide. None of you have any need to concern yourselves with the level of supply." If only these fools could know or even imagine the extent of all that has been prepared for them all in turn.

CHAPTER 2

To consider the road is a dream
Yet to keep steps upright shows truth
What shall become of me
In what direction will I go
Am I to be a follower
Then who will lead me
If I am the one in the front
Who are they that come for guidance
Most of all can I protect them

"Mister, Mister!!!" As Nathan looks upon Beatrice to find the cause to wake him from his slumber. He notices that her eyes are wide open with concerns and fears of an unknown reason.

"Yes child. What can I do for you?" With a somber tone he greats the child on the new morning of the journey.

"I heard you mumbling something. It was pretty like a song my mother would sing. What means the words?" She sits in childish anticipation for him to explain what he was saying in his sleep.

"It was an old saying my grandfather told young men who came of age. Anytime I feel lost I would say the words whenever I needed mental or spiritual help." as he looked upon her he realized she understood yet looked a little different than she did two days ago. As though she is transforming into something else entirely.

God! I have been helping this child search for her parents

for two days. Now sitting here in this empty hallow which was a favorite liquor store I would visit. The shelves are a ransacked mess of what was ones a well-kept store within walking distance of his office. He used to get his coffee here between court times.

Can there be anyone left alive or has it become like this store. Looking around I see the chaos that has consumed the world. Broken glass and scattered cans losing all sense of order like hell's fury hit this store with a vengeance. I really hope the owner was able to find a sanctuary during the madness. Yet for some reason since I have been with this girl there is a connection that I can't seem to understand. As though it is a unification of blood.

"Beatrice empties your bag so we can take some of this food. We may have to leave the city. I know of a play that can be a safe haven for us both." Her eyes looked upon him as if he was her father now to depend on him. She seems to sense the connection between them as well but a single thought still remained within her.

"But mister we didn't find my mommy and daddy yet."

Damn it how can I explain to this kid her parents are probably dead in the blast. This fucking sucks! Contemplating all the possible outcomes to help this one kid is insanity. I just hope she understands what is to come with the journey that must be made. Nathan you really stepped into a shit storm now!! How would grandfather explain to a young child life's sorrow?

"Tunnelwalker come look at this." As he approached a sense of curiosity filled every part of his being.

"Yes grandfather! What do you want?"

"There beyond the cedar trees. Do you see the wandering calf?" As Nathan looked over the crest of the small hill he noticed the direction he was staring at for some reason.

"Where?" He always had difficulty trying to see such thing in this forest. The trees always seem to block a great deal.

"Looking as the forest eyes and you will know the forest river move." Grandfather would say. Suddenly I noticed a shift in the brush and a young calf emerged. "Oh, look grandfather is that the one?!"

"Yes boy!" Looking up with grandfather smiling down in an overwhelming pride for seeing the calf.

"Grandfather where is the calf's parents?" his child like mind could not understand why they would leave him alone this way.

"Did you here that noise earlier?"

"You mean the ones that sounded like thunder through a rain storm?"

"Yes!! That was a hunter's rifle. It was not far from where we are now. That calf's parents may have been killed protecting him and now he must survive out here all alone."

"But grandfather it is just a baby!!" His eyes began to well up with tears for the way the forest life is for all nature of beasts.

"Yes I know. The old spirits have their ways in which all things must take and educated turn in unknown forest. Just remember boy that much is gained when you are brave enough to take a new path."

The city of glass and steel so high I can barely see the tops. People so oblivious to the others walking the streets with them. Why am I here? What purpose must I find myself in my time of dreams? Yet it seems so familiar to a place I have seen or been to before but why am I here now.

Oh, Great Spirit why do you bring this to me, or bring me to this place? Must I do something here in your plan again?

Wait, this is different than before. Why? As I look around I realize Nathan is with me. He was never here every other visit to this place. Why does he look so nervous? I have never seen him like that in all my life that I have known him.

Now I can see this must be his home in the city when he got that job as a lawyer. Only problem for me is the fact I have never been to the city or this apartment in my life.

"Nathan!" Perplexed he tries to get his friends attention.

"Hey Nathan can't you hear me?" Oh yeah this is just a dream and he is not really here with me. So he will never be able to reply to my call of his name.

What a day this is turning out to be. The sky looks thick with bad air; nothing at all like the reservation doesn't the wind ever blow away this muck

Suddenly streaks of fire break the very peace which allows me to accept these scene's from the Great Spirit. With a flash Nathan is running ahead of me to some unknown place, but I can notice that he only ran like this when he is scared. Within some of these building people stare to the sky with unbelievable fear. Why?

"Michael!"with his heart pounding him slowly turns to face a voice he didn't know.

"Who's calling me?" searching about the origin of the voice is not seen. As though the very wind itself has spoken to him.

"Michael I have a purpose for you. I have brought you here to see the coming nightmare." Confusion fills his mind trying to think if something like this could really happen in the world as we know it. But how do we prepare for this.

"What are you talking about?"

"Turn around and see." As he peers over his shoulder to see what further is to come. With great hesitation he turns and faces the destruction of the once magnificent city laid waste. Within the chaos a single form emerges into view. My eyes are frozen upon her amber eyes as she speaks. But what does she want of me.

Within the inner workings of an ancient library of the

histories of social existence he studies. Determined by the desire to protect all who lay there life blind to his orders work against this coming darkness of human corruption. His robes fashioned with crimson tassels upon the waistline of a purple and black robe. As were the ancestral monks which walked the halls of this monastery of the old brethren. Every time I peer upon the sleeves I am reminded of my humbling oath embroidered in gold. The eagle is the ever present strength on my left, to my right a dove which is the peace we strive for in everything we do. Yet as the chain about my neck is the emblem of an open book succumb by a hedge of flames.

Could I have believed as a boy that such a historical order would ever be necessary in all my wildest dreams? Yet we are here to maintain the order of the world that is constantly in a state of flux. How the many times we have faced the vipers of time in search of a new hell on earth. But there have been great sorrows among the terrible conflicts. Oh, how the histories have enlightened the generations of our order. Yet my age is amidst the great books over the stretch of time men would not believe.

Part of our story is never to be written within a single page of the histories of ages. Only the few who have been chosen to succeed us elder are told of the chambers which the codex is placed under ancient guard. It was retrieved in one or the great conflicts of old. The purpose of these artifacts presents its keeper and the destined longevity of life. For some reason few have the genetic code which has the purpose of being called in time of need to protect the world.

Long have the vipers of time hauntingly rose to change the world from light to shadow and each time the destined have prevailed. My fear is will it continue or will someday the shadow take its place as leaders of the world as we know it again.

"Mirauthor we have needed to speak with you. It is of great

importance" as he raises from the table to place the scrolls and books back upon the shelves he faces the young paladin and accomplished brother.

"Of course. I was about to end my days work anyway." his mind could only wonder why they needed to meet with him and the others today of all days

"Splendid the others are on the way to the evening meal where the meeting is to be held."why of all places does it have to be held there. This must have to involve us all to need to hear what is needed today.

Why would this be so important? Our great meetings are usually held in the grand dais. The value of the meeting must be truly grave for so many members and paladins are in need to hears this and prepare. Last time a meeting like this was held the shadows were beginning to rise for power.

Why do I dare to dream? Every time I close my eyes it's the same dream. My brother and sisters have all seen the same as we slumber. For the few of our people have been born to answer an unknown call. As the days go by they come to me more and more, what is there meaning? Why do I have them, I hope the answer comes soon.

There have been stories of dark days in the history of man that a handful of warriors were born with special gifts to defend mankind. It appears to be linked with the arrival of some monk-like individual almost like druids. Yet I can't tell if it is true or mere legend.

It is almost time to set the next part of my plan in placing my brethren under my pure control. No longer shall I stand here and share the power with these fools who believe that this world can be shared. I will be the dominate force of the people with no other to present me with any complications.

The dark corridor echoed on into a sense of endless doors as if one has entered hells labyrinth. A place such as this can cause a man to question his own sanity. Still for my own twisted existence this place gives me a comfort from all the many trips taken to the very depths of these dark halls. I only hope today that Volta has good news for me with those ancient scrolls my father presented me upon his deathbed. To remember that day I smile for the fact of him being so blinded by age he could not tell I was not my brother who he so loved. Especially since both have been destroyed by my own hand.

Hearing his last breath was my greatest revenge.

CHAPTER 3

"Michael you must fulfill the destiny laid before you, but Nathan without question is to accompany you. The world is consumed by blackness, both of you have been marked from creation for this time as many others before you."

"What?! How can this be? I am just a man like any other. Are you sure I am the one you are looking for?" He could hear his heart pounding in his chest greater than he has ever heard before.

"Yes you are one of the people we are looking for and you're not like other men. There has been a power in you from the beginning." As he faced the reality of his life Michael began to accept what he was told but a hesitation still remained till full proof was given to his purpose.

"Does Nathan have something in his destiny like me or have something in his body like I do?" Rethinking his comment he began to feel a little awkward having to think it was like some kind of substance of disease.

"Yes. Only his needs to be awakened by an artifact. I will guide you as time needs be set."

"How will I know if I am on the right path?" Her eyes held the resemblance of peace like no other he has ever seen. He began to relax realizing that the spirit would never let him down.

"Head east to the lake of the wolf inside the base of a mountain. The keepers of time shall be there waiting for you."

As she stretched forth her hand I felt a stir in my mind. Images of the trail I am to travel unfold before my very eyes. All I had to know of the path became clear as if I have been there many times in my life as well as throughout the existence of all mankind. My only desire was to fulfill my sudden quest of the medicine man.

God I wish Mike was here with me. With him around I could always make sense of things without a sense of fear. Now I have to get out of this city and back to the reservation. I only hope that it is still there after such an attack.

The dusk came hours ago so I had no choice then to hide inside of this wrecked apartment down the road from the store Beatrice and I were after collecting some food supplies for the journey. I just hope the people who lived here made it out of the city unharmed. Above even that fear there is the chance marauders might be roaming the streets looking for victims. The future days ahead will be tough especially with the need to protect the child plus myself. What more obstacles will I face as the time goes by?

At least we can rest for the evening in a shelter. May be in the case of Beatrice's parents I will let her know that the possibilities of finding them alive are slim. She will just have to come with me to the reservation. It is so far from here and I can only hope I can find other survivors on the way so strength of numbers could be utilized.

I feel like I am in a tunnel similar to the one that I got lost within the snake mountain by grandfathers house. Man these walls feel so damp with a frigid touch all the time like water is being sprinkled down from a leaky faucet. Where is grandfather?

"Nathan!"relief washed over him when he heard the calling of his name by a familiar voice.

"Grandfather?"

"Nathan, where are you?"

"Grandfather I am here. Help me!" His rescue was at hand.

Suddenly hands reach out from all directions trying to grab me. There could touch was just like the cave walls. They are all pulling me in every direction as if they want to tear me to pieces. Without even understanding why a light of some kind appears like a ball of fire from my own hands which forces them to release their grip.

"Mister! Mister!" At his eyes opened to the welcoming sight of the child. Her tiny hand gently shacking him awake from the dark nightmare or vision who could tell anymore.

"What! Huh!" With the confusion of the dream still apparent in his mind of the dark feeling of those hands upon his skin sent shivers down his spine.

"Mister wake up!" The signs of fear had shown evident upon her face.

"What happened?" his mind raced thinking some type of danger was close to threaten their hiding place.

"You were screaming and it started to scare me." realizing she was the cause of her fear he tried to quell her fears.

"Oh! I am sorry Beatrice I just had a bad dream. Just go back to sleep. We still have a couple hours till sunrise."

"Can I sleep here with you?" as her eyes gleamed like orbs of earth he could feel nothing but a fathers compassion for her.

"Yeah sure." as Beatrice moved close to him she seemed more like his own child he wish to have some day. Looking down upon her small figure he could only wonder how he could ever do anything but protect her with his life.

As dawn broke we prepare to leave for the walk to come in the need to leave the city and its possible dangers that linger in the shadows. Yet I have to see this little girl with the facts that her parents did not make it through the attack upon there once fine city. I just hope she can take it at this young age. But my heart goes out to her for the truth she will now have to face.

“Welcome Mirauthor I am glad to see you join us for this contingent meeting.” as he walked into the room all eyes were upon him. It appeared his very presence was a great necessity for this meeting of the brotherhood.

“What?!” why would my being here seem so important above everyone else.

“Yes, you heard me right. The time has befallen us again. We are to awaken the warriors to stand against the madness once more.” the shock of such words rippled through the room like a wave upon the shore. All he could recall was the last time of the call of the chosen to stand against the shadows of evil that once attempted to conjure the earth for their greed of power.

“But that has not been carried out for a least a millennia. How do we even start to look for the warriors of old? Must there be some way to begin our search for them?” with the shock of all that has been said he tries to rap his head around the chain of events that has led to the line of action.

“Keepers prepare for what is to come. Return to all I have assigned you to do and I will call when it is time to make the next step. Mirauthor walk with me if you please. We have much to speak about my old friend.” as the rest of the keepers rush to their assigned duties the two headed out to memorial hall as they have done for years to have their own time to speak alone. Yet something was different as he looks upon his friend.

“Yes, you’re High....” as the cold stare of his old friends eyes turn to him as he was beginning to speak unto him.

“Don’t you even dare call me that in front of the others? You know I am as simple a man as you.” seeing the old smirk cross his face as he has done every time before when he wishes to challenge his friends whimsical comments.

“Why not? You are of high royal blood since the time of your ancestors and the chosen leader of our order.” while the echoes of their boots flowed down the hall with an rhythmic balance.

"I know but I am not of any more importance than you Mirauthor."

"Then what should I call you? You always know I try to honor your bloodline." with a glimpse of a teasing smile revealed upon his face Mirauthor finally realizes that he is being taken down a hall he never knew existed in the towers. "Mirdan like always you are a stubborn old goat. You never wanted to accept your title as it should be." as laughter thundered from his youthful soul. No mortal man would believe after looking upon Mirdan that he even live upon this realm for centuries as he has. Yet this simple monk elder has lived my length of life many times over due to the abilities of the codex. With blond hair, a face appearing as though sculpted form marble. His very eyes feel as if he searches the depth of a man heart, every time I stare at his face the very color appears as moving smoke.

"Why do you look at me like a ghost my old friend?" Mirauthor quickly realized the fact that he was staring and turn his attention to the direction they were going in the towers.

"Well there are times I remember you are much older than any of the keepers. I guess it is because I envy your youthful look."

"You shouldn't let that bother you so much. Now to the reason I wish to speak with you privately. As you heard earlier the time has come to face the madness from those that chosen to live for chaos. I have a specific task for you to accomplish."his eyes had the look of concern as he spoke of the having this unknown task. So my mind swam in the many possibilities of what this could mean as the halls grew darker and darker.

"What must I do in the service of our order my friend because you are starting to speak in riddles like you have done when something is of the greatest importance?"

"My understanding Author is that in this time signs of distinction only few realize, can guide each of our very actions.

Your task is the direst to our needs and that of mankind! You are to find the chosen."

"I am to do what? How do I even start looking for them? They can be anywhere or anyone in this world!" does he realize this is an almost impossible search of the chosen warriors.

"Calm yourself old boy. I had a dream that shows one coming here to our lake of meditation at the base of the cliff. He will lead you to another. Just know all hell will break loose to stop you from finding the other. They seem to have some kind of connection that draws them to each other but that connection may also lead the vipers to them as well. So be ready for anything." both went into an air of silence that was unnatural for them both.

Something has changed as the sun rises upon the new day which seemed hard to explain. The clouds have grown dark with hateful spirits that have come from the depth of the underworld. We dance the heart of a warrior to life while the wind cries. Our people keep the mother from sorrow for the sake of her children. However, as she weeps we comfort and protect her in the dark times. She calls us to keep the long promise of time

As the long days and night flows in the current called life I bear witness to the ceremony for protection. Everyone prepares for my long walk after speaking with grandfather about the dreams and visions I have had about what must be done. He did not seem surprised about what I told him. All he could say was "I knew the time for you to hear the spirits would come my boy. What it said is true that you and Nathan have a destiny. Now go and fulfill it because there is a lot at stake here now."

As the drum beats pounded their way into my soul with the charge of the old songs I feel a frenzy of hope cover me for the days to come. My eyes begin to let loose the tears I can't hold anymore for the feeling of fear as the traditional dances circle me. They call the spirits of our ancestors to be with me on the journey. As I close my eyes I can see my people all the way back to the beginning. Such a bond of blood and spirit that will never be broken.

As the new dawn breaks I am ready to leave the res. Yet I exit my home a feeling comes over me as though I may never return to this place. Grandfather stands near my truck as I approach. With a smile as large and the night sky.

“Young man remember to listen upon your walk of the medicine man. The spirits will protect and guide you as is needed. Never forget that son!”

“Yes grandfather you have my word on it. I will listen as you taught me. I just hope I will make you proud.” he comes close and embraces my as he has done since my youth whenever I go on trips. Although this feels a little different than usual, I wonder why?

As I am about to jump in the truck I turn to say goodbye to grandfather yet he seemed to disappear before my eyes. That is when I noticed the gift he put in the cabs passenger side for me, an old medicine man's bag. Without needing to open it I knew all I needed lay within as is the tradition of our people. I smiled within my heart as my truck roars to life on my way on the long journey. I can only hope Nathan is alright when I get to him.

Entering the dark pool area of this labyrinth as my father called it I prepare myself for anything. My only hope is to receive positive news from Volta.

“Volta! Where are you hiding?” as his voice echoed upon the waters. He searched about trying to get a glimpse of his minion whose ability to understand an ancient language is exquisite.

"Here my lord Darius. I know you are in search for more answers to the scrolls and I have much work to do but there may be some good fortune." as a door suddenly opens from the far right. The dim candles within Volta's hand to guide the way in to his private study.

Volta always in his little sanctuary of knowledge translating ancient writings from the old scrolls of people lost to history. A disgusting troll of a man with such an appearance of which others of the league would consider vile to look upon him. He is a stocky little man hunched over for most of his life by a childhood disease. Disfigured from head to foot by skin lesions and deep scars that he has received by some society who feared his appearance. I noticed the layer of books, scrolls and a wide range of items across the room. This was the one place I could tell he felt most at peace was in this room surrounded by the length of knowledge as limited as it may be since the last conflict, but many have even been written by his own hand.

My own father seemed to be disgusted by the fact of me even bringing him here to this ancient hall. Even with all his deformities I believe he could be of use to us with his skills of languages. I even remember the time I began to train him without my father's knowledge or permission in the science of the dark craft. Later as time passed he seemed to have a great potential in a greater range of all things. I commissioned Volta after the death of my father to be my personal linguist. He has proven himself time and again with every ancient scroll he has decoded for my personal use.

It has been months since I had anytime to see his progress on the ancient scroll which I found hidden away. I even stand in amazement at eth experiments he engulfs his entire being for the sake of my kindness or favor in letting him live. With every new discovery my power grows over the counsel without their very knowledge. Only if he knew that I would dispatch from him without hesitation if he would become of no more further use!

"Now old boy what progress have you made on those scrolls? Is there any information that I would deem valuable." as his minion scuffles about looking for the notes he has taken from the study he has been performing. He retrieves a book at the far table near his nest like bed which contains all his progress and returns to where his master stands. He quickly clears a space on his work bench and opens the journal.

"Yes my lord! Look here this scroll tells of a time long ago when your family ruled the known world. Much of it was in chaos due to the lack of food unlike today." Darius removes his long coat and sits on a bench next to him for a further look.

"Really!! Tell me more of this history." as look upon the vile of serpents eye sitting above the journal. An ingredient of great importance in the making of poison and paralytic agents. His mind was a whirlwind of thoughts on the information he is receiving and the uses he could conjure with that ingredient. So he focused himself at the task at hand and that was to hear of the history of his family's power over the world.

"Well it speaks of your great house and a power unmatched by any other known to be made by human hands. The power was due to an artifact found in molten spire. It seems to be the source of all types of mythical abilities with speculation that it was not from this world. It was called the "Koda". Unfortunately that is as far as I have gotten, there's still more to study Lord Darius." the frustration building from the long wait he pounds his fist upon the table and stands near the door. Volta jumps with the sudden thud and backs away. "I will work harder lord but there is so much to read."

Damn! That's all you have you vile little troll. Why can't you work faster I need to know more of what is in those scrolls. Do I have to wait longer for this shit pile of a man to finish translating the scroll? Fine at least there was some good news for me but I want to know more of the artifact.

"Very well Volta continues in your work. I will send my

servant with the supplies you asked for the last time I was here. Just do the translation as fast as you can I need that information soon." Placing his dark robe upon his broad shoulders.

"Of course my lord just remember they are written in a language unlike any before seen on our planet. It is like they were written by the sky people my parents told me about before they died and I was left to the streets" he raised his head in gratitude as if he was looking upon his own form of a god.

The streets continued to be void of life with no sense of ending. At the once famous news station seem to keep a vigil watch for any signs of help or danger. As the days and weeks seem to pass since the attack happened no one can reconcile that life has changed forever.

"Jen I think we should make some kind of plan on how all of us are going to survive. We just can't sit here waiting for help to arrive. Who knows if there is really anyone left to help us?" Adam stares out, yet is fearful on the possibilities of what must now happen for all the survivors.

Sam never too far away from Jen sits silently grieving for the great loss of those friends he had with him when the attack happened, as well as how many have suffered around the world. Somewhere deep within his thoughts he felt a time like this would appear in which he was born for, with a lifetime of dreams for a day fire would fall as a fortune teller once told him many years ago. To him it's like a dark pool of secrets swirling in his soul where the demons wait to be released.

"Sam can you try to reach Jen? She is not responding to any of us I think she is in a state of deep shock with all that has happened. You seem to be the only person who can get her out of this trance." as he looks over at her and noticed she was very disoriented with all the havoc that has happened with the attack and the questions left to be answered.

"I will try but no promises since she has not recovered from all the trauma of the attack. Whether physical or mental it is hard to tell with all the corpses she has seen being cleared out of this area." I don't think I will ever forget them myself. Those casualties will haunt my dreams forever, I may have seen a lot of tragedies in my live with the wars I have reported but this one was too close to home.

There are even times I try to consider the facts that I survived the blast when others didn't. Maybe I should have taken my father's offer to work in the family business, but I really didn't feel I could fit into a business lifestyle like his. Even now his voice echoes within my head with the promises of wealth, power and all the crap he kept trying to sell me on. I have to get my mind on something else than the corporation my father runs.

"Adam how are you feeling right now? You have been pretty quiet most of the time." as he see the approach of his friend in the tattered slack he so favored come into view. With his shirt soiled in blood and dirt of so many days without change.

"Better than most Sam. I am a little tired and hungry but I can keep going." as a small chuckle filled the air with all the thoughts of sorrow around.

"Good! Can you help me move over by Jen? I'll need to see if I can get her to focus on something other than everything that has happened." as Adam helps me get closer to Jen my body starts feeling the pain of my injured leg all over again. I can only hope it's not too bad all we have now is each other and maybe some hope that few may have survived the carnage.

CHAPTER 4

To the holders of truth is surety
Yet the times breathe and flow through all
Marks are placed to each soul
Chosen are they marked by the angels?
They are ones to do the work
As demons rage in the darkness
Make them stand for the soldiers' creed
Soul eaters scavenge for prey
Seek the marked ones
For the light and darkness have a chosen
Though in slumber they wait

Something is coming like a dark cloud flowing on the horizon. Do I want to believe the ways of this world will ever be like it was before? As the rock towers come and go through the journey my heart weeps for the wanting of the olds way. When man and earth were truly one with each other.

Michael stares at the road thinking of what waits at the hills coming. His spirit flutters like a wild fire searching for a gulp of air that shall come with a coming wind. Knowing of our life's travel never bring peace. Yet with all that has happened peace is so far away to try an attempt to grasping in with his hands.

There is a battle about to be waged and Michael understands just a fraction of why Nathan is so important. When he reaches that lake the spirit directed him to go. However it seems there could be anything waiting for me where I am going but I do not fear what is to come.

As the road stretches on I begin to see the effects of the destruction to our world. It appears my journey may have to continue the way it used to be when cars did not exist. "Now my heart feels the rush of the unknown future as my ancestors did when the white man came. Grandfather may my prayer reach the great spirits for my protection and wisdom."

"The time has come brother to send the message of refuge and help to the survivors. Let us see the masses bend to our will and join us." as Darius mind races in the dark glee knowing he would soon seize power all for himself.

"But Darius we do not have sufficient man power to guard our stores from the horde of people that shall come." as the room fills with bickering of the league members on how they will present themselves to the starving. Darius sits annoyed at the very sight set before him. These members of an ancient league squealing like swine before jackals. I will enjoy the day I am able to dispatch these bastards from the constant doubts they have with the search for power over the people.

"SILENCE YOU BASTARDS!!! Did you believe we would leave ourselves unprotected? As we set the world to chaos I called our connections in government to set a select group to guard the supplies. Remember brothers when we stretch for our hand we can affect everything. Now let us prepare the next phase of our domination with assistance from our military contracts." while the league members calm themselves they realize the truth in Darius words.

Later that evening Darius sits in the presence of Volta to receive any further interpretation of the scrolls. Blood rushing through his cold views anticipation of a greater secret he has ever received when became an apprentice in the league. Thoughts mixed with madness in a hunt for what all crave more power!

"Volta have you no more message of the scrolls or am I

wasting my time.......” as he thumps his fingers on the table in anticipation of the information he has come to receive on the translations.

“Yes lord Darius I have much to tell you from the scrolls.” as his face flushes in the fear of upsetting his master. “I have seen an inscription stating of a conflict between the league and a group never seen before the time of your ancestor Ulvey. Even with minor battles stated time and again this group turns the tide with power unmatched by our collective.” Darius eyes grew wide with the anticipation of this news.

“How was that possible?” for a brief moment rage and fear mixed uncontrollably within Darius mind. Though his face stayed stone, never showing evidence of the turmoil in his own soul. His thoughts then cleared to release the newly set commission of dark wards for his own protection from the other members gaining any advantage.

“Master Darius there is another bit of news for you to hear.” his attention returns to hear the extent of what Volta is about to say.

“Speak of this new or still your tongue.” as Volta places the scrolls down before his master he reveals a vital part of the tale to the lore. “Look here the group was lead by one of extremely powerful mage. If this is true I may have a way to find them. I only beg for time to see these details out.”

“So be it! You have my blessing to seek it out.” if he wasn’t so valuable he would already be dead. Volta should thank whatever he believes in for his very life.

The keeps walkway to the depths of their centuries old castle seemed to go on to eternity. Consumed by this news Mirauthor has received of looking for people which have not been called forth in a millennium. Suddenly he realized his leader was taking him to a part of their dwelling horribly foreign to all the other places he has roamed in the keep.

“Mirdan where are we ....” as his old companion silences

him before a great wall of stone. Confusion crosses through his very soul with the secrecy.

Within a flash the lead keeper's hands touches the hard granite wall. He appears to be focusing on a single section for an unknown period of time. As this area seems dark as pitch like nothing I could recall. Before a word could be made to question the reason for him to come here a swirl of wind moved in around us. Swiftly to follow was a frightful crackling sound like wood to a flame, yet to my surprise the sheer face of the wall split into a passage way. "Enter my friend I have much to show you." grabbing my shoulder Dan guided me gently through the opening.

"Where the hell are you taking me?" looking at the surroundings I recognize the making of the elders marks. This is the catacombs from which this very order was born is it not old friend. How many have we lost through the pages of history? For what purpose have we entered the sacred and treasured hall of the elder, surprisingly a central chamber unveiled their secrets. "Author I have brought you here for a specific purpose. Look upon the floor and recognize your gift."

"Gift?! What are you talking about my dear friend?" as he fearfully stared at the floor and wonder what this was about. Even with all his knowledge of the order he did not wish to accept the facts he was blessed to find the chosen. Yet he must awaken something within himself to achieve such a task. The price feels a little too high for him yet he will do his best to succeed.

"I know how you feel Author, the one price is a complete change to yourself. I must leave you for a while so you can face your own image. You must succeed or die. Once the self-challenge is complete I will release you from this chamber. Forgive me! This will be the only way you can unleash the truth our greatest power. Let me show you what I mean." as he lifted his hands and the entire room engulfed him in a sphere of light and dark swirling about his body appeared to lift him from the floor. My chest pounded with anticipation of that balance of power. Then he left sealing me in the chamber. I only pray I survive this test.

Several hours have past upon the fourth day as Nathan remembers his need to reach the cities edge. Contemplating Beatrice's wish to find her parents in the ravages of the city. Yet she must accept they have probably died. Our lives are at risk the longer they remain here.

"Sir I think we should leave now." a sense of urgency racing through her eyes. "What is going....." she places her tiny hand over my mouth to warn of danger that is coming. Slowly she peaks out the window. It has been days we have traveled without seeing a soul. Now just outside our nightly hiding spot a large group walked down the street with hideous markings spread across their bodies. They didn't even look human by the ways each was moving. "Sir the scar me. I don't like them monsters out there."

We stayed watching them from the window trying ever so hard not to let them know we are here. I can't tell what they would do if they saw us here. This would not be good if they turn out to be hostile. So we wait and see what will happen as they pass.

Despite all that has happened we now must deal with this beast. Can there be more of these creatures in other parts of the city. "Sir what are they?" before I could answer my attention was caught by a survivor down the street who just seem to appear out of nowhere. My ears tang upon the screeching cry of the beast's as they went into pursuit of their so-called prey. All that I feared seemed too appeared to be manifested in them monsters.

CHAPTER 5

Within their safeguard the once well-known news crew must consider looking for supplies. Conferring this dilemma with each other on who must go scout the area for possible food banks. "Someone must take the opportunity in recovering a minor amount of food and water. Is anyone willing to attempt what we called in the military terms as a recon mission?" Adam sits consumed by his thoughts while Robert babbles on about his wish for volunteers to search for supplies.

He appears to be reliving his days in the wars when commanding troops. Every day he would just go on about all the times he came near death, plus all the action he would take to assure his survival. Raising his head Adam notices one of the interns lifting his hand to volunteer. "Good young man! You leave for the search in two hours when dawn breaks but you must not go alone. Is there anyone else willing to go?" many hands raised up but only a select few were set in pairs of two for each direction to search.

Majestically dawn rose like an old friend greeting us with warmth. Michael was engulfed by its touch as though he was seeing an angels face. This reminded him of those days with Nathan camping in the mountains.

Preparing a fire to conjure something to eat. Along the way of cooking he starts chanting what could only be interpreted as the days welcome. As soon the meal was consumed thoughts flowed in concern of the spirits quest he was on.

He even contemplated when the spirit would speak with him again. But he knew she would appear at her own leisure.

In preparation the young intern was advised by Robert on the necessity of caution as he searched. “Remember son locate the areas we could find the supplies. Consider the injured as well for medical supplies. Be careful and don’t get in trouble.”

As soon as there little meeting finish he departed out the door without his companion. God only knows what could be waiting out there for him. When everyone focused on him I decided to leave myself to witness the mayhem. Passing out of obscurity like a phantom.

The day passed on like something out of a bad dream. Although this is reality of senseless destruction. Aware of my surroundings I sought shelter inside an empty toy store. My eyes were amazed by the sudden grotesque figures passing my hiding spot. Each seem to present the image of dolls whose been placed near a fire and their skin bubbled.

Suddenly I heard what appeared to be the leaders make some type of loud noise alerting the others. With astonishing agility they raced in a direction which made little sense looking after them I realized they are hunters.

Has everything I once knew changed so quickly. Did the essence of humans change by an act of utter violence. Noticing those poor souls made me realize that I must change the way we all live as people. If those beasts are out here I need to go warn the others before those things find them.

Just when Adam was to leave the minor sanctuary of the toy store a quick movement from an upper window caused him to reel back into the shadows. With a heavy sense of caution he set his eyes to the window to spy out what may be hidden in that room. Moments later two figures appeared to be surveying the area. They have to be checking if the streets are safe to come out as he is. Both figures were a great relief to know others have made it through the bombings. I need to get in contact with them; it seems like a father and his daughter. Now I can have a little hope for the future of us all.

"Beatrice I think it is safe for us to get out of here." while they prepared the needed supplies Nathan took another glance for extra precaution. As his grandfather had trained him, Nathan pays close attention to every little detail of the street.

Moments later they descended the stairwell to the main street. Just as they were about to step out the door Beatrice noticed the man stand in front of the old toy store. "Sir look it's a ...." Nathan jerked his head in the direction she pointed to see if it was another one of them creatures. Uncontrollable rage rose from deep within believing he needed to prepare himself for a fight... By the blink of an eye there was the knife he took from the apartment within his hand. After evaluating the unknown man he placed his new weapon back in its hiding place.

"Hey! How long have you been standing there?" Nathan couldn't really believe someone other than himself and the child survived.

"Not long. Just taking whatever measures I can to make sure I didn't come out to soon. Did you see those things a moment ago?"

"Yup! Those beastly things were chasing some kid down the street. Poor soul I only hope he can escape them somehow." as the final word left his lips a loud cry broke the silence like an animal being torn apart while it is still alive.

As the day wore on the group moved on to find another shelter in there trek. Each seems to explain the circumstances of their understanding of what has been happening in the world.

By mid-day Adam revealed that he was one of several survivors from a news station. With greater relief Nathan could only hope that others could make a possible contingent to get the hell out of this city.

"Adam do you think the others would want to leave the city. It just doesn't seem safe to be here anymore."

"Don't know! But when we explain what we saw with those things a few hours might convince them."

"Well let's hope! Those things scared me!" as I looked at Beatrice my eyes bared witness to the utter fear she felt. I can remember my childhood in which I was exposed to such a feeling. By the time I could even think my hand reached out to Beatrice like a father comforting his own child. "Remember little one I am here. You have nothing to fear." the day was nearly one in the time it took them to reach where the rest of Adams group was residing.

My time in this place is a dark nightmare that I can't wake up from. Looking about the walls with my hands a great sensation envelopes me like a wave. Do my very senses deceive me or does this place reach into my very soul. Where am I?

Realistically my very spirit needs to be invoked to even begin to understand. Setting myself in what I believe is the center of the enclosure I begin my meditation. Countless amounts of time dwindle away like the seasons when no one cares to notice.

Abruptly the room reaches back in my direction with the glow of an ancient script no man has seen in the great scheme of existence for some time. Although they reach to me I must not lose myself to them. My flesh grows cold at their beckoning to reveal their grave.

Depth lying upon depth to press on me like a cave in, but what is the purpose of this? Focus you old fool this can be withstood but keep my mind focused. Instantaneously a storm within me raged uncontrollably fighting back there bone like touch upon me. How long will this last my mind is losing itself. Yelling breaks free in the core of my soul, like an injured lion. Then I see a figure in the edge of the darkness watching me silently.

"Yes old boy, your weakness is the force which feeds me and your pain brings me so much pleasure."

"Who are you? I thought I was alone in here." as he stared trying to figure who it was in the room with him. The agony grew as the time wore on.

"Huh! You are never alone. In the darkness I am always watching, waiting for a time like this. Above all people you should know this being here for so long."

"For what? What in creation are you?" pain riddled his body every time he tried to speak.

"Soon you will know what I am. There is much more for you to learn Mirauthor."

As I looked harder to study my dark companion pain within my chest throbbed even more like being pierced by a scorching blade. "See old boy it has begun. Look for the answer of the riddle."

"Who are you? What riddle?" saying anything caused the pain to increase. "Listen and know for the answer will come. At that time we can reveal the name. Now search old boy." do with me all that you can oh wretched one. You will soon see I am no easy prey.

As the countless days pass, while the earth and sky passes in time with all the mayhem that has happened. Michael reaches such a point of fatigue which could not be ignored. Noticing the remains of an old motel he chooses to rest for a night. "May the spirits guard me as I sleep..." before he could even finish his thought a shuffling curtain caught his eye.

Taking a closer observation he hoped another person may have escaped the destruction. Still I don't want to take any chances. So he took the rifle from the rack in the back of his truck's cab to prepare for anything. After careful inspection Michael's tension eased slightly with the evidence of the building being abandoned. In his search of the surrounding area he caught sight of an old fire pit in the back of the building. He prepared a quick meal.

During the arrival of twilight a fire was set to perform his people's spiritual cleansing ceremony. Such a heaviness felt layered upon his soul, there was only one re-course to free himself from it.

"How can we set the faithfulness of those loathsome masses to my will….." as Darius contains himself with the confines of his sleep chamber a sudden knock on his door interrupted his thoughts. He turns to face the door as it opens from his servant's entrance.

"Great Darius I have brought the items you have requested. Shall there be anything else my lord." a dark sense of satisfaction and annoyance boiled within. "Very well, place them upon the table there. I shall deal with them in a moment."

Humbly obeying, his servant entered further into the room and places the items upon the empty table by the window. Though the building was strategically untouched by the bombings, the evidence of the new holocaust can be seen out stretched upon the horizon. "Will there be anything..." with sudden rage Darius forced the servant out through a cold stare that could freeze the blood of any man.

Examining the items he arranged a subtle concoction which aided his need for rest. Caution was needed in the preparation, too much of any given ingredient meant death just like he gave his brother. Oh, would he relish the thought of seeing the others die so painfully. Securing his door he proceeded to consume the contents of the tonic. Reveling in such devastation where for the world sees itself could only be succumbed by his desire to rule it all. Although much was still left to be done. "In the morrow I will call those wasted masses unto me." a dark smile crossed his face in the thought of how many may consider him a savior.

Amidst the shadows of illusion Darius turns himself over to awaiting slumber. Setting the welcome for the meeting of dreams.

Revealed to him or the subjugation of the world which he finds himself in seems different. Communing with the humble servants fulfilling his every whim, yet an underlined chill crosses his mind for the fear he will not accept as his own.

Even his very fantasy that would be for only one king in the world. Looking over at the dark halls lays a blight of his perfect rule. Just beyond the ability of lowly sense of sight he sees a figure.

Within terrible whispers that grasp his soul he listens to this overwhelming presents that shakes him to the core. "Now I shall be your master." Immediately Darius feels his spirit shrivel like prey before the hunter's strikes. "Remember the price of your rule that I have given you." cupping his ears the rasp continues to grind his very will to dust.

"There is still much to do till that time." waking with a start Darius looks frantically for his nocturnal pursuer. Realizing the sleep was not peaceful, he attempted to return to the slumber yet all would come in time. His mind continuously ponders what has just happen but the answer is like the wind escaping his grasp, but the time will come when he knows the meaning.

Looming within the League's servants a keeper sets in wait of orders to return among his brethren company. Foreseeing the planned meetings of the vile filth of existence he goes on observing their actions.

While in the chamber he was assigned by the very leader of this group. "Darius has set a pride to his own destruction." stopping to be certain no one is spying upon him he continues his report. Assured he is alone he goes on with his conversation with Mirdan. A gift of birth was his ability to build such technology that could not be detected by normal human means.

"They speak of how they have caused the attack and how they wish to control the world's population. If they have any changes I will advise you as soon as I can. Darius seems very protected on what he wishes to say to the others so it is hard to know what he plans." for this is the way of us all may to succeed in stopping them. I can only pray faithfully that our order is able to find the chosen before it is too late.

CHAPTER 6

Concluding the receipt of the information from the infiltrator of his very enemies. Mirdan contemplates the next step in there plans to stop the darkness of the League's mind.

How will this affect our search to bring this world to balance again? He is appreciative of the advance of technology for communication yet with all of the orders has to use in there needs to stay ahead of them. Still he has knowledge of a power that surpasses anything as the greatest gift of the creator.

Days have passed since he has been able to check on Mirauthor. Returning to the fountain he checks the progress of his longtime friend. Dan then realizes the old being that once tested his soul years ago. "Please Author find the secret which all men find in their souls. You can do this like other test before." whispering to himself he felt a tear track its way down to his chin. Wiping the semblance of compassion for his dear friend he had to accept that the gift must be found. As did many others have in the long years of the orders existence, yet so many were not as successful.

Unyielding vigil are the destined
We beguile ourselves to Gaia
Her words burn our blood
Stand does the called
The tide of shadows comes
Surrender yourself to her touch
For she is waiting

As the conclusion of his prayer of purification Michael sets himself down for the eve. Knowing how tomorrow is the setting of the next steps of his journey. Belief in the spirits pull is the only reason he holds on too.

Before he sets his final attempt to rest a barricade is placed to give him a defendable domicile. Looking out through the window he takes ease at the lack of any possible looters that may be out there waiting. Upon falling into deep slumber Michael realizes the lady waits for him, yet he is startled by such an appearance within the dream world.

"Michael is weary of the moor drake. They have awakened for this time. There only purpose is to hunt down anyone who may cause there masters a challenge in this rule." puzzlement crosses his face as he considers what they are.

"Huh! What the hell is a moor drake?" Suddenly she shows him an image of the creatures. His heart dropped with the sight of its dark figure.

"An ancient evil born of shadow that thrives in misery. There sole purpose is to destroy anything of flesh and bone."

"But......."his words are caught within him as the confusion consumes his mind.

"Just be ready I will send you a familiar to assist you in the next part of the quest. When you wake he shall be waiting for you. Now is the time to continue to the lake and he will guide you without the vehicle. You are to walk from here on out to the lake I showed you."

Volta seeing the need to expand his search of the past records confines himself to his personal library. Hours earlier he cast the spell of awakening to his mind so he may be able to grasp the knowledge at a faster rate than he normally does.

Make his way to the wall opposite the entrance to his private quarters. Pushing a stone latch the secret library of all the scrolls opens. Each one a potent force to bring all the world to ruin. "Where is it? I know it's here somewhere it has to be."

working his way through his sources of knowledge he finally locates the prize upon the far shelf.

Tearing through the ages of secrets Volta locates a treasure his master may deem suitable. The legend of dark hunters specifically born to hunt any precious treasure. As he continues reading he spots a script that surprisingly has been unnoticed for some time. It speaks of the moor drakes'ability to hunt an ancient enemy like the mage who defeated his master's family so long ago. "How did I not see this before? This shall be quiet valuable to or cause." he continually engulfs his mind to the words without much want for food or water. The secrets fuels his hunger for this moment greater than any other thing in the world could do.

Rising within the dark morning Darius prepared himself for the coming chaos of dawn's calling. As the sun crested the distant hills his minions were dispatched with word for the military actions of the day. Within his mind he could calculate those who would bend their wills for the comforts of food and shelter, if they wish to live this would be a good choice. If they only knew the real price of the precious supplies they may not have gone for it.

My destiny shall be fulfilled this day. The world is but at trophy to be claimed. Within he permits himself to feel the satisfaction of what is to come this day of control as all the food has been treated with the additive that shall be an addiction to the masses.

As Darius prepared for the hopeful simplicity of those weak minded bastards to set delegates into order at the storage facilities. Within his dark understanding of control he believes them to be spineless dogs.

How can I consider them equal to me? They seem to have little sense of the power to even be part of the counsel that shall rule this world. As the day drags on, he convenes the cohorts which command his military support to a meeting.

Looking at the men who sit before him Darius evaluates each in turn for any sign of weakness. Testing the extent of their personal standing in command of such a force. Without hesitation he expresses the need of the work each must maintain. In turn each commander explains the logistics of their own units to do the job.

While Darius listens to them, his mind is entertained with the control he is achieving over these men. All seems well in the meeting so he silently contemplates the information given to him by Volta on the scrolls. Power must be tipped to my favor; I will let nothing stop me. As the commanders finished their list of needs the meeting was concluded and his personal assistant was given the task to supply them with these needs for the moment.

Several hours later he sits alone reflecting on the next course of action to the plan. As though two opponents quarrel over a global chess board moving and countering for complete dominion. Yet the greatest question is who may the phantom be he has challenged and when will he make the next move.

"Insanity!" I have seen many things in my time but none like this. As members of the league sit in wait to consider the next level of action. As Darius seats himself in the prestigious head position of the counsel table. He is explaining to the others of the meeting with the military officers to commence with distribution of the supplies to the survivors. If any exist, yet others of the council consider it's a preposterous notion to partake in at this time.

"Why did you not consider our presence in this meeting brother Darius! We have much to gain as you do with the plans that must be carried out." each bickers in turn to what has happened earlier that day.

With fierce hatred to contestation of his action he faces is a brother to impose their positions on the decision. "We have discussed this before to bend the wills of the survivors, and you should recall volition was set forth. Our will is in affect to rule the world. So prepare brothers for our next step in the plan." delving deeper into his conscious use of the word brother tasting bitter upon his palate. Utter despise for them coursing through his veins like acid.

"So be it Darius! But there shall be an observer needed to record our great course of action." Soba as outspoken as always to challenge Darius. For such insolence he craved to set against those who considered themselves his better in all things.

As Soba expresses his point when one of his personal aides enters the chamber. Receiving the dismissal of the others he exit's the chamber knowing how it would enrage Darius. With extreme sense of inner glee he marches out of the room. As he hears the heavy door of the chamber slam shut behind him.

Soba makes haste down the corridor to the lower levels in which his personal chamber is stationed. As he enters the vanguard of his private intelligence bowing in respect to his lord. Wearing the crimson breast plate of the dark vanguard which he established some time ago under his direct order to serve as watchdogs of the corporation.

"Lord it is of great importance we leave this place for you own safety. There are plans amidst plans against all the members of the counsel by Darius himself." tearing all sense of formality out of the comment made by his most trusted servant.

Being of such an age greatly held by the bonds of youth this young warrior excelled rapidly in Soba's favor. Peering upon his featured bulk within his upper torso, his aquiline facial shape would disarm any man. Skilled through years of weapons, plus hand to hand combat few could stand against him. Yet his loyalties run deep for his lord Soba alone. It is even possible that not even Zeth could stand against him.

"Give me your report and we shall consider the next course of action. Till then we must do what is needed to remove Darius for his position. We must not give him any reason to begin his plans early or have him doubt anything I may do." with an air of confidence he stares his great guardian and chief spy.

Michael wakes upon the new dawn interpreting the dream of the ladies words. Peering protectively out the window to avoid the chances of being spotted by marauders that may be roaming the streets.

Hopefully relieved there is no evidence of hostile individuals he emerges from the temporary sanctuary. Stepping through the door a sudden movement caught his attention. Preparing for a conflict Michael investigates, yet surprisingly waiting around the corner was a young coyote. It has a peculiar group of markings revealing this is not an average breed, his mind considers if this was the guide the lady promised for him to receive.

Standing before my so-called guide I begin to consider the very essence laminating its very skin. As our eyes meet they present a murky pool of mystery which has seen countless days. The very coat contains a titian design so brash the lady herself seemed to create him. Without a hint of warning he walks unto the long valley stretching far beyond my eyes.

We have far to walk my brother may the ancestors protect us both. While the thought of my ancestors crossed my mind the coyote looked back as if waiting for me to catch up with him. So as I hurried to get to his side I wondered if he would tell my thoughts were drifting. Then something I didn't consider happened to my surprise.

"I am your ward young one. I have been here for a great time waiting for your day of the journey to begin. Can't you remember long ago when you were but a babe? The one who plucked you from the river after you fell in and couldn't swim." he goes back to that day when his family was out camping and he wandered off near the river just to fall in, yet there was someone or something that like just like this one pulling me from the water. As my parents run up to get me the animal ran away.

The words that struck my ears sent a shock through me as

my eyes rushed to look upon my companion. "have you spoken unto me!" Michael's eyes filled with a mixture of fright and joy to see that he was more than a simple beast to guide me.

"Yes young one we can speak and we listen to the hearts of men that is why she chooses you."

"Then tell me your name my brother? I feel it would bring us closer together." Michael walks with anticipation to know he is guided by the spirits in true form.

"I don't have one. We are like moving shadows with a specified purpose. Once it's done we are to return to the void between time and space. But there are a few who are allowed to stay on this side of the wall."

Shall this be given to you to stay here amidst this plain of existence?" he looked with anticipation to know if his companion will be permitted to stay.

"I don't know." whispered the coyote. "Some say it is the choice of the one who can say. Yet none of the others understand what this means."

As the two journeyed on the vast horizon stretched on without end. Michael perplexed by the words of the others was a profound revelation. Silent of words between the two of them left great opportunity to let his memory surface the continuum of the past stories and the present living. Having remembered story upon story without ceasing for all to bury in our hearts.

Without warning a deep sense of euphoria surged through him like a great wave. Michael seems to realize all his visual surroundings appeared alien as if in some time or place lost to the world. "Coyote where are you?" Michael was in a state of inner panic as he noticed the shift in his senses.

"I am here. The feeling will go away." as his mind spun he continued to walk on through the mixture of sickness.

Looking to his immediate side he could believe the sight that greeted his very eyes.

"Can you really stand me old man? The times you have

stood against me you realize your no match for me. We have been waiting for this day when we would meet her. How have you lived without me all these years to help?"

Yet the chamber feeling of loathsome hell which could not be described in mere words. This place the cradle of unknown fears and a personal hell I wish to leave but how. Think old fool remember something that may free me

As Author leaned upon the sudden existence of training within the order how an old intuit told him. "The day one faces the dark mist or shadow of him is painful to accept. Just look hard and know a balance of two contentious minds would open the inner dimensions of the hearts power."

Without even realizing his own self he looks throughout the darkness. He has determined the key of freedom was always within his reach. "This entire riddle you seek has now been revealed old man." I have come to the will of al you have sought.

As he attempts to stand before the shade of his confinement. Despite his location Mirauthor can feel as if the world falls away within their merge.

Shear pain envelopes him like a raging turnout of waves upon the shore. Agony upon agony which forever seems to consume his soul. Within him a soft voices whispers to bare your rebirth unto the end of time. Ongoing misery revealed as memories hidden long ago resurface, yet there visions are as if another bring in their own dark nightmares. Perception of his thoughts blur with combining of him and the shade.

His body slowly returns to a sense of ease as earth seems to rise to gently cradle the new oud-rah. As his eyes slowly open to welcome the warmth of approaching light he was grateful seeing the kind face of Mirdan before he relinquished himself to welcome slumber.

Amidst the village below the keeper's towers, virile men awakened to the change in the wind. Hearts set ablaze as the generations before the heed the monks call. Shouts of celebration rise unto the heavens as though there purpose for existing has been unleashed.

Upon the heights of the towers Mirauthor awakes within his quarters to see Mirdan standing by his bedside. He ponders on the aching that surges through his body. As his eyes come into greater focus he realizes his friend apparently speaking to the physician attending his wounds.

Seeking answers Mirdan musters the strength to question the two of his conditions. With sudden attempt brought a look of utter surprise on the healers' eyes. "Mirdan how long...." with faint whispers to extent of his ability to find answers

"Rest my old friend. You have been through so much within the chamber. I will explain all when you have recovered enough. Let the time pass in dream while the healers work their magic to get you back to normal." as Mirdan was forced to turn away as the unbearable sorrow flowed as tears. He alone knows the extent of physical and mental torment that is presented while the test of ages commences.

"Tell me Dan have I succeeded in the test." his friend could only chuckle at the question with innocent laughter.

"You stubborn goat you would not be here if you failed." as Author succumbs to the elixir given by the healers to place a resting sleep upon him as Mirdan walks from the room.

Looking back at the old keeper within the bed Dan notices a wide smile cross his beloved friends as he drifted off into slumber once again. "When he is ready notify me at once healer. There is much to do and he has a right to know the extent of his purpose."

Rushing out the door Mirdan hurriedly down the ancient corridors of the keep down to the courtyard. as the fountain of mercy comes into view the bronze figure of the women appears. With a kind hand reaching to touch the head of a crying child representing angelic comfort. A testament to Shao the wife of the first keeper at the first calling.

Peace settles in his heart staring at this relic of the honored past. A sudden movement then caught his eye noticing an errand boy upon his daily task. Mirdan calls unto the boy to approach him. With reluctant fear the boy hesitates at the call then realizes it is the orders highest keeper. Wide eyed the young lad is covered win sweat he looks about the yard to be sure it was he who was being summoned.

"Yes lad I am speaking to you, come at once I have a job for your ears. No do not fear me I mean you no harm." as the lad approaches he quakes with fear to wonder what job is to be done. In his young mind no memory exists of being summoned by the high keeper. He only wonders the purpose of the task to be done.

"Ease your fear child I mean to give you a simple task. What I have for thee is of great importance. I know you came from the village below the towers." as the boy relaxes he is amazed to see that he knows where he came from.

"Yes my lord." stated the boy with a great sense of pride of his heritage.

"This is what you must do for me. Go back to your elders at the village and tell them to wait. I know your people have felt the oud-rah has been reborn." observing the boy's face the could see the lad could understand.

"That is true my lord. My people are linked to the change in the earth. Even now our blood is set ablaze to do battle for the oud-rah." as the words flowed the lads eyes began to show a sense of courage born to his line.

"Good boy there is still much to do so have them do as I said. When the time comes to battle you will be sent again to tell them. But for now have them just wait then return to me at once." with extreme honor and joy the lad rushes off to deliver the message to his people.

Looking to the fountain Mirdan sits upon the stone bench to reflect on all that is happening in the world. Searching deep in his thoughts on the next step needed for the chosen's arrival. The only problem is finding them before the darkness can attempt to save the hope of mankind.

As Michael slumbered her voice echoed in his ears like a memory of the past life. Though he could feel the touch of her skin against his own. To hear her voice was a sweet comfort to his soul in this time of confusion and loss with no set course to travel.

Dreams of the dance of ages and Gaia swirled throughout his heart and soul. "What is this to me? How am I to change the course when I don't know where I am going?" while he pondered the vision after vision. Yet he can feel something else coming that brought fear he could not explain. Still with all they joy Michael knew there is always more than the happiness in life. Just then he listen s her voice spoke again.

"Yes my dear rest and remember what you see. As you have lived we have been with you each step of the way to guide you. It is not only your life that has a purpose to fulfill but several of your kind. You are the first of the chosen to become what is needed for the coming battles against the darkness. Listen to the wind with pride and look to the mountain with faith for we are there in them. It is part of your strength mixed with the beating of your heart. A new day rises through the darkness of night. Follow grandfather as he leads you to the brother of the new conflict. God this is the way of the reborn...." then the ancestors vanished like mist before the wind.

Gently waking form his slumber he saw what appeared to be grandfather. When his eyes finally focus all he could see was the coyote waiting. Michael attempted to recall his dream or was it a vision of his mother's spirit long past. Making sense of these times was always difficult for him except when grandfather was around. Wait! Didn't she tell me to follow grandfather, but the only one with me is the coyote.

Eyes wide with the sudden realization that his grandfather's name at the ceremonies represented his totem. With his guide in sight he understood part of the dream that he saw. Michael joyfully shouted his grandfather's name. "Painted coyote as the name echoed in the distance his guide turned and gave a quick nod of its head.

"You have finally remembered my name boy. Now it's time to continue your spirit walk to fulfill that dream of yours. Just know our path will split again. But do no fear for you will have brother to lean upon and strength unseen for a long time." Stated the coyote as he began walking in the direction of the rising sun which revealed the mountain he was to reach.

Rushing to gather his things and catch up he knew life would never be like it was before. As he approached his companion's side a strange sensation manifested upon his forearm. As he rolled up his sleeve it revealed a mark of the earth and wind guide markings which was not there before. Looking closer it represented the bear and the eagle totem.

"Yes boy you are looking at the mark of the chosen. Your mother was as the eagle and the bear is your father's totem each holds great power." Michael looked back at his path after his companions' words which made sense to him revealed a greater sense of honor to his calling. Now is the time in which the path truly begins.

CHAPTER 7

We who stand on the precipice waits
Yet as one who dare the fates will know
For he is hell bent on power
Kings bear their heads to his might
A god of men born of blood and bone
Stretching forth his arm to consume
Ashes left to reveal his presence
Sorrow upon the few left whole
Timeless are the shadows
Dark is his stare and empty is his soul

How is it that I find myself here again? What is the purpose of it for me to stay here?

Walking as if he were continuously trapped in a nightmarish castle. To every step echoing in the distance of the dark hall. As Darius attempts to find balance within him to go on within the dark corridors he wonders of its calling to him.

I feel like this place should be familiar to me somehow yet he can't see how or why. Digging deep into the dark memories of his life he cannot get past the sense of truly knowing this place he finds himself. Eyes which can pierce the abyss of shadows which stretch endlessly around him resemble the confinement of a tomb.

Though he believes himself to be alone, but the pressing weight of a presence is evident. What it may be escapes him at the present time. All he can see is what candle light bids him see which in not a great deal.

Searching about Darius hopes something can awaken any clue to where he truly is at the moment. Taking his time to venture his gaze unto the worn pillars and tapestries positively decade by insurmountable time passed since any have laid their eyes upon them. Yet he cannot find himself to understand the sense of being here before in a past life or something.

"Welcome necromancer! It has been ages since you have been back here in this castle. I have waited for this day you would come to see me again." the voice caused his flesh to run cold like ice had formed in his veins. Still the voice had a great deal of familiarity to his life long ago.

His very ears felt as though a course fire burned him from the depths of hell itself. Yet as wretched the sound he suddenly knew without even turning its appearance would be worse than the sound. Was this his own inner demon made real?

"Turn and face me boy! You at least owe me that much after so long." Darius then cringed at the sensation of his mind being torn asunder by a blunt knife. As he attempts to focus his mind he sets a barrier between the voice and his flesh. In doing so he felt relief from the tormentor but it was short lived. Instantly he remembers this place of despair from another time in his youth and the barrier wavered in strength.

"Finally you recall where you are, don't you boy." the voice seem to hear his very thoughts even with the barrier up. How could I be here at this time?

Within myself there is a certain connection with this place that surpasses the very stretch of time he has tried to stay away. Have I been here from some time long forgotten? Just to walk amidst the shadows like a childhood memory. How do I know this place? Why does the voice call me a necromancer?

"Come now boy and remember your birth right long passed down the line of your own family. For you were meant for more than flesh was ever permitted to know. You must know that your life is not like others on this world you exist upon."

Chilling to the very core of my soul his words continue their penetration deeper into my mind. A dream which feels like a never ceasing nightmare comes true. But my presence here must mean something to my future. I must remember a name or I am finished.

"Michael looks upon the horizon trying to know the beginning of your true destiny. It is there upon that precipice a truth shall be revealed." hearing grandfathers words help me realize the reason of my walking with the ancestors calling my soul. I was always told there is a greater purpose to some that are born this time, but only the ancestors know who shall be called for their cause.

Setting my eyes ahead my vision was obscured by the sun to realize the definition of a towering fortress of sorts that is laid into the very mountain itself. Yet what lies within the walls shall enlighten his inner curiosity. The only mystery in his mind is how this could have existed without anyone ever finding this place.

Bestowed upon me is the opportunity to make an impact upon mankind. The world seems to be in chaos with countless people are being lost, possibly fearful of a future event that waits to be revealed. Beyond this point my life had little meaning for me to consider my course. With the appearance of the maker I believe there is no turning back upon the events to come upon the horizon of time.

Searching out the landscape of the mountain I can't understand how it can be so lush with foliage especially after the devastation everywhere else. So staring back the utter desolation seems to run rampant beyond some unseen wall. If this is just one part of my world how does the rest appear in this valley?

"Grandfather what is this place and how can this place seem so different from where we have come from?" Michael's heart was beginning to race as he got closer to the mountain. Taking a sudden glance he noticed his companion was missing for some reason. Frantically scanning around in almost a blind panic. Instantly without notice a voice called out to him in a soothing tone catching his attention. “You are safe here Michael. Thy so-called grandfather will return to guide you the rest of the way shortly.” as he turned in the direction of the voice he noticed a man dressed in an ancient cloak. He could not see his face for the cowl that shadowed his face. All be it, there seemed to be no sense of danger in the man’s movements.

As he took in the scenery it unleashed an inner awe to the depth of his soul. His first glance of the area didn’t permit him to notice the enchanting falls that was apparently fell from an unknown source of the heavens. In spite of the serene visions of beauty before him something was not exactly right. A sense of deeper awareness brought a need for defense which could not be explained. Within the blink of an eye the figure standing before me seemed to morph into a grotesque beast of dark origins. His worn robe seemed to appear to be tattered from numerous conflicts which did not only rip away pieces of fabric but the underlying flesh as well. Within the exposed rips of the robe revealed the gray ashen skin and rotting muscle. It seemed as though this poor wretch was nothing more than the walking dead. It moves like a puppet on broken strings.

“Ah you finally see what is to come of you boy?” Michael’s understood he was not meant to be here at this time with this creature. The very image of the falls he was exposed to was mere illusion. What greeted him now appeared as scorched earth and torment. No sign of life anywhere like he has entered the very pit of hell itself.

“Grandfather help me!!!!” fighting out of the deep slumber Michael could feel the sweat drenching his clothes. Looking about in fear he noticed his companion lying no further than an arm’s length from himself. His entire body seemed taut with the need to fight away the darkness. As the adrenaline surges through his veins. He began to breathe trying to control his inner fears from the nightmare, yet it felt so real even the scent flowing upon the breeze.

While the day waned on Michael continued to recall the nightmare that haunted him. I can understand that my road means facing my inner demons but that appeared to be something completely un-natural by any means. How can anyone face a beast such as what I saw?

"Are you still contemplating the vision you saw as you slumbered." grandfathers voice seemed to soothe my mind. "Remember there are far greater obstacles to face as this road continues. The vision is extremely different than what a normal medicine man would ever face. Just believe that your destiny will change the course of events set into motion by the catastrophe." the words fell upon his mind like a great weight upon his shoulders.

My hope is that I can be ready to face the coming darkness. Wandering the endless plains of the desolate world his mind recalls the joyous past. His greatest memory was Nathan and himself coming of age to become men of the tribe. Tears and blood shed amidst the ancient rites of passage. Now he sees those tests are nothing for a journey of life and the real trials yet to arrive. Come what may I must stand my ground.

Darius awoke from his restless slumber to hear a vigorous rapping upon his door that could not be explained. Relieved to notice his personal servant wake him out of that darkness. Yet he must never show fear amidst the others to do so means his own death as the leader of the league.

Eventually he knew that when he closed his eyes again there would be no telling if he would return to that place. His mind swam within the beasts words of a birth right of unknown origins. But its name continues to escape him, with time who knows if he can remember the name.

As he sets himself to focus on the next stop of his plan, there is a sense of a spiritual cancer eating its way through his dark resolve. It seems the very foundation of his dark heart's desire. "What shall become of me from that demonic vision? Does that creature really have any power to affect me on this plan of existence or can he cross over." mumbling to the fact of what the night has revealed. Gawking a quickly at the expanse of the room to see if any could hear his ramblings.

Staring back at the documents set before him to examine his detailed action needing to be set forth rather quickly. As an instant sound at the chamber door to the main hall suddenly opening. Darius witnesses Soba enter for an unknown purpose. Without trying to hide the utter disdain in a stare at the youthful member of the league.

"What do you want brother Soba?!" with a dark edge he inquires of his entrance within the hall.

Soba peers at Darius with a look of false gratitude to witnessing his fellow member viewing the plans of the previous day yet he contemplated the predictability of all his meticulous planning of every step of these endeavors. "I have come to perceive the next action of the prior days plan. It has been days since the last bomb fell upon the city." as he sheepishly tilted his head trying to sow a mask of innocence. Although his mind is a maze of deadly intention for the en of Darius reign. A heart pounding for the bloodlust of a reaper seeking his next victim.

"I know not the next time table for a coming action. There have been reports of an unknown beast roaming the city causing havoc for our troops. They are a formidable fighting force yet the sounds they make is quiet un-nerving to the troops by the recording sent for my examination." playing the recording for the first time he had to discontinue his attempt of examination due to its piercing frequency.

Soba had an inner sense of satisfaction knowing his creation was a thorn in Darius side. Although he had little control of them himself he relished the fact they were causing his greatest rival some discomfort. Still I could present myself a god with control of the onslaught after that old bastard's death. Yet to prepare the cause would be an under taking which requires careful timing and constant planning to succeed. I just hope he does not discover my agenda for him to soon.

As the days wore on Nathan and the others made their way out of the city as fast as possible. Though the continuous need to elude those demonic creatures posed a constant problem for all he survivors.

Fear was a thick fog which seems to hover over them all. With the unknown gun battle appeared to burst out from time to time, yet who were the combatants. Nerves were frayed with each furious out cry of weaponry. Suddenly the battle seem so close the group almost abandoned the attempt to leave the city all together.

What seemed worst was the scarcity of food along the trek. Will there be enough hope to carry on to the end. Looking at the reality of devastation disheartened Nathan from time to time. Yet he can sense within that he can lead these people to safety. To just feel an aching fire flow through like a river carrying a leaf in its flow.

I can remember grandfather once tell me. "Life is like a man in a boat. We know not what waits around the next bend. Just let it take you to the wakening of mind and spirit." how could the world fall so easily. Is the horror of the darkness been unleashed to torment the innocent? Nathan only has the evidence of a mad world having stared him in the face.

The past weeks have loomed upon his thoughts like a never ending nightmare. As they take refuge within an abandoned sports store seeing it as a sole representation of shelter for them all. As he explored the area a modest quantity of supplies were set within the back store room. Everyone was distributed a generous portion of food to sustain themselves for the night.

Jen I believe that was her name took it upon herself to use some med kits on the minor casualties we had in our midst. She seemed to have extensive understanding on medical techniques with such limited supplies. Some of the others were designated for construction to make shift stretchers for the seriously injured.

Dusk rushed upon us while we considered our plight to escape this city of madness. Some of the group made preparations to the idea of leaving before dawn, yet few had no inclination of departing outside this city so soon. I even feared this may tear our contingent of survivors apart.

While the silence reached a feverish peak a sudden noise broke out behind the counter of the store. Much to everyone's instant fright we realized it was an old radio. It appears Beatrice's curiosity assisted in finding the only source of news from a wide spread broadcast.

Seeing that our state of knowledge of the present events was greatly limited so we all listened. The broadcast stated "We have reason to believe much of the world is lost. Presently military forces have considered marshal law. Anyone who has survived please make you way to the central arena. Food and shelter shall be provided to all who arrive. All those who do not comply will be taken into custody. Further news shall resume at dawn."

Darius made his way to Volta's chamber to receive any news interpretation of the scrolls have been discovered. Yet his mind remained on the reverberation of the hideous creature his forces were encountering. As he descended the stairs his footfall produced an ominous echo that followed him. As it reverberated from the marble was which swelled into a cacophony of explosions with his ears. Darius mind drifted back to the very conflict that is engulfing his city.

He was so consumed by the event that his very surroundings seem to transform around him unnoticed. Ultimately by the final step of his descent he realized that he was within another corridor of the tomb like castle. Yet his mind seemed to guide him without rational thought as though something or someone was controlling his footsteps. When his mind cleared, he realized his whereabouts.

Peering about the large chamber was endless shelves full of books and scrolls. In his dark heart he realized this to be the location of his family's ancient archives. The black hall of history where he sat for hours studying scroll upon scroll, but it seems so old. Why can I remember this place so vividly? "Because boy this was once your home which has now become a tomb of memory." as the dark entity followed in his wake.

During the time Darius stood there he did not even feel its presence. Was he so enamored by the room to the point that nothing else mattered. "Who are you?" he asked with such control of his inner fear of it. "Come now boy remember. I stood day after day in this chamber. Watching you as scroll after scroll you studied your birthright." stated the entity with an unknown ease in the rasp of its voice.

Instantly as the beasts name surfaced within his memory of only one who stayed with him in this chamber. "Lilith!!" slipped through his lips like a puff of smoke on the wind.

Cry as a mother to the hill
As her children listen hard
Does the earth bleed in vain?
Come to her aid
Hold her from the darkness
Angels of mercy while we stand
Let no demon ravage her beauty
Chosen by heaven to ease the pain

Having the rebirth of the oud-rah has unleashed the blood fire of the village. As the keepers messenger arrives his eye become witness to an ancient ceremony of ages. Bonfires blaze, great squalls of chanting erupt upon the night sky as shadows jumble about. As he gazes at the freedom of the villagers in such an awe inspiring yet fearful display of joy and savagery. It's like time has stood still here as the world evolved.

Although the villagers frightened him by the traditional chants he had no choice but to deliver the message. Emerging from the tree line in the garments of a keeper's steward he could only hope for a peaceful meeting. The moment he reached the fire light cheers ascended unto the heavens. Elders approached without delay to greet him with gladness. His heart eased with a merciful sigh of relief.

Many rushed to present food and gifts of welcome unto the messenger that has arrived. Yet in kindness he addressed the elders with his master's message. Without hesitation they agreed which left him perplexed on why they would listen so quickly.

As the nights festivity word on them presented a feast of such that he has never known. Each of the houses begged him to stay and rest within their homes as if he were a king himself. On and on the celebration continued as songs where sung and stories told of his master, plus the connection with this village people. Open was his mind to the unfathomable history these people have passed down. Generation after generation waiting for the one known as the our-rah to return. I took it upon myself to speak with the elders to learn more about my own people since I have lived a long time in the towers. Instantly my eyes opened to a history of my life that my dear mother never told me. These people and I are kinsmen. Their blood awakened to a power that has slumbered since the last call to a battle. Endless stories were told and my heart broke, but was renewed with my own ancestry.

"Elder you have shown me a valuable honor I did not know even existed for me through our people. My blood feels like the flame that burns before us." with an uncontrollable grin he stated his understanding.

"We knew who you were as you approached child. The mark on your neck is the same as our young warriors that have been given at birth. I also knew your mother." as the elder looked upon him with such approval. "What do you know of my mother? I would truly like to know more if you can tell me." with an eager hunger to know more of her.

"She was a true woman of honor. When she passed the village mourned for three days to remember her. I was pained greatly in my heart like any father would for his child." just as the words spilled forth from the elders lips the young boy was shocked to his core. "You mean I am your grandson?" his eyes still revealing his sudden emotion breaking forth like a rush of rain over an exposed face. "I will reveal all in time my boy, but now let us continue in the celebration." The elder then set his mind on the dance which honored the sky spirits.

In respect the young boy set no further thought to the news of his heritage. He just marveled in the evening's events as a new bird that has learned to soar on the wind.

While Nathan and the others continued their trek from the city it presented a world of utter desolation. Having come from a lively place to what is now a living hell full of death and destruction. But what shall come of them? Days have passed as they left the sports store they rested in for a short sense of safety. Some of them now armed with simple rifles hoping it would help. Beatrice by my side let me focus on something other than the decaying bodies. Somehow she has become a little more than an orphaned child I took in for protection. Her mind was presenting awareness greater than any natural person could have. Just to think anyone so young could have such a gift seemed to keep us one step ahead of danger.

To recall the other day she told me we needed to find shelter without any real reason why. I quickly question her wish to fine a hiding place she only stated "dark things are coming!" while I stared at her face a realization of fear streaking in her eyes pushed away the doubt I had.

Mere moments later the area was filled with a sound of high pitched shriek echoes in close proximity to our location. Whining the matter of minutes after entering an empty apartment complex those hideous creatures enter our line of sight. Many were shaken to their core to lay an eye upon them. Just the minor hope they do not find them all was racing through Nathan's mind.

Weapons at the ready some of the men who claimed to be excellent marksman to aim. Instantly the seconds of thunderous combustion accompanied by the flame of burning powder. Each striking its intended victim with such furious vigor. With a final shrill cry the beasts died a well-deserved death reserved for such animals. Looking back at the child my mind could not fathom the recent awakening of such a gift. Later that night Nathan came to her just wanting to discover how she knew they were coming.

"Beatrice could you tell me how you knew those creatures were coming. It seems you have some gift that is beyond any one else's ability." with a sheer appearance of curiosity crossing his features. "Well the lady told me about them. She has been close for the last couple days." with a child's innocence which is undeniable.

"Lady?! What or who are you talking about? Am I able to see her if the time came?" my thoughts wanted to imagine this could be real but it was hard to take such information from her as anything but fantasy.

"Well I don't think so if you're asking me about her. She looks like an angel so pretty and shiny like a star in the night." she giggled as she thought of how he was asking about the one help she was given. Time will only tell if this is real or not.

"Can you speak to her anytime you want too?" Nathan tries to dig deeper into the mystery of the lady that seems to be helping them on their journey.

"Maybe! The lady even knew who you were when she came to me. She told me that we were meant to make it to some place but I forgot." with her eyes becoming heavy Nathan set the young child to rest close to his side.

He contemplated the information this little child presented to him. How can anything exist to help them escape those evil things? Suddenly a consuming need to sleep over took him. As he slumbered a dream came to him like a welcomed friend. Walking alone in a forest area next to a sublime river bed he has never seen before. Staring out at the appearance of a woman arose from the water like something out of a story book he read a long time ago.

Nathan felt himself slip into a sense of surreal existence that he could not explain. Peering out unto the water the angelic figure rose with ease from the depth seemingly with his eyes needing to realize why he is here. Her very appearance showed to be ethereal as the being Beatrice spoke about when she warned of the beast's that were near them.

In the character of her approach she moved like a smoke like mist in the wind. Mine own eyes were trapped in the glace with the windows of blue eyes she had which searched my very soul. What is happening to me? "Nathan I am the one who bears you safely within a purpose yet to be revealed to you. I have known your life from the very beginning of all things. The source of your strength is bound up for such a dark hour as this. You want the others must head to the towers of the keepers. As a guardian of the little girl there will be many who shall seek both of your demise if they knew what you two were destined to become." listening intently as I did my mind could not help but be enchanted by her voice. It swept over me like a sweet song carried on a gentle breeze.

Moments of exquisite joy filled me to the point of over flowing with such a feeling. But my mind paid close attention to the details she beard to me as this dream or whatever it was continued to drift on.

Within an instant the lady vanished into sheer vapor.

Dawn broke with resounding swiftness and her last words echoes deep in my thoughts. "Michael is waiting for you and I will be watching."

Setting out to the new dawn the survivors seem to have the fear of what may be waiting for them out in the world. In spite of all that has happened Nathan feels an awakening within his very soul that cannot be explained with ease.

It is like a raging fire burning deep inside his veins to fulfill an undeniable destiny; he never knew shifting of his very being it did not consume. But the lady of his dream has remained a never ending echo.

With exceedingly insurmountable wonder he realizes this place is not where he belongs. Yet he had a duty to the others as a guide to safety. Above all that he understood Beatrice was sent to him in some peculiar way for his protection. "May the great spirits guide me to my true self?" as a self-prayer the words floated from his lips as a whisper of wind. Looking back at the child he could see she was different from everyone else. But he would have to wait till he could really understand why this was so.

Darius jolted form his slumber sweating extensively from the dream. His time with Lilith provided him with a sense of his true nature and identity. To explore the dark world of the dead brought out his great need for power. Strolling through the soulless world of waste and despair his entire gifts were released. Longing for the endless pit his ancestors relinquished dark knowledge of these studies to the new overlord of the world.

Wave after wave of dark power and history flowed straight through him. At the times he even felt a loss of his very identity to this insurgence. By the final touch something seemed to be extremely wrong within the world of the living he could not place his finger on the problem but it bothered him for some reason. Looking about his quarters with blurred eyes he continuously tried to contemplate the pestering question in his mind. As his servant arrived with his morning meal he could not release it. So he decided to let the answer come to him on its very own accord.

Days have been ventured and Michael was push to the point of extreme exhaustion. As the day break showed its face he could not tell the length of earth he has traveled. The world has appeared to lose all semblance of it in the way of marking the terrain with identifiers.

Having made an account of his supplies revealed he had maybe a day or so left to go on. Although these hellish winds whipped across his face he went on with the journey. Deep within his mind the darkest doubt crept inside like a hunting bear after its prey. Nothing has ever pushed the soul of a man as much as a spirit walks. Mid-day approached the distant horizon revealing a welcomed mercy. Far before him laid the sight of a forest he never knew existed especially in this part of the world. Yet how could this be within a wasteland.

"Grandfather do you see what I see or are my eyes deceiving me?" with extreme wonder setting forth in his tone Michael examines the site before him.

"Yes boy that is the next step of your journey. You need not fear anything in those woods that lay before us."

Reaching the outskirts of the trees they welcomed the cooling shade of the area. As the old coyote ventured on he guided the boy to a small stream to ease the dryness of his thirst. The cool fluid was a wonderful sensation renewing the weary soul within him. Doubt gently subsided to a short meal of dried fruit and nuts he had gathered.

After a short rest he pressed on toward the setting sun. dusk fell rather quickly to reveal an unexpected glimmer of light from a fire just set. Thunderous drumming preceded a moment later, chants floated on the night air like an inviting friend. But Michaels eyes looked to grandfather for a sign of warning yet he saw none.

For some unknown reason his companion was nowhere to be seen. So Michael took it upon himself to the edge of light for a quick glance. To his wonderment grandfather was within a village of peculiar people who has appeared to continue in an ancient way of living with few modern conveniences. They live as though locked in time of the old ways where technology has no meaning here.

Peering at grandfather approaching a modestly young man dressed in some type of monk's robe that has not been seen since a long way back in history. As far as he could tell they seem to know each other laughing and having a conversation of sorts. Before he could understand their eyes met and he was beckoned to enter the village where they stood. Timidly he moved forward into the fire light so he may be seen by all who inhabit the village. Few people paid him any attentions as some type of rituals were being carried out.

By the time Michael reaches the tow of them he noticed the young man's welcoming smile. Feeling grandfather place a reassuring hand on his shoulder the tension subsided. "You have little to fear here my friend. I have been waiting for you Michael." the emblems on his robe seemed so familiar to a distant memory. Yet Michael could not place where he has seen them before. All that he could think of was the ceremony taking place a few yards behind him by the villagers.

"What is this place?" before any real thought the words rushed from his lips. He could barely believe a place like this could even exist in such a time.

"This is the true beginning of the life you were meant to live. You are one of a cadre know to us as the chosen who were destined to save the world from the darkness. All you knew of life will be changed forever you young friend." with a profound appearance on the man's face Michael could realize this to be one of many changes for his very existence in the world.

Nathan stood next to a crumpled wall that lay as a

temporary cover from anyone who could pose a threat to the group. His very heart pounded inside his chest like a thundering drum resonating through time. As the others were left behind to wait for their leader to return. Moments before this venture someone projected the idea of finding a transport of some kind that could take everyone out of the city. While some agreed few dared to take on the task of searching with an overwhelming fear of what was outside to greet them. Frustrated with their lack of courage he personally volunteered to go at least he could have a little while to think. All the worries of the group clouded his mind for any sense of peace.

Being out here gave no semblance of mercy to his mind or any thought that the humanity of man could survive the attack. His blood raced inside his tense muscles and fringed nerves. A sudden glimpse of a truck appeared there best chance to escape, but he realized a second vehicle would be needed for all of them to be carried out of here. Yet above it all would they even start to work at all for them.

Rushing back to his sanctuary in a need to reveal his findings of the scouting mission. Turning the corner Nathan found himself facing one of those grotesque creatures from the days before. Instantly wanting to flee something deep within awakened for a fight that has not been felt before. Even though he could only see one there was a likely chance others may be close by to attack as well. All he could feel within was what could be considered as being engulfed by some type of warrior spirit. Fire burned in his stomach churning over and over like a volcano ready to erupt. Before Nathan could even realize he launched forward with uncanny speed. In an instant the gap between the two collapsed with a battle that ensued. Fiercely the two struck each other with powerful blows hoping the one before them would shatter. Grabbing his opponent Nathan finally felt a dark flame unleash itself through his hands.

Shrieking in agony the creature attempted to break free with no success. In mere seconds all that was left were bones and ashes. Quenching the inferno seemed a struggle in itself, yet a peace somehow enveloped him soothing away the fire. Looking at his hands with shock as well as wonderment broke forth as to what just happened. Maybe the lady will reveal its source in time, still at this time I have to make sure this power does not get out of control.

As he hurried back to the others Nathan had to consider what to say about what he found. Noticing all that has come to pass he noticed they were going the right way. As he walked into the building Beatrice stood at the door with an awkward smile he has never seen. She appeared to be someone with a secret waiting to be told.

“You woke up today huh!” with a whisper as though stating a new fact for what has happened. Then softly she giggled like the happy child she was. Yet I couldn’t understand what she was talking about. “Beatrice please tell me what you mean by me waking up?” taking a quick glance around hoping no one could hear their conversation.

“I mean you woke up just before you came back. I can see and feel the real you who was asleep inside just waiting to be called upon. The lady even told me that I would know when it happens.” letting the words just spill forth as any child would do with a great deal of honesty that actually left me in awe of her lack of fear now.

CHAPTER 8

Dawn broke as Michael stepped from the dwelling provided by the villagers as a place of honor. As he peered out unto the rising sun the shadows of his new companion met his eyes.

Much to his bewilderment he could not tell if he was even moving. Approaching the man he began to hear a slight chant that seemed to flow from the man's lips. Finally seeing the man's face sent a shock through his very soul as nothing in his life has done before. To look upon the oud-rah's face seemed to be white in tone like a deep fear entered his own body. I had no words to even try and break him from this state of being in such a concentrated form of meditation. "My friend will you be alright?" Michael's words were a sheepish attempt at reaching him. Yet he supposedly understood the young man must be in some form of prayer in his people's way.

Trying to ultimately fathom this complex circumstance that has lead him to the present destination. In spite of all these changes Michael explored his inner soul in a ritual of his own taught to him by an old medicine man in his village a long time ago. Though the day began bright and calm darkness seemed to absorb the peace which flowed through the township. After completing the morning ritual one of the townsman came to retrieve m. as he approached I hoped he had news of their oud-rah, but looking past him I could see there was no change do his demeanor. This left me to wonder what this day would bring for his spirit walk.

When this boy revealed his face I was awe struck by the

scar across his jaw spreading past his throat to the left shoulder. Locking eyes with mine he gently beckoned me to follow him into the village. Without hesitating I fell into step as he led me into the center most part of the village unto a greatly adorned hut which I could hear the echo of more drumming and chanting. As I entered everything seem to stop for some unknown reason to me while all the eyes of the people inside fell upon my entrance. One man stood out amongst them all although a small man. Even to look at him I realized that he must be the leader of them all.

"Welcome Michael." with a kind smile he stood up as each sinewy fiber of muscle flexed. To even believe a man of his age could have no sign of degradation to his physique was amazing. My mind was a torrent of questions of this man and his people who have escaped all notice from the modern world.

Looking deep within his eyes wisdom could be seen that surpassed any recollection. My greatest curiosity caused me to examine every line of his face, yet the only sign of his age was the streaks of gray down the center of his hairline. "The oud-rah requested we speak while he travels in the other side of life. So please sit with us for the possibility he may be a while."

Slowly making my way through the crowd I sat in a space the old man had set for me. Moments after getting comfortable some of the young ladies entered with a wide assortment of foods such as meats and fruit I have never seen before. I could only contemplate this as a common morning feast for these people.

"You are an honored quest so out of our hearts we present to you a feast of brotherhood." placing a hand on my shoulder he reached out his other hand to the air. Making a gesture which seemed quiet foreign to me as he made a comment. "To the spirits of the ages we welcome the lost brother chosen by time to the coming battle." in the time he spoke the words I noticed the oud-rah entered the hut to join the feast. But with all the hustle and bustle Michael could tell something was happening by the look on his face.

Hovering amidst the borders of nightmare and life one could only imagine the shift of power. The very ripple of its release could be felt by Lilith like a distant memory that she would rather bury away forever. "How could this be?" speaking softly to the emptiness of her domain. Looking back upon the past when she was roaming the world without a care. Persistently tormenting simple village folk with a display of merciless power. Yet recalling the sensation of such a power that trapped her in this place so long ago. They shall be found and this time we shall rule over the world. Who has the gift which is the birthright of earths chosen guardians?

"Darius must be informed of the temporal shift that I have felt. If one is stopped then the threat shall be over." as she entered the very chamber of scrolls which had the little information of those wretched bastards who raises the fires of hells hatred.

Seeking the reprieve of all the reports coming in from his military advisors about all the conflicts with those beasts. Darius ventures to the catacombs of darkness where Volta awaits with further understanding of the scrolls. Yet his mind continues to wander unto the sickening feeling which seemed to vibrate through his entire being. How can his soul overcome this internal conflict?

"Must I suffer the madness of my dark kingdom? Memories of the past confounds of my mind like a dark tidal wave that wishes to crash upon me. Maybe Lilith will ease my confusion upon the next meeting in that other world. But for now I have other things to consider."as he turned a corner from which few know of in this place.

Suddenly seeing Volta at the fountain of reflection brought anticipation for a good word. Although a look of consternation was apparently revealed upon his face. What has it that has caused him to be doubtful of his skills I have never seen him in such a befuddled state. Has he found something within the scrolls which demanded further thought only time will tell?

"Volta!! Why have you requested this place for our meeting? Have you discovered anything of interest?" with the tone of evil determination resonating the sound of his voice through the basilica shaped room. As he turned to look upon his master with hunched shoulders it was undeniable to witness the fear and sadness within his dark eyes. Has the studies of those ancient scrolls reveal a dark path or was it just the feelings that surged at the beckoning of his name. Only time will reveal when the news is cast like the die of fate which few seem to survive.

Sitting within the village Michael became very perplexed at the look upon the oud-rah's face. As though he has been shaken to the very core of his being. Only asking may seem a bit ridiculous for me but it is the only way I may learn the answer I am seeking. Even thinking of what to ask was difficult to fathom at this moment.

"What is your question Michael?" with calm eyes staring at him he felt shaken himself at the response. How could he have known what was going on in his mind. "Well!" still hesitating as a child before a parent he began to sink within himself. Desperately trying to find the words to the question within him.

"I see much you do not understand young man." with a calm demeanor was that of a tree calm with deep patient roots. But can he truly see things I am thinking.

As memories of his youth trickled into his mind. Oh how I miss those days when life was innocent and I could venture into the world. As a child he would walk along the rivers after a strong rain overflowing the banks. His mother would know and chase him back to town. Yet it always was unnerving how she was able to find him when no one else could.

"Well boy she could see with more than her natural eyes. She bore you in her heart every moment of the day. But my sight is that of greater calling few can really understand. We have much work to do a little time which to complete the task so we must hurry!" searching the oud-rah's eyes showed a great sense of urgency which I did not notice before. As though all humanity counted on what needs to be done. Rushing from the hut the two made haste to the towers of the keepers in which to reveal the purpose of his calling. For the eyes of death search for its reign.

Soba amidst his cohorts a shadows blood ritual was being held. Each placing their own portion of blood to conjure a forsaken entity. "Whose time has come for a new lord of the counsel? He has outlived his usefulness and his family must pass completely from existence." swiftly his cold words spread like the chill of death gripping a man from within his soul. None of the others dare look at his face for fear of the dark eyes attempting to penetrate their thoughts. Fear was the greatest threat to them all for Soba's cold vengeance.

Setting all their spiritual potency of a wish for power or at least the knowledge on how to rid them of all who stand in their future. As the voices set there rhythm of summoning the myriad. As there castings stir the depths of the mixture of hatred, the flame rises from within like a demons rage that one dares not awaken.

"Who dares summon me from the depths of hell fire itself? For few are worthy to stand before me. How is your cause worth my attention?" as the voice crosses the very boundaries of human and beastly sounds. Suddenly the essence of a dark nature fills the very room as if to choke the life from the world. Instantly within the darkness of the room a figure appeared. Hunched over as if a withered man battered by age.

Although to look upon his eyes the purest form of hatred was revealed to all. Without thought one of the members stood in defiance to this new presence. His blade within his grasp to find off the demonic form. As a flash the myriad struck separating the man to his very bowels. Fear subdued the others from the sight to believe this may work. Although a great deal of apprehension remained within their minds.

Setting on a quick pace Nathan begins the trek outside the city hoping not to be followed by anyone or thing. Everyone was stressed to continue the pace which he set for them all. It was highly unlikely that any normal human could keep up with the speed he was traveling but nothing could be helped to stop what must be done.

Accustomed to the ease of society many were not able to hold up for very long with him. Instantly a sound of horror the sounds of grinding metal and screeching tires following at a distance. At once the group examined the surrounding area trying to locate the origin of the sounds that were coming. Not wanting to waste his time looking around Nathan focused on his plan. Setting his foot to the gas lead the run of vehicles away from the noise. As they made haste the first blasts of the cannons commenced. Attempting not to be struck by the shells all the vehicles separated hoping it would minimize the chances of anyone getting hit by the blasts.

As his blood began to boil, he could feel the sensation of a rising tide of flames engulf his very soul again. Without a word he turns the vehicle into a spin causing it to stop dead in its tracks. Nathan steps out to face them as the explosions of rockets continue to be fired upon the group.

Stepping forward like a man who has lost his mind with all that is happening. Raising his hands a shimmer of light formed upon the surface of his hands. As this started to going on the others stared in wonder of what is to come of this event fearing they may lose the one they considered the leader of the group since he knew the way they needed to go. Bursting forth as a wild torrent the flames consumed the air before him laying waste to all the munitions in flight of the directions of them all. None could understand what just happen but they took it as a miracle striking them with awe.

Each dared not approach where he stood fearing that they may be consumed as well. He peers upon the horizon which stands the hunters of men. Built upon the machines and training designed for nothing but destruction and death to any that may challenge the new order. The soldiers halted as they recalculated their means of approach of the people attempting to escape the mandate from the corporate officials.

"Sir what the hell was that? I have never in my life seen a single man have such ability." eyes left wide with fear to even get close to the group. The military vehicles halted their pursuit as a single officer sets his gaze to his enemy. Moordra ventures his mind on the past when men knew of such abilities that have long been absent to the world. Though he appeared as a modern man he was far from such truth that few dare to know. Emerging from his personal vehicle to walk upon the ground before his men. Surveying all that has any true meaning in his dark mind not to give any ground unto the man he would continue to pursue. Suddenly he cocks his head to the side as though measuring an unseen danger while a smirk crossed his face. "Men fall back to the city I will handle this alone." setting his words upon such a grotesque tone.

"But sir we are not authorized to leave them alive. You know our orders...." the words spilled forth as the soldier shook with immense fear of his commanding officer. "Leave now!! You can let me worry about orders and protocols. I must deal with this one alone as I stated before." without the slightest hesitation Moordra presented his pistol aimed upon the one who challenged him and fired a round executing him in sight of all the others.

Without further contestation all the vehicles pulled away

leaving the commander behind. Alone he began to consider his worthy opponent as he released his gun belt from his waist. As a demon of habit he preferred an honorable form of combat that could be done hand to hand. But having such a craving can cause un-needed time lost when the outcome is left in the hands of fate. Moordra's lust for blood was only outweighed by the desire to test a worthy foe that would consider his personal attention. Yet it takes a madness of a fighter to take such a gamble to challenge the unknown combatant. Taking his time to measure the extent of the blood fire of the one standing before him.

Nathan stands his ground to the last soldier left behind to guard the others from whatever may come. Yet he can't understand why this one stayed. This makes no sense for one to stand without help in case he needs assistance. Confused by the bravado of this man he took little concern for any possible threat.

A strange sensation he has never felt began to flow over him that he has never known before. Looking around the area suddenly changed to lush green woodland as the wasteland was washed away. Daring all he called out for the others who flocked to him in haste greatly worried for Beatrice's safety. The fear in all the faces explained the mood of the groups' thoughts. As he was preparing to speak a soft voice called out from behind him. "Hello Nathan! You have no need to fear in this place it is a neutral plain of existence. I have brought you hear to protect you from Moordra." with such a beauty she spoke as the lady from before in the dream.

Yet in the back of Nathan's mind wonder why he needed protection from whoever that was left behind. "Actually you did need to be protected for good reason. Moordra has a power that supersedes yours right now my dear. But you will be ready in a little time for the war to come you just have to be with the others." as confusion spread extensively in his mind as he began to truly wonder what was happening in the world.

"What do you mean a war? The world is already in a state of war and chaos haven't you seen that from here. I am just hoping to survive it and get to a refuge away from the madness like I was told, I am no warrior meant for conflict."

"Then follow the child for she knows the way unto the keeper's towers who will assist you. Her destiny shall begin there. Many have been waiting for her arrival for an ion." with a look of utter joy and mercy apparent on her face they knew the importance of the child's future.

Yet my mind wondered as we dwelled in this dimensional sanctuary as I recalled all the madness of the past few days. It is all a complete blur of chaos. Although I am grateful we have escaped the city of shadows as grandpa once called it when I was a child. My thoughts go to that one man who stayed behind as the other military men left back to the city.

Deep within my own flesh I could feel the cold fire brush against me from inside of my own soul that I have never felt that before like a warning of fear and danger. Last time my body had felt like that was in my childhood facing my first mountain lion. Somehow like magic someone comes to my aid just in the nick of time. Every time I was in danger someone was there like a guardian angel, was there a purpose for the protection of his life. Although I am still curious what the reason was to keep him alive and what has come of the soldier that stood alone in the open field.

Moordra stood as his eyes lay witness to the victims he has chosen to withdraw from existence vanished. While he watched he knew the temporal beings had intervened as they have since the beginning of the war for dominion of all who have existed in this world to be there pawns to play with as they choose. "The likeliness that any have a choice in the matter is a complete fantasy. We were all born to this and nothing can change it." as Moordra stands ranting to himself moments after the one whom he yearned to fight disappeared.

"Calm yourself Moordra this shall get you nowhere in the cause." as the voice seem to come from within as a small guiding voice. With a sudden shock he remembered the sound of the voice.

"Neil?" with a sense of relief flooding in his mind.

"Yes it is me." the answer echoed in his mind like a ripple of water after a stone has been tossed into it depth.

"It has been so long since I have heard you speak to me. Why have you been so silent for the past century?" with a sense of gratitude washing over him. Memories from the past which Neil would always share his guidance in the deeds he was to accomplish.

"Though you may not hear me I am always watching over you my boy. Since I have given you the name you have lived by I have watched over you like a father." all sense of being human going to the wayside Moordra stands with a twinge of pride welling in his chest.

"A father?! You have been so much more to me than that. You are a God to me Neil creating the new me from a broken shell of a man into a spectral weapon. The growth I have achieved as a sub-sapien was much more than I expected." with little care for his emotions he smirked in satisfaction of seeing the release of an easy fight.

Michael seems to feel the days pass like a blur wondering what he is waiting for while the village continues to go on. The town was a constant buzz of activity from the fight training to the weapons making. Even the kitchens were busy with the preparation of meals all day long. Setting his mind to relax one of the member of the village approached dressed in ceremonial war armor. To look upon it shows the humble nature of the people yet there was an underlined ability for destruction of an enemy that he faces. Even this young man appears to have strength beyond the normal capacity of any man outside the village.

"Well brother I see you could use some company for a moment. Would you consider we speak of what is to come?" as Michael looked upon him he considered what they would speak about as they sat below the trees of amber colored leaves."

"I wish to tell you brother; I am honored to be in your presence. We have been waiting a great time for the return of the chosen as we have been here." perplexed by the young man's comments of his arrival, Michael prepared his mind for what is to truly come of this turn of events.

"What did you call me? I have never heard someone call me that other than my grandfather." confusion crossing both of them was facing trying to understand each other's position in the events to come. His whole world is changing in a way he really doesn't understand.

"There is a legend passed down the endless generations of my people to a group of people which are to come upon the rise of the oud-rah." his mind raced as he attempted to perceive what he was told.

"Tell me more of this legend I am very intrigued. For I have much to learn while I am here preparing for is coming." they both lean into the trunk of the tree which seemed to give them a great sense of comfort. Mysteriously Michael felt the tree seemed to form around his body like the arms of a mother cradling her child.

"Do not fear brother this tree is an ancient relic which has guarded the village from the beginning of our existence. When we sit before her she speaks to us as we are comforted." now a sense of true amazement filled his soul with these people and this place. He was starting to believe he has left the real world and entered a dreamlike world left to fantasy.

"Tell me more of the legend? But first what is your name?" waiting for a reply Michael could feel himself go deeper into a relaxed state where his eyes closed as if going into slumber. At a certain point of the decent of a pure slumber he could feel himself become part of the trees soul.

"Welcome Michael! I will guide you on the legend of this world. But walk with me for a while we have much to talk about." as he searched about he could see a lush plain similar to the places he had seen as a child.

"Who are you and where am I? This place seems so familiar to me." searching for a sign of movement Michael feels himself ease into a peace as a women appears like an angel from the horizon of trees.

"I am a Sharilyka who shield my children from the corruption of this world. You are destined to be part of a long remembered prophecy foretold from the first magi's in existence. I will bare unto you the past and what may come if any of you are lost before the awakening." Michael stood in awe and wonder of this prophecy she speaks of, but what more could he do but sit upon the ground and listen like a child was being told a story.

"It's beginning was some time ago to your peoples standards but a sheer moment for myself. A threshold was set about five hundred to a thousand years ago. When society was in the stages of change caused by the darkest of forces that hungered for nothing more than power. There leaders hiding in the shadows close your eyes and I shall reveal the time of madness." as he closed his eyes again within the dream he could feel a shift around him, quickly snapping his eyes open quickly he noticed the field has gone and a city stands before him.

Society stood in flux as he watched countless people pass in fear of a militant patrol lead by a fearsome beauty who evil was to know boundless infliction upon any who stood before her agenda. Just seeing the furousity as she dispatches those who she chooses to suffer a worse fate than death itself. "What is her name? She seems to be one person who has let power overwhelm her very soul." as he stared at the woman's composure with all that surrounds her. She revealed a distinct distaste for a world she lived upon. How can anyone ever really live in such a way?

"Her name is Zeth, leader of the elite guard who sole purpose is to control anyone who may pose a threat to her master. Her very soul was corrupted by a shadow of your own history that few dare speak of anymore. None dare to challenge her less they meet a fate worse than humans would want to imagine." Michael looked in awe as he attempted to visualize that such a person was full of such hatred of others. Still there is a struggle that is so hidden from all, but to look upon her eyes it is so apparent.

"You see it don't you?" with a great shock Michael looked upon the lady to see if she knew his thoughts or did he speak it out loud. "You cannot hide your thoughts here it is a place of joined minds. Everything is shared here with me not even your destiny for I see the trace in your blood sapien child. There is great power waiting to be unlocked from within you." he doesn't really understand what she means by the terms "sapien" but I guess time will reveal the truth. As he continued watching this so-called Zeth unleashes a new terror upon a new area as if time fast forwarded to a later time. Wearing a crimson overcoat opened to reveal an ancient blade accompanied by a large pistol with the look of being on the hunt.

"Does this woman have some great connection to the circumstances we are dealing with today?" with such wonder Michael searches for the truth of what he is seeing. Looking upon the spirit which seems to guide him through some distant history lost or hidden from the present society or what is left of it.

Blurring through the time which seems to pass before him he begins to understand the visions he has received in his dreams with more clarity. Yet there is still a question that lingers within the distance that he feels the answer is not ready to be delivered to his mind. Having seen the history of man Michael begins to return from this world unto his true sense of consciousness. Heavy is his heart for what the lady's last words she stated so he would remember that his greatest friend is linked to the purpose in-store for him.

Nathan awakens within the forest expecting to be somewhere in his home preparing himself for another day in the court. Although his eyes are met with the lush green of ageless trees that surround him like a great wall made to protect him and the others. Suddenly he realizes Beatrice is nowhere within sight. This began setting himself for near panic for the fact he feels responsible for her like a parent. "Oh shit! Now where did this kid run off too? She is so adventurous since we got here but compared to other girls she is so different. Must I be her guardian or can the lady choose someone else?" walking through as he does speaking his thoughts aloud. It has been a habit he has had since his youth.

"Nathan!" as soft as a feather falling the lady approaches with the semblance of a smile. His tension seems to relax once she approaches, yet he could never truly understand why. "You need not worry about the young girl she is by the lake with Cobble. He is a dear friend who has resided here for hundreds of countless years. I have confided in him about the many events that has happened in your world."

As they have walked by the great trees of splendid arrays of colors unlike any seen by the eyes of men. They softly speak of what has happened and what may come to occupy their minds in the needs of companionship. Finally reaching the lake he suddenly sees what appears to be a strange looking dog, yet its head is much larger than normal.

"Oh Nathan! Sorry I walked off I just saw this doggie and wanted to play since no one else wants to play with me. What's funny is he can actually talk to me. Just try it yourself talk to him and you'll see." with such oddities he thought what could be the harm in trying. Coming close he knelt down by the calm waters and attempted to speak with this so-called Cobble trying to understand more about this place. Many times he has seen places like this in his dreams but never realized that it could truly exist. Continuing to look about Nathan sets his mind at ease. He finally believes there is nothing to fear for any of them. Now is the time of contemplation of what will become of them all when they return to the world of darkest nightmare of reality.

CHAPTER 9

Michael wakes to a day fresh with understanding for where he must go. As he was barely walking out the door of the room he has been given awaited a young maid to care for him.

"May I prepare you anything my dear brother? I believe you may have a deep hunger after speaking with Gien." his mind raced when the name of the spirit he spoke to was mentioned. Yet it seemed so familiar like an ancient memory come to life once again. Suddenly a strange sensation engulfed his arm of which the markings lay like cold fire rushing to the surface. "What is happening to me? I feel something awakening in my very soul like an old familiar memory resurfacing. Do you know of this kind of feeling?" she looks upon him with gleeful splendor as he describes his change.

"Yes I do it is called the burning blood. Many of us have heard stories of few over the histories of our people that have this gift." hearing her words seem to bring a greater curiosity of his destiny and the path his future choices will take. Although he feels even more that it shall be a long dark road.

"Author! Can we speak a moment my old friend?" as the high keeper walked into the main hall of the records to confer with him about the present events.

"Yes Mirdan I am hearing you. What do you wish of me although I have an idea of what it may pertain too." having such a familiarity with one another they quip themselves for a bout of mental chest as they have all through the early years of their lives. "Well my old friend you think I am here for a story do you!" with a slight chuckle freeing itself from his lips. The mere smile alone portraying the game is afoot. Mirdan looks upon him testing the waters of Authors move to come.

"I am not you father and you are not a young boy. So tell me what have you come for then. I have much work to do." setting the scrolls upon the table he set his work to order. Detail upon detail he ponders the chosen's legend to know what must be done. "What are you searching for now? I have known you a long time and have never seen you so determined to find something as you are this moment." not even looking up he continues with his work. All intent on finding the breaking code to truly unlock the ancient abilities that lies within the chosen's blood.

"There is something I remember about the blood memory and the unleashing of their inner power." as Dan stares in awe how he considers the unleashing of the blood memory. Yet they both know all the chosen must be together so the ritual must be performed. Continuing his research Author looks upon the dais of Corinth who has described the details of unleashing the bloods abilities. For much of our lives we have tried to understand how to control this gift, but now we must unleash the unbridled ability that the chosen are born with. It seems the way is shown through the connection between them who were chosen by birthright and the koda's existence as a tool to awaken what is hidden in them all.

Nathan considers how all of them have escaped the dark world once again but considers the idea of the past. Of the simple pleasures of life in a modern world where no end seemed in sight just to have the simple comfort of a shower seemed like a dream now. His visions of a women he has never known in the office giving him a smile as they lived in a harmonious world or the apartment he wanted to share with her but who is she now and what has happened to her in the world that seem to end like a seductive nightmare come to reality.

He sits at the edge of the lake that stretches out before him like a still mirror on into eternity the trees reflecting there great majesty from a time long forgotten. The serenity of a soul can be found here again to the man who has lost his way. Looking upon the waters he sees the face of another man to represent the past of his bloodline to some kind of place he has never seen before.

"WHAT THE FUCK IS HAPPENING TO ME! I DON'T SEE WHO YOU ARE AND WHERE I AM!" he yells to the point of madness looking at the reflection within the waters looking back at him.

As he stands before the image he feels a presents behind him like something he has never felt before in his life time. Turning slowly to face the possible entity waiting to be noticed by his eyes. "Look son you are not the only one who has wondered of their origin when they come here. You are a represent a long line of guardians from the sapien world long lost centuries ago due to the hunger for power. Now you stand before the darkness that has consumed our people and world which is continuously seeking to overthrow all who stands against them. You have been chosen to be a light in the darkness for the lost." his face seems to examine the man's face with a curiosity of a child for the fact that he looked so familiar to him.

"Who are you? I feel like I know you from a distant memory of my life. But how can you be here. Do I know you?" his soul stirred with constant wonder of the man or entity that has taken form from a nether world or past vision from a long lost memory. "You are part of my bloodline young man and I have long waited for you to arise in my stead for such a time as this. I am Sebastian! I have come to provide you with a glimpse of the past which our people have lost since we have come to this world and have become a part of this society that now lay dying from madness."

By some reason of respect Nathan sits with him by the shoreline speaking of what has happened and what may come to pass is he does nothing. Like an ancient grandfather sharing stories of life lessons needing to be told. Hours have passed by with little recognition to their eyes as endless histories is passed to him by Sebastian waking a longing to do what he believes is right upon the path he was given in his true youth. "I tell you this for the morrow you will return to your world and begin the journey meant for you to travel and a friend waits for you at the tower of the keepers. They will awaken you further for the battle yet to come upon the world and the darkness will stand against you attempting to control the hearts and mind of many. You are part of the key to overcome them but most of all the child shall be the greatest part of this whole war. Guard her with your life she will be the greatest light to all who is truly lost for she was born for a purpose of ultimate manifestation to the glory of our people and the humans." confusion crossed his face as the words flowed like a wild river from his lips.

"How will all this come to pass? I am not the bravest man out there surely someone else can care for her. What is she because I know she is more than she appears to be?" hoping against all odds for some kind of answer or clarity to what the child Beatrice truly is to be.

As the twilight spread across the lake in a shimmer of light from the strange moon that shown overhead. He sat alone of a moment trying to think of all the things that may come to pass in the coming journey as they return to the world as they knew it. When shall he become more than he truly is and what is next for this transformation of his soul. Beatrice holds the key to all that is coming and now Nathan considers the fact that he must protect her. Does he even believe that he is worthy enough to complete the task laid upon his shoulders. All he can do now is admire the beauty that lie before him upon the waters and hope that all shall be well with the girl.

Returning to the camp with everyone that was brought here rested given by the spirit of this world. All were asleep but Beatrice she seemed a little scared by the night so I set myself beside her to ease her fear. As I leaned against the stump of a tree she rested her head upon my lap and seemed a little at peace by my presence. I sat and watched her fall into the land of dreams as grandfather would say all children went to see awaiting friends. Within a matter of minutes I could feel the waning rest call upon me which great fervor so I gave in to a well needed sleep hoping that when I wake I will be home and all this would just be a long forgotten nightmare. Yet time will tell what shall come to pass with the next day's events I can only hope that life will return to normal. Although a good night's rest should do all of us a world of good.

Michael follows the oud-rah up the steps leading to the height of the mountain which lead to the tower of the keep. His mind a whirlwind of wonder what is to come of the ascension of the stair to all that may lay hold within? The view of the world below stretched for endless miles in all directions, yet he wonder how all this can lay hidden from the known world. What kind of power can ever be imagined in life do such a great thing?

"Where are you taking me now? It seems that I have been exposed to such wonder I have never seen in my entire life." just setting his mind to anything new revelation of who he is to be or what he is to do next.

As he sits in his chamber contemplating the darkness he will wrought upon the world he seeks his own personal solace upon the night. All the news he has received from the scrolls Darius hungers for the power of the artifact that Volta has revealed unto him. Where can it be and how much power shall he gain by it being in his possession? The night consumes him like a dark comforting blanket of darkness looking out at the night sky as fires still rage in the distance from the battles with those beasts who roam his streets.

All he can imagine is how this has come to pass as he seeks to know every little bit of information of the activities of the world. This must be someone's plan to unravel his domination of the world. But who? As times before he drinks his elixir and slowly sets himself to sleep and maybe find himself some moment where his personal torment does not hound him in the world of dreams or spirits where every he may go.

Nathan and the others wake upon the new day hidden from sight not far from the city views. Knowing now all the events were no dream but a dark reality and remembering the task set before him to complete. Setting the group in order to continue their trek unto the towers which Beatrice apparently is the only one who knows its location. Walking endless hours upon the scorching daylight sun upon the highway.

"Hey fearless leader we need to rest. Can you seem to find some idea of where we may find some sense of safety out here or are you lost?" he keeps himself from a momentary spark of anger realizing that it would be a good idea to take a time of rest. So he searches the surrounding area and finds a convenient shelter in a highway station no more than a couple hundred yards away where they may find food and water for all of them to re-supply. Plus a time to attend to the injured will be necessary for them to keep up on.

Seemingly Nathan has been on edge since the return of the forest unwilling to accept what has come of his life and to be called the leader was a burden he did not think he could bare alone. Upon a whispered breath he calls the only name that would have been a great ally "Michael I really wish you were here my old friend." as though lost to the thought of saying what was on his mind Beatrice smiles as she tugs on his shirt. He looks upon such a child and could not believe that she was so peaceful in what has happened.

"He is waiting sir. Don't worry so much." confusion surged his soul like an unknown wave wondering how she knows such a thing about him when he was not even sure his good friend was even alive with such a darkness befalling the world. As they make the approach to the station the take a quick glance around to make sure there is not possible threat to them staying for a while to rest and re-supply. I minor sense of peace gave them hope that they would not find any type of danger from the beasts he encountered in the city.

Dust laden countertops and ravaged shelves seem to be the norm since the attack upon the world but there seem to be something of use so they collected what they could and took a few hours rest within while some of the group went about attending to the injured.

Nathan stepped outside to take a moment to himself from the madness of what everyone is doing. All seemed lost upon a hope for help he knew nothing about led by a child that seemed even more bizarre than most children he has ever seen. What is she really? Contemplating the possibilities of her existence he could tell she was much more than human but only time will tell what is to come of her. Now is the time of riddles that no one could solve with the greatest of minds searching the answers?

Michael looks out form the towers at the world beyond thinking what he is to do as the oud-rah approaches from the stairs that lay behind him. He is lost in the thoughts of the past when he and Nathan used to play. Most of all he remembers the fights they got into over the years guarding each other like brothers. With all that has happened he can only hope he is okay till they see each other again. Yet the idea lingers if his dear friend would survive the journey to the towers and safety.

One memory comes to mind when they used to fight over a girl that seemed to have all of their attention. He chuckles to himself on the blood they shed for her and found out she didn't like either of us. I guess that is nothing but a fond memory now to his friendship with Nathan.

"Ah the memories of the past they are such a comfort to those whom you hold dear. I see you worry of your friend but I know he is on his way here with a group of others and a special person we have been waiting for. You and he have such a destiny that with the others will bring a change if you succeed. The prophecy is been with us for such a long time and it seems that it may come to pass if the one of importance arrives here unharmed." Michael looks at him with such bewilderment at what has been said of the prophecy. Many times he has heard from these druids of a prophecy but has taken little notice of it till now. How can such an old prediction lay such hold on their lives that all else would be of little importance.

While his thoughts wonder he thinks of the people he met in the village and how they prepare for a battle that seems to be unknown with the arrival of the oud-rah. Will they also be a deciding factor of all that is to come? To have trained with them lets him learn that there entire life was hidden from the world to contain the spirit of a warrior. They all have a power untainted by the very world that has changed all the hearts of man to stand for something greater than them. His people have been the same way losing the spirit of a warrior that has been the root of their own existence.

With all that has happened he now believes that it was a sleeping wolf waiting to hunt once again. "Can you tell me more of these prophecies and the people which are to fulfill them? What is it we are waiting for and how shall we be able to stand against the darkness that is coming. You seem to have all been preparing for these events to happen. I can only wonder what shall come to pass as the world seems to burn waiting for us to take action."

He falls back into the memories when he was with his people taking the ceremony of manhood at his thirteenth year of life. Having to stand alone within the woods with little more than a spear to defend himself against the animals. Nathan was with him as he went through this rite of passage. Seeing the movement of the trees swing in the breeze just brought a serene wonder to our eyes. Yet it has been so long since I have felt such a peace that encompassed my very soul.

"Ah! The memories of youth long lost to the world and time but held by those who have lived them. Life is such a journey young man that we all must take some are for the good and some turn us evil. Yet all must make the journey and discover the role they shall play in the world. We have a journey to make as well for a needed ally who lies a distance across the waters. I know he will be a great factor in the need to change this tide of darkness." as Michael looked upon him he can see the distance stare he lay upon the setting horizon of the sun. Who could this person be and what importance does he have to the coming struggle. As though we are looking for a warrior of unknown destiny. A Lancelot for the round table is the only thing he could imagine this man to be.

"Who is this man we are to seek out and what purpose is he to fulfill in this battle. What is his name?" more questions was aroused in his mind to think of such a person would be vital to assist in this fight. How long will this journey take us to complete. I am just curious because I thought we had to be here for the others arrival." the oud-rah contemplated all he has said and seemed to be in a state of concentration of the journey of an inner thought he was not revealing yet. A man if he could be called that of few words that hold great importance to all who listen. Now I see the strength within this one man who has been given the duty of guiding us through this time. So much rides on this prophecy he speaks of but will they live up to the demands needed.

"The man's name is what you wish to know ah lad! He is the descendent of a long warrior tribe that predates the people you met in the village. His ancestor was there at the first battle of the dark battle against the dark lords. He is not even human but the blood of a race long forgotten by the likes of men. The power his blood holds almost equals that of the chosen so we must find him. It will be a journey into the darkest part of this world men dare not go for fear of what may become of them." looking upon the oud-rah Michaels mind began to race at the possibility of ever finding this man. Could such a task be achieved in such a short time? " When will this journey begin my friend. For we already have little time to search for such a man."

As the dusk approached they considered there plan for the journey and the number of others that must go. The our-rah described the extent of the journeys dangers and what is expected when they find this Damian. The supplies have been set and all will commence in mere hours for them to go east for the dark waters forest. They walk upon the shadows to let no other know they are leaving to find this man that he deems necessary. They know that this may be the first test of their spirits in this long journey to which the outcome will not be known. We can just hope that this man chooses to join our cause. Now we head unto the mystery of this conflict the only wonder at this moment is if this man even exists anymore.

The group traveled through the briars vain behind the towers as the moon rose into view. Sounds arose about them friend creatures that Michael has never heard before as though they have come from the darkest pit of evil. "What is that sound? I have never heard anything like that before in my life." the oud-rah looked upon him and motioned him to be silent as they ventured through the area. His eyes scanning the area like a hawk to be sure that they are not being followed by anything or anyone.

During a night march all of them were in total agreement to stay silent as though all of them were aware of what was in the area in the fact of danger. His heart seems to thump in his ears like thunder with the stain of what is out there. Without warning some large creature burst out before them with a sense of madness. It almost looked like a bear but the scales upon the ridge of its back seem to show the difference within the hair on its body. As the warriors pounced upon the beast attack they seem to know what they were dealing with. Having seen the lack of fear for any type of conflict. Seeing them move with such speed seem to be un-human the streak of the blades and spears striking the from all sides like lightning. Just to watch such movements seemed unbelievable by any human means but now anything seems possible since the world has changed in such a short amount of time.

Having to stand there seemed a waste of his presence but the oud-rah held a hand before me beckoning me not to interfere. Watching so closely he noticed him raise a hand towards the beast and it became encompassed by a sphere of smoke like power stopping it from moving to harm any of them. Though it struggled it was of little effect the trap appeared to shrink as the beast lay within like into a void of existence no one has seen before. Then like it started the danger was gone so suddenly.

CHAPTER 10

Soba sits in his private chamber contemplating all that is happening within the plans of the League and seeing a way to dispatch the leader of the council. His heart black with hatred for any who deems themselves his better waits as patient as a grave for the events to come. A rap echoes upon his door rousing him from his thoughts of conquest. "Enter" with a foul his he deems the disruptor to set forth unto his presence. His mind a raging whirlwind of vial filth to any who may come into conflict with his plans to rule the council.

Looking at the books that litter his shelves remind him of a time of his life when all was simple before the new leader was announced when he felt he was truly a leading role for the group. Now all he sees is the betrayal left upon his family by Darius with the death of his father which no one's was found responsible. As he himself looked into it he found signs that Darius may be to blame for his father were the leading contender for control of the league. He could see the figure of a man who was in the service of the council bringing him a message sealed by the ancient crest of one of his own personal guard. With haste he approached the man and grabbed the letter from his hand and beacons the servant to leave with wretched annoyance for being disturbed.

As the servant left he tore open the letter and began to see the report of his servant: My lord we have made progress in our endeavors to overthrow the Darius. Our creation has force many of his defenses back. They have no idea the origin of the creatures so we are prevailing as planned." Soba gave himself a moment of revelry yet he made every attempt not to show signs of it on his face. As he prepared for a night of his own choosing for the arrival of one of the concubines which were in his service as a member of the league. But he had one in particular that he deemed his favorite of all the woman. She was a vile as he was in her soul who feared nothing let alone death.

Moments later she entered to his approval a figure of dark desire that would let her soul unleash all men's desire. He approaches her like an animal at the hunt of a prey yet she does not step away. Standing her ground she reached out to him seductively pulled him close passionately kissing his lips as though she could love him. Removing the robe from his shoulders exposing the flesh beneath covered in the scars she left the last time she came to pleasure him. While his heart is as the blackest of all that could be imagined he would let himself be the animal of nature as he let his dark desires loose upon her body. All manner of pain and pleasure was indulged as Soba spent hours with her to his minds content.

Looking upon her bare breast heaving from the time they have spent seemed to unleash a greater sense of euphoria from their sexual encounter that he has never felt before. His mind would fade into the freedom of thought that all was right for him even if it was just for a moment. Continuing to stare his mind returned to his dark intentions of destroying Darius and his control of the league. She looked upon him and could tell that Soba was his dark self as always with little else to care for as much as she wanted to have him love her. Though she was a concubine she had a fondness for his lust for power that lay evident in their encounters that none of the other members seem to show in all the time she has been in the league's hold. She then dressed herself and left by his command with an emptiness he could only fill, so exiting the door she contains herself from the pains of not being the part of Soba's desire till he finishes the plans he may have within his soul to complete.

Of all people she knew that something ate at him like a demon who torments him till it is released him from its hold. As she returns to her chamber contemplating what she must do to free Soba from his torment so they can start a life together.

On the dark isle he walks through the trees seeing a change in the way of nature that has not been noticed for many generations. All nature speaks to him of the turmoil which the world is suffering in the wake of evil. He is emerging the out of the tree line to see the little cottage made of store and wood which has been his home from his childhood. Centuries his family has been upon this land preparing for any change in the world but there is little use unless called upon from that world which has banned him to his solitude for the fact that his form was not even human. Teeth which are as sharp as razors pointed at the end eyes black pitch which seemed to dig into the soul. To look upon him one would believe him to be a beast form hell itself.

Damian's own people have been feared by man for the hellish deformities brought on by a mutation caused by some unknown force. Still the memories have been with him since he could remember of all the centuries of history laid upon his own mind. He has wondered how such a thing could be that his mind would have such a memory like he has lived hundreds of lives himself. If only someone would show him the reason for such a curse that has given his family such ability. There have even been times that he believed it was just his people who have been given this ability for the mutation which they suffer from. Yet like the others he has even greater achievements to his other siblings. By his own family he was marked the Benoni of all his people to be trained for the sake of war and to read the signs of nature that only he could understand.

For now he is but a servant to the nature that many have forgotten from it separation through all the achievements they believe they have made as men. Although his own bloodline has remained as close to nature compare to those who live in the other world far from this solitude he calls home. From all the ones born like him he is the only one which survived the life of battle. Trained by the many elders given the duty to train him in all manners of living he stays alone with little more than his thoughts to accompany him. In a couple days one of the masters shall come to him to provide his supplies and work with him on greater skills of war for his destiny shall be determined by the coming of years when he is tested.

Looking upon the ending of the day sitting upon a stone removing his great boot to feel the earth below his feet as a comfort. Continuously feeling more like a force of nature than an outcast from normal humanity. Someone he holds to his sense of peace within himself for the time he shall see the shedding of blood which he is soon to see for the darkness he is to face. Dream upon dream he is exposed to a nightmarish reality that he will stand with a group of people greater than himself to tip the balance for the lives of innocence that are lost. Does this time and day what has been foretold of his kind that one shall stand with the keepers of light to protect the world. How can something like him even protect this world when he is considered an outcast by all the so-called normal beings that wonder this world?

A life he has seen holds little interest for the fact that his appearance causes the strongest of men to tremble from their souls knowing his purpose. He sets his way to the door and enters his place of solitude he calls home. Many just refer to me as the son of sorrow for that is all I am made for to bring death and sorrow to those who stand before me, yet I remember the time when a young girl silent as rain approached me and with innocence in her eyes looked at me. I saw no fear in her from the very moment she was near me and put a medallion upon my next for the protection of the old gods whose protect many of his ancestors long before his arrival. One of his only fond memories of his younger years before he was brought her. Alone since the death of his wife by the attempting to have his child but he knows now that lose shall never leave him.

As they make their way up the cliff face they consider how the journey shall go once they reach the great waters to find him. Michael looks upon the distance which they must climb and ponders the very likeliness of the situation all of them are taking in the search.

"How will we know if we have found the right man when we get there? Is he supposed to be some type of mythical creature?" as the silence flowed from all the others he heard the wind in his ears. It rushed over him like a rampant tide which brought the memories of his youth. A great storm which wash over his valley stirring the ground to madness. He focused himself back from the thought to focus at the task at hand to get upon the precipice of this mountain and hopefully see how the darkness has taken the world we travel. I just hope he tells me why we really need this man.

Making his way up he can feel his body go through the fatigue which he has never felt before as thought the life is being drained from his very soul. His companions seem to feel little affect from the climb. The sun crest the horizon as they get to the extensive part of the climb when they pull out ropes from the packs as though they have all been here before. Suddenly he felt himself on the verge of blacking out. Moments passed and he awakened to the oud-rah next to him giving him a type of elixir which refreshed his strength to an extraordinary level.

"There's you go. It seems I should have paid more attention to you here. This place is known for taking the strength of a man. You have not been tested here like the many generations who have come here before from the village." as Michael regains his footing he sets with the others to challenge the shear face of the cliff wall. A daunting task to say the least by the very look of it. "How many have been lost to this place over the years. It seems like it can take a man's life just by standing here next to it."

He places his hand upon the stone and could feel it speak to him like a living being which feeds upon him. Yet as what he is all he has been shown in life is nothing compared to the wonders of this place that is hidden from the rest of our world. A name comes to me as if it wishes me to know him like a yet it is hard to know such a name.

"You hear him too? His name is Hupia the spirit which lives in the mountain and is the mountain. He feeds upon the souls of men which is why we must reach the mirror rock on the top and speak with them who reside here. For they know where the Oubao-mion can be found and find the one who is to help us in the coming battle. If we tally to long we may not be able to leave here again.

As they make their trek up the dark surface of the cliff they feel a new sense of purpose to reach the top. Hope is greatly tested against the merciless face of stone that would drain the life from them to make them a long lasting member of the collective torment within the stone. Many have tried and failed to surpass the test of the dark mountains search for life which these people have come to know well. Muscles strain as the mere inches push them to a point of breaking into a shear fall into hell itself. Many tales have been told by those who have come close to being part of the mountains residents that it is a dark abyss which steals the mere essence from you within its caverns. All to see the Oubao-mion this shall reveal their destiny of a warrior. Yet the few who have come never return the same they once were shattered to know they were not meant for war like the countless others.

Daylight burns away with every passing moment to see the top of the mountain they long for. Michael seems to feel the strain coming to him greater than the others of the group since he was not like them changed by an evolution beyond anything normal man has ever noticed by science. His soul burns with a fire deep within he has never known existed even to him. With sudden fury he feels the mountains wish for him fall away in fear of something greater than he could imagine. The whispers reach his mind of what the oud-rah has spoken of at the towers of a group of people with gifts that are beyond true human understandings. Confounding as it seems a voice he has never heard before reaches him even further than he thought possible inside his mind."Michael you are a chosen son now I shall be with you till the end of this test for we have been destined. Now reach for me and strength shall be yours to call upon."

Michael expands his thoughts to the voice and he feels a torrent of untapped power unleash in his flesh like a great wave of water. He steadfastly moves up the rock face moving faster than any of the others with him like a man possessed by a force that few have seen in a long time. The others struggle to keep pace as his movements become more than they could fathom. As he goes before them the oud-rah calls out to him in great need for him to hear his words. Michael slows his pace and looks back to see his companions far behind him as he nears the top alone. He sits upon the peak and looks out seeing a land which could steal the soul with such beauty he has not seen in all his life as though it has come from a dream long lost. An hour goes by when he is joined by the others as the dusk reaches them all.

"What has come of you this day Michael. You have done something I have not seen in more than myth and legend. You move with the spirit of a guani as you climbed the face of the mountain. So now you see what is to come of you when the time comes for you to be joined with the koda. That is just the scratch of the surface of the gifts locked within your blood my friend. There is still much to do so let us get going for the time shall move swiftly now to the time we are to see Oubao-mion to know the path we are to take and it only comes upon the darkest hour of the night." each set a pace of madness upon the dark mountain top for the place he has never known. His eyes scan the surroundings to check for any possible dangers wanting to fall upon them.

Miles have been traveled upon the top of this place and they finally reach a mysterious fountain in the midst of a bowl like depression at what time has not been made by the hands of man. The water seemed to shimmer unlike any other type of normal water like it was part of a precious metal that no man knew existed. All of us approached parched by the need for a drink of the water that seemed to temp them all in turn. But the oud-rah gave us a warning stare as though not to drink of such water for it may be deadly.

"The time is not right to touch such waters from this spring for the oubao-mion has not come to touch the waters to reveal the truth for us. Stand back so I may do what is needed but it will take time for it to come. Stay out of sight so it is not feeling threatened by our number. It has a defensive temperament to any number or person other than one like me." all of us walk unto the stones in the distance and hide themselves out of sight and rest their minds till they are called to approach. It just seemed very strange for such a creature to exist in such a place to protect such a place like this and what are they to learn from it. Most of all what shall the waters do if we were to drink of it before the creature arrives.

Hours pass and Michael could hear the chanting echo on the wind as the oud-rah calls upon the oubao-mion to come forth. He looks to the skies for an answer from the brother stars he has searched upon for a dream of his life's purpose. I guess the dream has become a weird dream that may turn to be a nightmare he did not want. As the moon waned within the sky into the corner of his eye something in the air changed to a moisture that could seep into the very depth of his own flesh like nothing before and he could hear the chanting stop with a sudden halt that could not be explained like time and sound itself stopped. He could feel the urge to see what is going on but the voice spoke to him again to remain still that it is here and it could tell if something moves by the earth itself. This is his domain and he rules all that is here with a mere feeling in this mountain.

A grumbling sound started to pulse through the ground beneath his very hiding place and she showed him the appearance in his mind using the eyes of the oud-rah himself like he was permitting this sight. Grotesque was the creature's form of earthly much that oozed from every pore of its being like deaths mistake come to fruition. As it spoke its words seem to his upon the air with vulgar malice. Many of nightmares could not describe the form of this beast yet it was one of myth and legends that anyone would want to forget of after its meeting is over.

"You have come again oud-rah as it was destined many centuries ago by the very patriarch of you wretched watchers. I knew it would come to this again old vestor. You look for the one who shall join the coming shift of balance to your cause." rough was the voice that came from its lips like grinding stone against the bones of man to crush its life. Why such a need for us to see such a beast was and what could it really provide us but a nightmarish story to share with children for generations to come. "It is well known that you know the place of his existence and we have need of he who is to match that of the dark walker upon their control. There is no other choice but to have him upon our side before they stop us by any means at their disposal and the koda must not fall into their hands again. With it they shall be unstoppable. So much rides upon the need of one man's skills for we have but one chance for the chosen to succeed in the coming battle. Mithra you are the Oubao-mion's keeper but I knew you when we shared our lives among the eyes of man before you were cast into this guardianship. We were friends now I ask as a friend give it to me so I may fulfill this task and hopefully free you from this curse."suddenly Michaels mind was shaken to the core seeing that they knew each other in the past. How could this be for this to have come in such a path? Now they must trust a cursed beast.

"Then have him come forth for I know he is here it is to him that I am to give the oubao-mion to have in the use of it. For the price must be paid for its use. Taking such a risk must be set upon the waters as all is well preformed into our histories. COME OUT CHOSEN I KNOW YOU CAN HEAR ME." Michael's heart raced with his life being placed in such a position what is he to do. All the emotions a man can have is bubbling to the surface of his flesh thinking this thing could kill him with a sheer strike of its massive arm if that is what he could call it.

"Come on out he is not permitted to interfere with the prophecy in your life. You are given a task to fulfill now my friend. I know what is to take place and neither of us are permitted to do it only you." with such things said he stands upon his feet from behind the boulder and approaches the fountain which they stand next to. The beast comes towards the waters and sets its gaze upon it as though he mean to use it as a weapon upon him. Rumbling came from the beasts belly and the water began to churn like a fire within was about to spring forth but something amazing happened to the waters. With a simple word from the beast lips it shines of crimson red that has never been seen by his eyes.

"Now drink boy the blood of Kulmai she shall test your bloodline. It is the only way to get the oubau-mion which your people have brought here." a mysterious thing to say for a creature that does not even know his life. So he comes close to consume the crimson waters that brought a nervous shift in him like the test he took when he was a child to become a man. Deeply did he drink of the so-called waters which so resembled the blood of a man. While it flowed into his belly it churned like a burning fire that came from within his own blood. The oud-rah and the beast stepped away from him as a whirlwind surrounded his body raising from the ground like he could fly without control. His mind was consumed with memories of lives and people he never saw before. Hundreds of faces whirling about him in the wind that could not be explained. Her voice reached out to him again like a mothers caress. "You are to open you mind Michael please for the mind is the place of you purpose and the blood shall guide you. Hurry she will take you if you do not take it in to yourself for this is who you are and what you are. Child of the sapien people not born of this world but creatures of light and darkness choose now." screams rang out from Michaels lips from the suffering taking place within his flesh from the change the waters was causing to him. Spinning thoughts matching the movement of the wind. Without even a thought words spring from his lips like a rushing river that breaks the madness. "Mika elo saivenus devanus va!" all stops and the pain is ended dropping to the ground Michael lands in a heap before the fountain which returns to the color it was before. Crawling back to the water he drinks deeply again to refresh a thirst formed by the ordeal. Gulp after gulp he could feel the strength return to him from the much needed wonder of the water. Standing to his feet he could see a look on the oud-rah that seemed puzzling.

"You have done it Michael! You have risen from what you were to the being you were meant to be. Your eyes are something I have not seen even in the scrolls and text within the towers library. A sapian release from the bonds of human ties. You very eyes are that of your people." it was baffling to hear words such as those. Looking at his arms he could tell even his skin was reformed by mere color and much stronger than before. Silver tint flows upon the surface like he is made of a metallic substance. Yet he wanted to see what he meant by his eyes changing.

"What did I say when this was happening to me. I have never heard that language before." a rush of understand flowed into his mind and he realized he said his own name and lineage of his peoples title for him. Soon the other shall be ready but he was to be the first as it was meant to be. Nathan I so hope we can do what is needed for our people and the people of this world.

"You see that which is needed was not an object but the gift within a sapian man. The oubao-mion was the sight with you to use and shall find he who is to join your cause to war against the darkness which comes. You are that being which is given the gift Michael." he looked at the beast with wonder for what has come of him and what he is to do next. Hearing the voice speak to him and he hears her words guide his mind.

The day's activities shift in the wind like a wave of madness which cannot be explained. Moordra senses the change like a tingle in his body like a chiming bell in his very ears driving him into a rage. It has been his connection to the spirit world has opened him like a book of time. He can only know something new has become apparent in the world which may prove an interesting challenge to his very skills of death, but there is no telling where this new being may be. It appears clouded in the location of his present station.

Neil is apparently silent in the alcoves of his mind which leaves little assurance to what is coming or what this all may mean to him. He secludes himself in the darkness of his courtyard upon the dark hours of night when he feels at home in the pitch black as though he is in deaths presence like a reaper from the pit of hell. Walking upon the path to his reflective pool so he may feel consumed by the dark ripples of his mind which little need for the world is wanted or needed. Moordra looks within the waters and sees the scared and twisted form his face now shows from the years of hunting others for his master.

The memories are beginning to surface once again of a past long lost in time. Of a woman he could barely see now as more than shadow wishing to tear the flesh from his bones. A day he called his rebirth unto the man he is now. Yet he feels himself more beast than man to what he has done over the time of his life since he has lived far beyond the normal span of a human life. Countless corpse left in the wake of his coming with dark vengeance to the demons he thought he would free the world but has consumed his own soul become the destruction of all who stands in the path of his master. A weapon born of such battles that would shake the souls of any person who sees the carnage from those things he has fought.

His own transformation to the dark beast to fight is that of legends that spread across the world of a misshapen demon that searches out those with power not born to all men and women. Feasting upon there flesh like an animal who has killed a pray which is far from the truth as he believes it to be. As he hears the stories from his own men he makes every attempt for them to consider him ruthless upon the battle field to leave him when time calls for his transformation to a beast. He gives himself over to the carnal madness of the darkness he must become for the fight with those people that have the gift of the dark gods.

Moordra's mind tries to contemplate the origins of those he searches for and why are they hear but Neil tells him they are the enemy of man who wish to control the world. So he continues his work destroying all with the powers yet it seems there are so many and he will never conclude their existence. Although the thoughts of battle brings a dark joy for the challenge to come with such and enemy of his master. He sits beside the reflection pool and releases all sense of his humanity unto the water's surface as it roils like a fire started beneath to cause such a change. "No room for such thoughts and feelings for my mission. I am the weapon of fortune to better the world from the darkness of those who challenge my master's rule on this plain of existence." if floods from his body like a tide of madness leaving only the hatred for all the life of this place that has no purpose than to cause chaos.

As tendrils of darkness reach out to him they extract the humanity from him like an ancient creature feasting on his own soul. Feeding upon his pain and sorrow like a flower would feed upon sunlight to sustain their form in the waters deep darkness.

"Yes Danny feed me you pain and sorrow they are the nourishment to my existence." his dark voice comes to him with a wave of comfort knowing that his efforts sustain his lord's being. All he has gone through appears to feed that which formed him to what he is now but at what price has he taken this deed.

Nathan and the others have been walking for days following Beatrice to the mountain of unknown origins which the lady has told them to go. Entering a new town they seek out more supplies to aid them in their journey. All that he knows so far seems to boggle any man's mind having to follow such bizarre directions to find a haven of sorts. What is this towers that wait for them and the child most of all. His soul stirs with the changing of this world that cannot be solved at this moment like a quest that is all question and no answers yet.

"Mister do you feel that?" as his eyes raised from the ground he was staring at he could see Beatrice just standing in an open area of road with a strange grin. As he was looking upon her something within his body felt like it was vibrating like it has long ago when he was a child. What could this mean? Thinking back to his childhood he remembers this feeling with grandfather as they walked in the old woods on one of his learning trails. Walking past an old stone platform the feeling seemed to affect him and called to him as a friend. He approached the platform and a surge which awakened a vibration within his soul which told him when a change has come. One day he walked the path alone and came to the platform and it was different as he set foot upon the sacred ground.

The entire world faded away and he was face to face with

something he never thought was possible for a man to see when he didn't believe in the old ways. He felt the earth shift in such a way that he felt responsible for all who seek aid from the darkness. What he heard was grandfathers words "You will guide many from the tunnel back to the light young warrior. The child shall depend on you as will many others who follow. Face the darkness and bring them to light." his mind could not fathom its meaning now each day he sees its meaning as the world has apparently gone into a tunnel of darkness but how did he know about the child.

"He is ready for what he must do sir. I can see he will find the son of Minerva and be with you when the time comes. He has been waiting a long time for this time." with every word he grew more confused on what she was stating and who she was speaking of. Nathan took a breath then it came to him like a whisper in his ear by a loving friend speaking a name. It flowed from his lips like a silent breath "Michael" the one person he thought would still be on the reservation doing all he can to be a medicine man like he was wanting since they were kids. He chuckled to himself with the thought that he was some reason a cause for this feeling. What is next?

As the thought came to him screams arose from some of the others that seemed to come out of nowhere. Turning about to see what is happening then he realized they were not alone here. A number of men walked towards them with barbaric weapons made of simple rubbish left from the carnage. The leader was a small man which a fierce gaze that would make you think twice on crossing him in a fight. Quite fit with the small stature of his frame. Yet Nathan took nothing for granted so he prepared himself for anything.

His mind quelled with rage to protect all those he journeyed with to this place. Although what caught his surprise was only the leader approached him as they got within a few yards from them. "What are your intentions her? We don't want any trouble in our town." shock filled his mind as he could not believe that they were not meaning to harm anyone. His mind calmed and Nathan spoke as the group huddled behind him.

"We just wish to get some supplies and continue on our way. Our group means no harm and we have a great journey to make." his words flowed like a peaceful river from his lips to ease the man's tension for their arrival. "These people and I are traveling to a place called the keepers towers. If you wish you could come with us." the little man's demeanor changed when he spoke of the towers. Nathan could not put his finger on it but sensed this man had the same calling to where they are going.

"You are going to where?" suddenly the man's face turn to a state of shock when the words finally settled in his mind. "I had a dream a man would come and speak of such a place called the keepers tower. After so many days I never thought it would be real that such a place existed." the man suddenly began to smile at the thought his dream came true, yet what is next for them all. Nathan put a kind hand upon the man's shoulder to assure him of their intentions then a feeling came over him like a kinship with the man. They walked together towards the place the man's group was staying for a night of rest as he welcomed them to his town or what was left of it.

"I am Brewsenger yet everyone here calls me bruiser for short. I have lived here all my life and never thought such a thing could happen to the world. Days after it happened I had a dream someone came here and spoke of those towers you are going to and a lady told me that is where I need to go to unlock something within me. When I woke up I thought it was a dream and then you came." as he settled in a center area of the building everyone took a resting place and tended to the wounded as they have done many times before. Bruiser called some of his men who had medical training to help us care for them. It was such a relief to know the whole world has not gone mad and there is still some kindness left.

Nathan told of their journey and the creatures they have faced. Much of it seemed to astonish him as he listened intently of what has changed. Bruisers mind seemed to understand that this may happen or was told by the lady as he was told. They even shared their experience of the lady and what she has told them of the journey ahead.

"Well a couple days rest here should do you and your people some good. I will make sure we have men on watch for these creatures you speak of and the military forces that may be out searching for renegades like us. Don't worry you are among friends now." as the two of them set themselves to the task at hand dusk quickly approached once again. So the group settles to rest for the coming days of preparation. They spoke in length of the journey that is to be ventured such as the supplies needed and the unknown distance which is to be traveled. Bruiser asked a lot of questions on the lady and what brought them all there. As the day broke Nathan took some of the people out to search for supplies needed to sustain them all with an air of caution they walked the streets with the inhabitants of this city to know where the possible stores may be for the gathering mission.

Looking about they see they are not the only ones who have survived the carnage of the attack and feel grateful to still be alive. Bruiser himself accompanied him on the search since he knew the entire necessary place that could still have some things they all needed for the journey. Great doors stood before him with a gray twinge of paint that seemed to be peeling of from the bombardment made on the city weeks earlier yet still standing with a gaping hole which leaves them and entryway. Stepping closer they could see a dim light filling the interior of the building exposing a great number of shelves and stacks of supplies that could be used for the journey. While six of the group entered the building two stood watch outside to guard against possible threats by any other who may stumble upon this place in search of supplies like them. Each of them came across a large stack of mountain bags that could fit a great number of supplies for them all. Taking several bags each they went to the other stacks and filled them with water, food and medical supplies which would sustain them for several days. Nathan could only hope the next trek would have such a bountiful supply of goods.

Time seemed to stand still as they went through all the stacks and shelves of items that seem to be a dream come true to what they needed. This must have been a warehouse store for anything people may have needed for the basic needs of daily living which now has changed since the world has slipped into the dark ages once again. Their guards outside let out a shout of warning as the men inside gathered. Nathan and bruiser rushed to the door to see the reason for the shout and the two men lay in a heap of blood and broken limbs. Appearing to be attacked by some wild animal than mere man. Looking closer they could see large gashes lay across their torso by some claw like hand or weapon yet it looks more organic than man made. Apparently they must have been caught by surprise but how scanning the area around they could see not cover which could hide such person that would be able to do this to some of his best fighters. Nathan looked up and saw scar marks on the walls above the men like something crawled along the walls and fell upon these two and tore them apart.

Dread filled his mind as he charged back in to the building for those still left inside gathering. His heart pounded in his ears like the drums of war to his charge shouting a warning unto his companions. "Guys get ready for a fight something is here." looking up he sees the nightmarish beast that dispatched the men outside. A reptilian scaled monstrosity with a bat like head with fur and large ears. Getting closer he could feel a subsonic vibration penetrate the flesh of his body like some unknown machine he has heard about. Pulling the blade from his belt he launched it to the head of the monster burying deep into its forehead and a shriek that could shake a man to his core. While its body made a sickening thud to the ground crashing into the shelves with a large bang. His eyes frantically looked again for any other that may be left as the lady called to him again to search your soul and you will find the last of them Nathan. Closing his as after stopping something open in his mind like an unnatural sense of radar that drew him to the next beast that appeared to be closing in on one of the other guys in the far back all alone unaware of what is hunting him.

Sensing the danger was about to strike he felt the fire arise in his flesh again. This felt more like a welcomed friend whose help would be greatly accepted. Turning the corner his eyes fixed on the best about to pounce and he unleashed the burning rush of fire in his flesh like a whip aimed directly at its neck. Feeling the vibration once again he focused all he had to sever the head from its shoulders. It was in mid-air when he struck the beast with full force removing its head, yet it was already striking his friend with its body knocking him to the floor with its entire weight landing upon him. With a sickening thud they fell to the ground as blood flowed from the place where the beasts head was located. Making his way to the man he lifted the limp beast body from his friend and began checking him for injuries. Thankfully he was not badly harmed more than a couple scrapes and bruises. Raising the man from the ground he could see that he was in time for saving the life of at least one of them.

"What was that thing? Who could I have not known it was there it is so big? Thank you Nathan for saving me from its grasp." Nathan looked upon the beast to see if there was any kind of familiarity or if the lady would let him know where it came from but he received nothing.

Bruiser came around the corner in a mad rush trying to help with anything that may be happening. Looking down at the creature he could see that everything was in good hands. He placed his hands on his knees trying to catch his breath from the mad dash to catch up with Nathan which was pointless. "You are fast I have never seen anyone move so fast in all my years of living. What are you? No human can run that fast by any means." his eyes wide with shock at what he could do was more than the little man could take. He looked on the verge of collapse with the effort he put forth trying to keep up with Nathan. Grabbing him before he fell he could feel the connection again with the man as though it was a blood kinship they shared.

"It is time to get back! We have to get these supplies back to the other so fill you sacks and lets go quickly before more of those things come here." the group labored intensely to fill all the sacks they have collected with the goods in the warehouse. Much of it was preserved meats and water with dried fruit and nuts that would last many days. One of them grabbed some canned meats that could sustain the trip as well but few as not to cause the weight to be too great for who carries the sack. Emerging from the building the can see many hours have passed and the made a hurried trip back to the others leaving their fellow comrades bodies as they lay to return unto the dust of the earth. As they return to the building which the others were waiting each to a review of the activities of the battle and were grateful to still be alive. Still Bruiser was perplexed on how such things could exist in the world that has never had such dangers before. His belief of the world was irrevocably altered never to return to his level of normal. All that is left is the journey to the towers and hopefully safety.

CHAPTER 11

Darius walks the great isles of the store house with the general to evaluate the supplies needed to contain the masses control. Only he knew that the food had the additive that will make the people follow his control by the need for what is needed to survive. This change in the food is something he found in his father's journal on how they manipulated the food to have the world under his control during his reign of the counsel. His mind was a whirl of ideas on how he can get those masses to consider him there savior for the supplies he provides them.

Moordra approached from the back of the warehouse toward darius with such purpose in his stride. His face a stone of dark desire with such focus to speak with the lord of the league. Yet Darius can tell what he may want from his hand as a faithful follower of the cause. "My lord I am in need to have a word with you on the recent changes from the escaped people of the city. I can even tell something more is happening beyond the reaches of our city so I need some men to hunt down any who may stand against our purpose." he looked upon him to study his intentions and could tell he wished to face a challenge of unknown strength that has come his way. He contemplates the request and begins to consider the wish for hunt of such and enemy. Yet his mind knows of the beast roaming his city are of great disturbance that few can handle for his military men which are being overrun.

"You are of needed here Moordra but is this of such importance that we can bear little time to have you go on a quest.

There must be a good reason to go on this journey for us to have your services absent from our call." Moordra's expresses a complex look upon his face as though he was being chained to his master's house. His mind entered a torrent of rage at the fact he would not be able to hunt the new enemy which would present him with a proper challenge. He must take it upon himself as before to seek out this threat to his master plan to rule this world. It is time he returns to his old way of hunting for the blood again so all shall be set in the order to consume the world.

Setting himself within the confines of his residence he walks to the courtyard which he takes as a solitude of his madness reflecting on the actions which must take place upon this new enemy. Looking deep within the waters he stares into the void of his own being wanting more. The world spins around him into oblivion with the escape of thoughts to something so maddening for him to be denied. "You know what you must do my son. These mere mortals have no hold on what you are capable of doing for I am the one who is your one and only master." His dark soulless face tightens revealing the fangs he hides from all who set themselves as his lord and king. The dreadful fire shimmers in his eyes know the extreme amount of formations he may take to destroy anyone or anything. Reliving the past victims and the satisfaction he reveled in as their blood washed over him like a cleansing bath.

"To hell with Darius and his demand that I stay here to fight these mere mutations, his military can overcome those beast in time. Chanting unto himself so he may awaken the sensation of where his new enemy may be in this world. The shadows begin to shift in forms of the darkest of demons which may hunt the location of his prey. Emanations of his own dark will which shall go forth for him as parts of his darkness. Without even a word they set out to their task to hunt his worthy opponent.

Nathan slumbers restlessly with in confines of the domicile which his new found allies reside. As he dreams he sees himself with a dark garden which shows no sign of relevance unto him. Almost reminiscent of the labyrinth he wonders on searching for the end which leads him deeper into the darkness. Instantly he stands before a dark pool of water that reflects nothing yet churns unlike anything he has ever seen before. The very density of this pool reminds him of a tar pit he saw when he was a child. Gazing at the surroundings he feels the sensation of everything reaching out to take hold of him.

"You have come to me for thy doom." Turning to the direction of the voice he sees the origin of the voice. It was him again the military personal which stood against him before. Something was different about him at this moment. As he stepped forward his movements seemed to be unnatural like a mixture of beast and man. Nathan watched closely his movements to ready himself for anything he may do. The dark cloak he wore seem to shuffle like something was fighting to break free of their confinement billows of spectral smoke seeped out from the bottom like the fires of hell were upon him yet he did not burn. Slowly the cloak opened and his enemy seemed to split into many different creatures from some deep dark nightmare from hell. All mad of smoke with a formation of demonic best claws and fangs at the ready to tear him apart. Suddenly they bolted toward Nathan which awakened him in a cold sweat looking about hoping it was just a dream. Beatrice was by his side with her angelic eyes calming his fears as if she knew more than her innocent age was withholding.

"You saw him again didn't you sir? He will not stop till he finds us!" as she was staring into the dawn of a new day sun.

"How do you know this child? You have some secrets locked within your soul many man would kill to have. I am still wondering why am I meant to be your guardian and what happened to your parents!" as the sweat made its track down his flesh and his heart was racing from the thought that a fight was eminent. Nathan prepared the others to make their move to the next part of the journey that must come. Bruiser even prepped the mass of his group who he convinced to leave with them with the others who decided to stay behind. Those who stayed behind were special chosen to stand as an outpost for any others who may come that way searching for a refuge and seeking a short sanctuary.

Bruiser looks back at the place he once called home and worried about the men and women left behind to carry out such an important task. Walking forth into the unknown path of life sets his nerves on edge to the excitement and fear of what may come against them all. Touching upon the new precipice of a journey which all of us must now experience. With the day stretching before them the newly enforced group ventures out to the towers of the keepers which only Beatrice knows the way. Taking his place beside Nathan he stares at the girl who rides upon his shoulders searching out the horizon for any sign which may not even exist.

"What's on your mind bruiser? I can tell you are thinking hard on something it might help if you talk about it. Who know whatever god's existing to care for us may hear you." Looking up at the young girl after hearing her speak helped him see the angelic appearance in her eyes. She truly seemed beyond all human comprehension to her age and be so wise and attentive to all the things around her. She smiles at him to ease the apprehensive thoughts in his heart and mind. She turns her head back to the path before them as if something called upon her attention again. As countless hours and miles passed they walked unto the valley which stretched on without end. Desolation and despair greeting them along the way with the vision of abandoned buildings and ruined cars encompassing them.

Circling a corner of a building Beatrice began to tense as if she felt something dark approached the group. Nathan realized this and had everyone scramble into the closest building in search of cover. As everyone finally found a hiding place she clutched his hand with abnormal strength. This seemed different than the many times before when she feared something he could not see yet. Within the wind he heard the sounds of someone moving out in the unknown streets his ears attentive to the sounds of the movement. A familiar sound touched his ears of a shrieking madness that carried itself from a few blocks away. Something was different this time with the sound of their movement like they were much heavier than before yet he could not explain why. Nathan ventured near the window so he could get a closer look at what may be coming in the streets. As they seemed to walk themselves out into the open with no fear of what may be around and these were definitely bigger than the first he fought in the city. Even the skin of these creatures was darker than anything he has ever seen in his own life. Spectral pitch black like the sun didn't even shin of the reptilian type skin whose very hands had talons that stretched as long as a man's finger. Only familiar part of them was the sound they made shredding the very air around their ears causing a great pain. Trying to fall back into the confines of the building with his eyes on the beast Nathan bumped the table behind him causing a slight sound.

It triggered the beast into a heighten state of alert which made the others cringe in fear that the beast may find them here. Trampling down the street as they leaped into action closing the gap between them in what seemed a heartbeat of a man. Talons ripping into the concrete structure as if to gain a sense of balance to peer within to look for us as hunters in search for a fresh kill. Without question he noticed the beast have no eyes to see realizing they must hunt by sound in a way which reminds him of bats. Yet the sound they made was unbearable to all of them clapping their hands over their ears to muffle the sound with little effect. Enduring such torment was insufferable to many in the group some wish to flee when by sheer look a noise emanating from down the street caught the attention of the both of them causing them to seek out the origin. As animals in search of the next meal, although who would take the chance to produce the distraction. While the thought ran itself through Nathan's mind he lack any reason what someone or something would do such a thing and how did those abominations get so huge compared to the ones before. A time of answer shall come in time.

Soba stomps his way down the hall on his way down to his personal lab at the sub sections of his home. With a mind full of rage over the fact that Darius is still in the position of the league when he feels it is his time to rule. Approaching the entrance he places his hand upon the wall permitting the bio-scanner to read his print. As the temporal shift of the wall commenced he stepped himself through to his personal lab while the geneticist continued his test on his version of the beast they has been designing to cause chaos in the world for his own pursuit of power. Every day he looks upon him is like an insult to the memory of his father's right to rule, yet that bastard was the cause of his death somehow now I shall be the cause of his demise. As he made his way to the samples of the genetic material he is cultivating to make his thorn upon the side of Darius. Each seemed to progressing well when he heard the door open again behind him which was quiet unexpected at that moment of the evening hours.

Turning to face the possible intruder Soba prepares himself for anything that may come. Few of his trusted cohorts new of this lab which he did his most private work. He then realized who was at the passage way was none other than his trusted assistant who personally over sees his mutations. "What is the extent of the experiment these days have they been faring well with all the modifications you have made." As his assistant stared at him partially startled she began to brief him on the outcome of the creature's status from the manipulations they have made to their genes.

"You will be pleased to hear that the subjects are showing favorable signs to the coding we have done. We could never have expected such results so quickly to their destructive capabilities and the way they can be programed for combat. You can see from the reports this next group will be ready within the day. Some have even grown larger than we could imagine with a mental capacity to understand the instincts to hunt by mere sound. Tolerances to pain are off the chart, some even seem to be impervious to pain which will make them hard to stop in a combat situation sir." Slightly grinning to himself he looks upon the charts of his latest creation. All his plans are coming to fruition for the sake of his family who would wish him to control the world as they wanted for many generations of league members.

Prepare yourself Darius the house of Ul-vah shall rule as it was meant to be for I am the rightful heir to your throne of power. "Fine what of the beast we have unleashed upon the city to keep the military busy. Are they showing favorable signs as well?" Looking upon her stumble for answers she seem to show herself quiet capable of working for him. "Well sir they are revealing above average results with all they are doing in the city. Yet we have a minor problem with a couple going off the grid to other cities which seem as though they are hunting some pray that we could not understand. I have noticed that a couple of the specimens have a greater awareness from the samples we have spliced into them. We had a bearing on some of them by their bio signature but were lost. I can't understand how anyone could kill them. I have sent a seek team to investigate what has happened, as well as retrieve them if they have been dispatched." Soba was shocked to hear that anyone could defeat his beast away from this city since the military was only located here.

"How is that possible that our creatures have taken any

choice of their own to hunt or even leave our control grid, do we still have some of them out beyond the city limits?" Soba secludes himself in the vault of his lab looking upon the specimens created through years of research to create the perfect bio-weapon. Each like one of his own children with only one purpose which is the subjugation of death upon any who stand in his way to rule the world in his own way. Somberly feeling the amulet hanging about his neck reminding him of the time his father would take the time to teach him of the honor and heritage they hold within their own blood. It was so much more than that as well to him embracing every inch of the amulet, he knew there was so much more to it than just a trinket of his father's love. Going deeper into the recesses of him mind he could recall such memories few could even fathom to understand its surface. The day he received the gift Soba remember hearing a slight incantation of sort fall from his father's lips and a fire like sensation engulf him to the very core of his being. From that day a great door was opened unto him that revealed the very origin of his people he could barely understand as a child.

Walking the great halls of this once renowned family home his own father would explain the history of our people and the power we each are entrusted with from birth. The day after my awakening he showed me my own reflection and all I could see the change in my eyes that seemed almost un-humanly colored and detailed. Time past on with greater training by his sharing the understanding of his own abilities of controlling this birth right. Much was to attain in controlling the manipulation of everything around us as though it were a game to be played.

With all that was done he continually revealed book after book of what our people had endured from the death of our home world and all we were capable of doing here mixed among the humans. Years went by which shed much wisdom of our control by our abilities. One day I entered our home to see my servants tremble in fear for something I did not notice till I entered the family library to see the bloodshed spread upon almost every wall of the room and my father lying in an unrecognizable heap upon the center of the library near the table I received many of my lessons. I wailed unto the heavens in such agony that many within the house cringed from the possibility of what I may do to them all.

As I kneel over my father's body I didn't even notice Lord Darius enter my home? As he looked upon the carnage he commanded my servants to remove me from the room. Stepping closer he could see what has come of my father vowing to solve what has happened. That day he took me unto his care in an attempt to honor my family since my father was part of the league. Little did I know at the time he was the conspirator of the act against my father. Spending my time within his home I took every possible moment trying to find an answer to what happened to my father.

One day as I walked passed his personal study I could hear voices speaking of what happened. "It feels so good to know that Soba's father is dead. Now my family will have out right control of the counsel to do as we wish. You have done well in dispatching of him. I never thought you would make such a gruesome mess of him. How did you get him to be so helpless, there have been rumors that he had abilities few could overcome?" The servant in front of him merely bowed humble to respect Darius in a manner which only a personal servant would present. As I watched he places a journal which I knew belong to my father which contains many of the notes to articles placed in his care to discover their purpose. Most were found in desolate areas of the world few dared venture into.

After hearing the news from his own lips a silent rage flared inside Soba's heart to know that the very man who took him from his home was presenting a rouse to keep an eye on him. While the years passed he became of age to return unto his own home where he would plan out the overthrow Darius and his family. He immersed himself in science specifically genetics to manipulate life as he knew it to his own demented dreams of revenge. Commissions were placed upon him by the league to take his father's place yet he would be in charge of the science sector to watch over the food productions with his ability in genetics to increase productions. In such a position he could fulfill his own desires with the possibility for destroying all Darius wished for his own power. All he needed was the opportunity and time.

CHAPTER 12

Michael and the others make their way towards the rising sun in an attempt to find this stranger which they have been advised to find for the coming battle. As he thinks back to what has become of him he can realize he is no longer the man he once was now transformed into something greater than anything he could have ever imagined. Staring at the translucent flesh which he now bears little is known on what has been unleash within. The oud-rah looks upon him pleased that one of the chosen has been awakened to his true identity without the use of the koda. Yet it still lies before them a task of such importance that failure would be catastrophic to the inhabitants of what is left of the world they dwell. Hours and miles pass with little notice till the approach a once illustrious city that now lay in ruin. Many thoughts run through his companions minds and he could feel their doubt of what may lay in wait for them.

As the come upon the first of many buildings they all look apprehensively around for any signs of life left in the shattered windows and empty doorways. Hoping against all odds that there may be some signs of survivors, maybe even somewhere they can restore the supplies to continue the journey they are on. Rummaging through desolate stores little is found to help them continue more than a day or two. Taking refuge within an old dinner each takes a table for a moments rest from the long trek taken from the mountain. Michael takes and old paper left in one of the booths and begins to read of what once was his life. If only for a moment he could remember the way life was just sitting in a dinner as people flowed in and out living life to the fullest with jobs and families surrounding him in a place like this, now it is long gone. A brief moment of sadness fills him know life will never be the same again. Two of the men search the back for anything of use as the oud-rah sits with him just waiting for him to be ready to speak about what must come to pass with the quest.

"It seems like a bad dream now! What shall become of us? Are we to change the world now like some of those stories my grandfather used to tell me about?" as Michael looked for answers in the eyes of the our-rah he could only hope he would get a straight reply. While he glimpsed into the eyes of his companion he could see there is little reassurance for any good answer. He could only wonder what would come next in the days to come. Just a sense of tranquility lay in his eyes like an unknown calm few have shown in all the chaos surrounding them.

"Little is known of what is to come of our actions. We only know the prophecy left by one of the great ancestors of our time in the scrolls within the keep. What I can say is that you have a great part to play in the coming days that may change the world for the better when you succeed, but you are not the only one who shall bear the burden there are others who will stand with you. Foretold many years ago by Sebastian that some known as the chosen will rise in the darkest of days to show a light to many lost and guide them to a greater future. Yet beyond that little else is spoken." Hearing those words only made him wish it was someone else chosen rather than him, but in the furthest parts of his mind he thought of Nathan and knew if he was one of these chosen he would not hesitate to act on behalf of others. As the others pack the sacks with all they have found Michael looks upon the oud-rah and contemplates if he was something different before he joined the ranks of the keepers yet relinquished the thought to focus on what must come of the next leg of the quest.

"Do you have another name other than the oud-rah I could call you it just seems strange to me calling you that." With a sheepish grin he received a slight sense of comfort came over him. "Yes in my youth I was known as author!" a heartfelt laugh escaped his lips which release a wave of great curious wish to know more of his life. Still to hear such a name brought him to chuckle a little as well reliving some of the tension he was feeling to travel with such a man so young grace with a wealth of knowledge beyond his years.

Making their way out of the doors they find themselves in the midst of a crowd he could not believe was still around. Glancing upon the faces of them all he realize something was wrong with them all. Eyes void of any semblance of humanity as all stand around waiting for some time of trigger to unleash a torrent of madness. Looking behind the group Michael notice something else approaching that did not seem right at all by its very appearance. The flesh was badly blistered and torn like he has seen a lifetime of battles that could not be explained. Walking with his back hunched the crowd gave him leave to pass through the ranks unchallenged. I guess this is the leader of them all just by the way they coward away from his path.

The very extent of his prowess could shutter the very soul of a man to his knees. He stood head and shoulders all the others like a beast from the pit of hell that I never thought existed in human form. Every sinew of his body flexed with layer upon layer of muscle apparently flawless if not for the scars and present injuries of recent fights. Staring into its eyes there was a dark desire of death lusting for mindless violence like a lion in the hunt of flesh and blood. Raising its mangled hand an un-human roar escaped his lips and he charged relentlessly at Michael's companion striking with extraordinary force sending him off his feet and back into the building as some lifeless toy across unimaginable distance.

An unbidden whirlwind flared in his mind unleashing a

part of himself that was never revealed unto him in his life. Pulsating light emanated from his flesh while the tendons tightened for a fight against this dark beast. He realized that was just the pre-cursor of the others to strike against them at once. Lunging forward he began to fight with unbelievable strength and speed that he attributed to his transformation into this new being. Leaving all thought in the recesses of his mind Michael just gave in to the battle at hand. Every strike was precise and deadly to the small members of the lost and he remembered he has to focus everything on the leader to defeat this mob. Aiming himself to the giant he begins to feel the rush of power beyond all he could think a man could possess within. Stretching his arm forth a swell formed in his hand like a wave preparing to crash upon the shores strike out at the leader forcing it to sprawl out after impacting the wall of the building. Crumbling brick and mortar fell upon its back causing it to go into a blind rage looking at Michael the source of its pain.

Returning to its feet signs of the impact was notice with a sign of blood seeping from its side. Unhindered the juggernaut leaped at him once again closing the gap between them in a blink of an eye. Attempting to strike him with deadly force Michael shifted out of the way with ease striking back at the new injury at ribs of the mindless man sending them both tumbling to the ground away from each other. Almost forgetting of his companions he noticed author holding them back with endless waves of magic as the young warrior fought with an ancient sword never seen by the eyes of man.

Each consumed by the need to live beyond this day he focuses back on his opponent that was upon him laying a devastating blow upon him sending him through the masses of mindless victims. With great resilience he stood knowing he could not take another strike like that again charging head long into the monster of a man hoping this would finish him once and for all. Collecting every bit of the power he contained into the focal point of his fist sending a stinging blow upon the beasts head with a devastating crack while his very hand sunk into the flesh of the beast skull causing it to collapse lifeless to the ground. Dreadfully fatigue by that last assault Michael can hardly hold himself to his feet crumpling to his knees trying everything in his power to stand again. All the countless masses look upon him standing over the lifeless body of their former leader which causes them to quickly run away from them as the final blow from the oud-rah and the young warrior shows we will destroy the very last of them.

Watching them flee in terror Michael notice a mark on the arm of one of them which brought back a memory of the past. His mind wondered back to the days back in his youth of a love that he would wish had never been lost. "Kassandra Molissette!" a silent whisper of his heart which could not be held back from the world anymore no matter how desolate it may be. Concentrating his eyes on the one who bear her mark attempting to see if it was her, yet in the midst of the mass of people it seemed impossible. Just a simple scar almost brought him to chase after her in the hope that he would truly see if it was her. Author was upon his side in an instant checking him for any possible injury from the blow he saw him take from the beast. Although when he looked into his eyes he saw something more dwelling deep within the chosen's heart from the tears that began to well in Michael's eyes. His head was spinning with thoughts that few could fathom a man like him would consider important.

"What has befallen your mind young Michael? You seem lost to some place you don't wish me to intrude upon. Have you noticed something we need to know about or do you need a moment to regain your strength?" as Michael continued looking at the people still within sight fleeing unto the dead city which they consider their home. Debating against the quest and the possibility that it may have been the woman he has loved all his life still alive here in this city. What has happened to her? Looking back on the memory of her was something he has not done in such a long time.

Kassandra's slender figure which made him believe that angels did exist in the world. Soft skin of velvet that could not be matched by anyone before or after the time they spent in bliss. As her hair that was dark as the twilight skies above the res feeling like a soft breeze on his flesh. A distinguishing mark was the scar upon her shoulder that she told me she had since childhood from the fire she survived. Every look she gave me caused me to fall into her arms seeking peace from her very love. Kassandra's heartbeat was a soothing sound like music to my very ears as I dreamed of us getting married and possibly having a family. Just like that it was over seeing her family drive away to the city for the start of a new life that ruined me for years.

"Author we need to follow them! I believe there was someone that was not completely consumed by the madness. We could possibly save her." The oud-rah looked upon him confused on how we are to find the one he speaks of in such a large mass of lost souls. With every moment that passed he could see Michael would not let this go till we at least tried. "Ok we shall try. Only thing is how are we to find this one you wish to seek out and how much time you think we will lose in our quest. I just hope it is worth it to our cause." Simply smiling he forced himself to stand up and begin walking in the direction of the one he was seeking. Pain riddles his body from the fight but he would not give in to it for the hope of finding Kassandra again. So he stumbled his way letting his body heal at a fast rate now for the regaining of his strength.

Nathan could tell something has happened with a shiver in the air awakening his mind to a battle unlike any he could understand. How could he feel such things now in this world yet anything may be possible to him? Looking to his side Beatrice had her angelic smile know something has been shown to me. The image of Michael flashed in his mind yet something about him seemed different now like he was brought unto a new plain of existence which could not be revealed. His greatest hope was to reunite with his greatest friend again at the towers. Just thinking back he could feel the distance between where he is and the place he once called home lost in the madness of a world torn apart. Dusk approached this day of the journey to seek a refuge for the night hoping they would not run into any scavengers like the ones they fought in the storage facility.

Heading into the midst of the city they could only hope of a safe haven to rest in for the evening. Bruiser knew this city almost as well as his own leading them to a coliseum that once stood as a stronghold for the favorite team he would watch on the cyber screen every weekend. Setting the way he eventually the little man observe defenses laid upon the road on the way to the safe haven. "What the hell is going on seems somebody in this area has set themselves as squatters in the coliseum. How do we expect to get into a place not knowing if it has become a stronghold for anyone left alive in this town" we must consider a way to approach and observe what has come of that place before it gets to dark. Two were chosen to take a look ahead at the coliseum to plan a way of getting in if possible. Guiding the group in another direction hoping to get their bearings on the city advantages till the scouts returned from the short mission they were sent on. Nathan kept a close eye one Beatrice for any signs of danger in her eyes like a beacon. Feeling an inner turmoil he continues forward with uncertainty of life's twists and turns especially now that the world has fallen into the darkness.

Taking the time to look back on his past to escape, he thinks of how him and Michael would go and venture out in the forest when they went camping with their families. Such a mischievous duo they were when no one was looking, what has come of those innocent days when life was simple without responsibility for anything? It was the way grandfather told us when we were caught that one day we would be world leaders someday to guide others down a proper road.

"Tunnel-walker this way quickly you need to hear me quickly. You are what you were destined to be in this world, but now it is time to enter here for the sake of the many in your care. Bring the child inside." Looking around frantically for the origin of the voice he could not resist but feel a familiarity with the one who called him the name he has not heard or told anyone in this group. Seeking out the voice the only person who would call me that was grandfather and Michael but how could either of them be here. Somehow that voice had a familiarity which brought him a slight sense of comfort. From the corner of his eye he glimpse a sudden movement which should not be there as he instinctively pulled the child behind himself to guard her from what may be wanting to cause her harm. Glancing at the figure before him struck him with confusion and comfort as he relaxed from the stance he was in for any type of fight. With a warm smile he beaconed Nathan towards him in a gentle wave of the hand, barely upon the second step Beatrice tugged at his shirt pleading with him not to go that way. He could not understand why she would say such a thing for a man he has known his whole life, although he has come to trust her instincts these past couple weeks and knelt close to her in an attempt to understand what she is wanting him see. Obviously with the tears in her eyes he could tell something was not right again so he asked what she was seeing in the man he was to believe to be grandfather. As she described the look of the man as having a mass of shifting lesions upon the body hiding his true for like a shape shifter his was told about in childhood legends spoken around the campfire.

"BREAK!!!!!!" immediately everyone capable of fighting place themselves as a defensive wall around the others who huddled together in the middle. Little time was wasted by whatever waited in the buildings around them as a horde attempted to overtake them. As each crashed upon them like a wave upon the shores of a distant beachhead. Once again he called forth the fire of his soul to defend them all.

"What the hell can't we have any time were we are not having to deal with an attack from these damn creature which have come into existence after the decimation of the world." Launching himself forward laying hands upon the closest to where he stood Nathan struck without remorse sending the beast into a broken heap motionless upon the ground. What felt like an eternity of fighting the conflict continued until what was left of the marauding beast fled in terror from the loss of so many in an instantaneous onslaught. While the shadows of night began to take hold of what was left of the day Nathan took it upon himself just to get everyone to the coliseum and hope that whoever lay claim to it will provide them a sanctuary for the night so they may all have a nights rest from the exhausting trip they have taken to get here. May we find some semblance of mercy from who may stand against the darkness as they have been attempting to do? Setting the pace bruiser guided the way towards the only sanctuary left in this place.

CHAPTER 13

Darius stands in the control room waiting for his servant who has the news of the prior event with the military conflict and the dispensation of the supplies to those who have bowed to his will. It has appeared to be a long night of turmoil with all that is transpiring. In the time it took for his servant to appear an endless stream of thoughts flooded to the surface of his mind. How can such a beast come into existence without his knowing of it unless they were here before he begun the world in which he could control with the new found science his council has created as a conglomerate company. Finally getting the chance to look over the reports Darius contemplated what must be done to subdue one of these beasts for study in his lab.

Sitting in the roiling thoughts which bring calls his personal demons unto surface of his dark soul. Hours pass while he receives the reports on the continuous onslaught from these beast dwindle the numbers of his soldiers he has sacrificed in the evenings battle. Seeing the battle in his mind unfold with all the pain makes him think how he could ever rid himself of these beasts to complete his plan. This is not the purpose he would have hoped to come to pass. All Darius can think it can he put this to his advantage to rule the world in the dark way he would have dreamed. In the new day he shall consider a secondary plan to find the origin of these monsters. He forces himself through the far doors of the chamber to his personal stores which contain the memoirs of the past leaders to the time of the first war. Every chance he can he tries to unravel the riddle of the koda which unlocks greater power from the small notation splinters off into another level of secrecy. As time goes by he attempts to decipher the meaning of the riddle in the scriptures of the ancient family journal.

Closing his eyes to find a momentary solace from the menacing conflict from what he has been forced to endure. Lilith appears to him as an angel of peace to give him the comfort he has believed stolen from him upon this endless on-slaught. Contemplating the sensation that the wolves lay at his door to tear the flesh from his bones. In the labyrinth of darkness where he and Lilith meet brings him a welcome feeling of home that permits him to leave the worlds madness of control he is seeking. Weeks have passed from the time the beast appeared after the bombings. Building a new kingdom under the powers he shall unleash to rule all as the new king of this world.

So long has Michael and author traveled into the boules of the city in search of the one person who may be worth saving from the madness. Following the sensation deep desire to find a lost love he thought was lost to death upon the scars of a world ravaged by the attack from some unknown enemy Michael's soul burned for the reunion with Kassandra which word could not express. Standing before a tall tower the band comes unto a stop while they stare at the possible end of this hunt for the woman. "She's inside! We need to look for her. I can feel her author like a part of me is being pulled to her. What does this mean to be lead in such a way for one person?" setting themselves to the task at hand into motion stepping within the abyss of the buildings dark interior carefully choosing each step with an air of caution to what may be awaiting them inside the shadows lusting for the taste of blood.

The warriors stand with weapons at the ready to combat any enemy who may wish to test their skills for battle. Michaels wonders if she will even recognize him in this new form and if he can save her from what she has become since the fall of humanity. Searching the inner part of his own soul he tries to feel her essence in the stagnant air of the rooms. The connection to her was unbelievable to fathom as he made his way toward the stairs to the upper levels of the building. Looking back he thought of the possibility of tempting fate for her to be saved from the darkness which now lays claim on her very mind and soul.

Placing his hand upon the door of the 9 floor he feels the souls of all the lost within hiding. She is somewhere within the midst of them like a trapped child wishing to escape. Sensing her pain his heart began to break know she was just there on the brink of humanity and madness. As they group together outside the door they contemplated how each must execute the necessary task in order to be successful in saving her. As the warriors thrust the door open Michael called upon his power to bear in order to gather the attention of all unto him.

Some scattered to the walls in an attempt to gain some distance from him out of the fear he caused after defeating the leader. Searching among the countless number of people in the room he could see her before him trying to flee like the others. Michael held her in place by the use of his power. A few lunged forward in a hope to dispel his hold on her yet the others fended off the blows of the clubs they held. Author came from behind him and took her from the group she was surrounded by in this room. Her protest to be taken causes some difficulty which brought the masses to frenzy as before to defend one of their own. Lashing out his magic against the likeliest of the attackers Michael pushed back the wave of these lost souls that were attempting to crash upon them all. Wails echoed in the stairway from other floors of the building with a thunderous pounding of countless people was making a mad rush to where they were in heavy combat knowing it was time to escape from a deadly possibility of being overwhelmed by unknown number in an attempt to defend this hornet's nest they have awaken.

Scrambling for the door author finally knock the woman unconscious to make the escape less of a struggle with her. Finding themselves cut off from the only escape they gathered together with the one they came for in the center of the room. Michael hoped on a way out of this trap which they have placed themselves in for the hope to find just one soul to save. With his power swelling within himself he thought of being someplace other than where they are. He was overwhelmed with a rush he did not understand expanding out around them all blinding the attackers with author turning to look at him with an appearance of surprise with the power he is presenting in himself. Their surroundings slowly changed as the light pulsated around them like the beat of a heart. As all that seem to collapse upon them with alluring contrast of swimming in an ocean of light and power which none have felt in all existence. A cascading affect causing him to collapse unto the ground without any sign of the other people lost from view. Author rushed to his side to check on him as Michael faded into unconsciousness from exhaustion.

Volta waited for his master as a sensation of power rushed through his veins like a fire from the depths of hell itself making him shiver to think that something on this world could have such a power. As he works upon the scrolls he relives the many torments which brought him to his present state which gives him a solace from the murmurs of his past demons which drive him to complete the task of interpreting the scrolls. His work was all he had left to make a purpose to his haunted soul's ability. Keeping a secret from his own master was the swelling fear which brought him to live in the darkest parts of the tower with nothing but countless books, scrolls and inventions to obscure his mind from his own pain wanting more than being a useless shadow upon the ravaged streets where he hears the suffering of the masses to the beast at hunt for blood.

Lost in the thought of a different life and the events which are taking place his door opens with little regard or warning. Darius enters his servant's room in a search for answer to what he has found in the decoding of the scroll of his family. Grasping his shoulder with great force Volta twinges with the severe pain which it brought unto his fragile frame nearly felling him to the floor with a possible loss of his senses. "What have you found? I have waited long enough for your work deciphering the scrolls of my ancestors." Looking upon his face Volta could see a sign of annoyance as he awaited the meaning of what was in the scrolls.

"It speaks of the chosen that shall stand against the darkness which shall fall upon the world. A special person will come forth to give light upon the world who is unknown by the ancient members of your family. This one led the chosen into a fierce battle of blood memory and steel. The two armies fought in a battle that lasted days upon days in the valley of Tomblay. I have never heard of such a place but somehow the dark leader shall face his rule with dark madness." His mind raced with the information he has received with little regard for an understanding glimpse of what may truly come.

With all that is happening Darius thinks of all that must come to pass with all his battles upon the city he claims as his own as well as rid of himself of the other members of the counsel to rule it all alone. Yet he considers how he should change the tide of the battle against those beasts. Giving Volta a quick nod he makes his way to the door and walks his way back down the corridor to the stairs which lead to his room in the hope to gain a little rest.

Watching him leave for the moment he closes the door and takes to his shelves in the back of the room retrieving a small satchel to look upon a book he has contained for much of his life full of secrets even his master would kill to have. Few could ever imagine such a book existed that could change the world with the secret history it pertains to of a world and people who lived off from this very place in general. He went to the page which explained the change of the world when they arrived with little notice.

"I could only think how much you would want this very book Master Darius and how could you feel if you really knew your brother my father hated you for all you tried to do to him. My dear uncle I shall hide in the place of a mere servant till my time comes to avenge my father. Prepare for the day of reckoning shall come sooner than you believe. Wretched Soba thinks that genetic formula was a mistake when he found it to make them beast of his, all the pieces are falling right into my hands. The only ones I must worry myself about are those damn chosen." as he uses the power of his blood memory to summon Neil to his presence in a report of what Moordra is doing to rid himself of the one who stood against him in the fields just outside the city. As the specter arrives from the summoning spell he considers the next part of his plan to be fulfilled. He sits upon his chair as the room grows into a silent darkness between the world of life and death where they shall confer unto the length of Moordra's task.

"Yes my lord you called for me." as the dark form of the specter kneels before him in the sign of his loyalty. Neil has been in the service of his own father in the past and now is his to command.

CHAPTER 14

Nathan and the others sit in a building to take a rest as the scots return with news that the stronghold shall welcome them to enter with a promise to resupply all of the necessities. They even report the provision of medical assistance for our injured as a group of doctors have survived within the protective walls.

Gathering themselves for the venture into the safety of the stadium everyone keeps a watchful eye on the shadows of night falling upon the city. Anxious of what else may come when they enter those walls Nathan confers with Bruiser and the others from the news station to prepare for any contingency that may come about. Approaching the ominous structure a dread consumes his soul with caution to anything that may be waiting upon the inner catacombs of the stadium. As the one who scouted the area lead them unto an obscure section to a group of peoples who welcomed them in with apprehension to the sheer numbers of their own group of refugee's to lead them into the sanctuary.

"We are pleased to see so many have survived this nightmare. The leading members will be excited to see some new faces after so many weeks of isolation and countless attacks from the marauders that are wondering the streets. By the way who of you is the leader here? They may ask to speak to you first alone when we get you settled inside a rest area." as Nathan observed the surroundings he can see the extents they have all gone through to survive in this place. Masses of make shift beds and shanties people have made for themselves to find a sort of home from what they have lost in the supposed invasion some time ago. Emerging from the tunnel they feast their eyes on the extensive array of people humanity infiltrating every sector of the interior.

The appearance of sectors with extreme compacting the severe numbers of people who have survived wedged in to such a place as this stadium. Likewise taking in the very semblance of animals reacting to a new prey entering there domain while the many began to surround to get any news of the world beyond these very walls. Nathan feasted his eyes on a group of children seeking a sense of mercy from them all covered with layers of dark dust and a musky smell of not bathing for an undetermined amount of time. Clothes in taters as left for a lost animal with few attempting to even care for them, Beatrice stepped her way in the direction of the other children laying a soft hand upon each kids head as wanting to give them a comfort they have not been given. Orphans made by the destructive madness that plagued the world now. As he continued to watch something within unleashed a savage quiver through his very soul in warning that they are not to stay long and these young ones are to accompany them to the towers.

He understood there is no telling how many may be venturing with them but these children are part of the reason they have come here. Only wishing the lady would speak to him letting him know if some sort of choice could be made for them but time will tell as they take a temporary rest here with assistance for the wounded. Bruiser was set to keep watch over those needing the medical attention as he has proved himself countless times over the past couple days of mayhem which has brought them to this place. Calling for Beatrice to return to his side she looked with concern for them all who have lost parents as she has to this dark time.

A large section was cleared for all of them to camp themselves for the time being till they have to leave. While the guide waited Nathan took this time to speak with a couple members of his party to see what could be ventured as an escape route in case the need to leave arises suddenly. Little can be told of what this counsel may have in store for us in the near future and to set a watch over our people as well. Turning back to follow him to the council members which govern these people apprehensively thinking to himself what must be in store for his new found tribe. Musky stench of so many have saturated every inch of this place wondering if water was in short supply as the guards seem to lead him to a make shift office in one of the locker rooms. Doors open before him with his eyes laying hold of seven individuals confer amongst themselves in silent whispers next to a radio playing the message of safety in the cities central warehouse. Fear was apparent in their eyes with the possible retaliation for them holding outside marshal law as it was not put in this sector of the world as well. With his mind racing Nathan could only imagine if the enforcement was planned way before the attacks on all the cities ever began forming life into a living hell for the devils to rule. Misgiving shutter came over his soul as a brief message states a minor part of unknown refugees when they shut the transmission down to inaudible levels for any of them to hear anymore. Now he truly believed that his cautious doubt of this place were probably a good instinct on his part. Searching each member stares told of the fate which was to befall his people if they were to stay here very long within the possible governing of these members of the darkness which now look in a way to survive. Speaking briefly about where they came from and what is the destination of such a journey which brought them here at this time.

Conversing with the leaders of this place made he notice even more about how they were to consider his next course of action. He was thinking of biding his time in this place for a short time period so they would let down their guard where it would be easy to escape all these centurions walking every part as well as let the wounded gain a little mending from all the injuries suffered in the trek. Countless hours passed as they question how they came to this place through such madness of marauder's and the mysterious enemies which had the form of beast which have not been seen in all of human existence. His mind swam in the lull exhaustion which overwhelmed his body to the point of agony.

"Look I have answered your questions to the best of my ability. Will it be possible I may get a moments rest from all this endless badgering. My people need me and we will need little from you for our journey." Conferring for the moment amidst themselves directions were given to return me to my place of rest with the rest of my group. As I walked back making myself look fatigued I contemplated what I will tell the others of our next few days.

Michael took his time in approaching Kassandra when she woke nearly a day after escaping the near trap with a miraculous teleportation he did not even know was a possible ability in his power. Author and the others lay a watch over the night to keep from any of the lost may try to hunt them for taking her. Seeing the fear in her eyes he reached out by calling her name in an attempt to have her realize who she was. A glazed look came over her face as if she was lost for words from the very existence of humanity in her soul. Sitting for a moment is could feel himself fall into a meditative state of rest in thought to see if there is some way he could bring her back to the past which they were once lovers.

Taking one last look at her before he was consumed by the need to focus himself to this new way of rest he noticed she mimicked the very posture he took himself with recognition to what he was hoping to connect within her mind. Calling forth the gift into a flicker of light upon his very finger tips he stretched his hand towards her which she was a little frightened to come close to after what happened earlier. Placing her hand against his own she seemed to welcome the gentle touch from him as a longing for connection to someone who reminded her of a life before the madness.

Intertwined by some unknown force of nature he sees the hell she has been force to survive since the fall of darkness on us all. She seems to be hidden here in the secrets parts of her inner mind where the misery has little chance to reach her. Longing for his very touch to unleash what has been locked away for so long in a nightmare of life. He can tell something different is happening which he did not expect to find within Kassandra's blood boiling like his own the day his new form came to existence.

Author stands at the doorway watching over them as they merge within the light of the chosen fire. Under his very breath he whispers a hope that he will complete what is needed for her coming of life. "Unleash her Michael for she is meant to be one with you as the warriors of this world to save us all." As a hope began to rise greater in his soul he could begin to believe that this world has a chance to come out of the dark from all that has happened. Now they must focus on finding the one on the isle which is to assist in the battle that is still to come in the coming of days. Dawn broke upon them with little notice when Michael woke with the love of his life in his arms having changed as he did many days ago. Watching her a moment brought back the old memories of time passed into setting into motion the next chain of events with little knowing what is to come with the time which has been returned with her return to his side.

Making hast to conclude the quest which they have first set themselves to complete from the towers each member gathers his gear and supplies after a quick meal for mysterious foods which seem to sustain themselves for a great time. Michael set to author's side to question what has become of the woman which they have saved from the lost members of humanity making her as equal to him from the activities which unfolded upon the evening. He enlightens him to the truth of her being one of the chosen as he was from the first time they were joined years ago to fulfill the prophecy set forth by Sebastian his forefather which wrote of a coming of life that would need a special group of individuals that were born to the purpose of saving everyone. "Generations of your people have been living here on this world in an attempt to change humanity for a better future but the histories reveal of a time when a great battle was waged for the many that were preyed upon. Manipulation and turmoil ran rampant upon the world as a battle was fought between two groups of light and darkness for many years till the day a shift in power awakened what we now call the chosen. In our records Sebastian speaks of a race called sapiens which from birth had a gift to control a power known as blood memory which permits them to do as you have done many times over to not only heal but so much more. Now you have given that woman the same return of what she was meant to be which I have sensed from the first touch I lay upon her in that room we escaped from thanks to your help." Michael's eyes presented a sudden amazement for what is his purpose in this life. Not only did he understand why he was treated like something different as a child but the name of Sebastian brought back an even greater memory like he knew him personally. Striding out of the city they realize that little challenge was made from any of the inhabitants which gave them a great deal of trouble the day before, yet this did not keep them from holding a guarded state of awareness to anything that may come out to greet the wondering travelers. Michael suggested that they take the time to look into one of the old markets that were still standing to gather water and some other items which may come in handy upon their quest if someone may be in need of some sort of help. He took the time to look out at the endless valley that stretched beyond the limits of the towering city at the devastation which spanned the very extent of what was once a beautiful world and hoped it could be again.

CHAPTER 15

Looking out upon the far horizon Damian considers the cause of his future and thinks how he was born for war. While the dark days of madness is laying its grip upon the world which sinks deep within his very soul few would be able to understand. Dawn approaches like a warm friend last to the cold night to return. Eyes searching the very distance for some sense to all the changes he must overcome in the struggle. Who is coming for him to join them in fighting for what reason may they ask him to kill which is what his mind considers his only purpose to the world. While the sun begins to separate itself from the earth on its journey across the sky to dictate the time passing from history itself unto oblivion, contemplating the long road his kind have made with bloodshed little reason is given to the facts so few of his kind are born and only at the time a world will shift from light to dark. Was he meant to be a judge of the sway of the world what real reason could it be that he is in existence to begin with how long must he wait for an answer since his village elders don't know.

Frustration crosses damian's face thinking why he was truly born and will there be an answer when the time comes for him. As the quiet steps of his weapons master to test his skills once again upon an cul-vien circle war. Few have ever had the ability to survive such a thing upon the precipice of a mountain side yet this small island had the gorge which the circle was placed with pillars upon ropes which a great deal of balance was needed to keep from falling. A couple of the students teacher put me against did not master the test falling to their deaths for lack of balance but at times like that I had to be cold and hard as stone for war shows no mercy to a conscience guided person. Only the deadly of mind survive this way and I seem to excide the test with little complication for what is coming or how many I must face.

Nathan dreamed of the once green fields him and Michael would play in for hours as kids getting lost in the innocence of the world which now seemed gone to memories never to be reality again. Contemplating his life on the once green fields which he and Michael played as children has him hoping even more of what is next in the hellish world of the now. Just the wandering thoughts that flow through his mind seem to torment him of what has passed now to show the skeleton of a beaten world for reality of madness we must now exist here and make our trek another step further to the towers. Beatrice stands next to me as the twilight consumes the horror in a shade of misery which cannot be pierced by common eyes.

I would give anything to return to the life which is gone. "She is waiting for us sir for you to make it happen again. What you hope for may return again but it will just take a little work as she puts it." His heart grows heavy with her words and is trying to realize that she is more than any normal child in existence today. What is she really and how shall she be the catalyst to this change? Spending endless moments staring out into the darkness which could not be pierced by common eyes leaving him with a sense of hopelessness on how is he to change the world back to what is was before. Nathan wished Michael was there to help him in this tough time like the many times in the past when they grew up on the res.

"You alright man? You seem to have a lot going on with that look on your face. Is there anything I can do to help you?" bruiser stands by waiting to hear his reply but hopes that he can keep him from falling into a dark place and being swallowed by the madness. Nathan looks back with a look which could be seen as nothing but an endless worry and longing for a change.

"I don't know right now I am just here thinking on what is next to come with all that is happening out there in the darkness." Trying to find the light to guide us back to a world which makes sense as it did before. With a heavy heart he stands in silence once again with bruiser and Beatrice close by just staring at him with silent wonder. The same thought flowing through them all in unison for them. What's next?

Michael opens his eyes with his beloved by his side held tightly in his arms hoping never to lose her again. With skin as ashen silver matching his by what altered them both. He takes this vision of a reunion to a part of himself that has been lost for so long to be found in the world of blackness. Thinking back to when they were young he could smile for life has prepared him to be with her forever.

"Appears you understand a little more why the journey has taken you both this way. It was meant for you to be with her as you have always thought young chosen. You two are part of a greater fate which will turn the tide back from where it is now. The archives have said two chosen are destined to be mated for the strength of the joined hearts will prevail. May the others have such blessing as you two have found." As he turns his head to the origin of the voice Michael was assured that the oud-rah was the source of those words. Finding him stand next to the broken window of their hiding space he was slightly relaxed with having seen them both at rest. Yet his eyes contained a greater sense of thought and purpose for something he is not revealing to him. Dismissing it Michael revels in the closeness of Kassandra's warm body and the touch of her hand upon his chest.

"What time is it?" hoping that he may stay in this place a little longer that he would not have to move out of her touch.

"It is almost dawn. The first light of the sun prepares to

crest and break this darkness so we may continue. I feel we are in need to change direction for a time that we may cut our journey a bit shorter to the sea. But a stop must be made for some reason that may provide a much needed gift to us for our purpose. The lady speaks of a way through a valley which exist a cave which holds an item of value to us for this next part of our travels." Michael looks upon him with his is perplexed with his eyes showing a mix bag of emotions. Who's the lady he speaks of and what is waiting for us. How will they know what they are looking for in the next valley. Doubting he would be told of what is in his mind he surrender's to the spirits of change to find everything that is needed for the coming war.

While the others wake for the day's march stores of food are gathered in a nearby broken store for them to eat. Eating a nutria bar Michael receives some type of food he has never seen before from one of the warriors. It seemed far superior than what he already had with little need for eating great quantities. Just to see himself in such a way changes him to the very core of his reality as he looks at the others consuming such a meal of mystery. They seem so simple but to have such an ability to provide sustenance which is far greater than all the worlds attempts to reduce the once abundance of resource which is now lost to the nightmare.

The sun crests the far horizon marking the beginning of the countless miles they must traverse to the isle which they must reach. Considering all they have been through what shall come of this day. Looking upon the oud-rah he imagines the type of life he must have had before this with such a wealth of knowledge to a time no man or woman left alive could ever know. Emerging from the shadows of the interior to be embraced by the warm sun gave a minor sense of comfort that everything is not lost with the world. Kassandra stands by his side holding his hand tightly with her eyes aglow with hope for what is to come being joined to her love once again.

She looks at her newly formed skin with awe that it shines

within the light of the sun like something out of a dream. Accepting herself in this transformation much of what she was begins to fade into distant memory. Walking down the ruined street she sees her reflection in a window that is still intact she is amazed even more that her appearance has changed completely from skin to eyes. All that remained of her old self was the color of her hair. She giggles like a small child in amazement to a fairytale change come true looking back at Michael who looks upon her with love that has been held just for her all these years.

As he thinks back on the purpose that is placed in his hands he begins to realize all the lessons of his youth from grandfather had been set for this time. Yet is baffles him how he could have known something like this would happen but the spirit of a shaman was more connected to the world that surpasses time and space. Now he must come to grip with all that must be done since this is his test for the same position of his grandfather as a shaman but now all has changed. He has a greater purpose than the simple position for his people.

She falls into step next to him as they walk their way on to a place never seen before in the likely chance of finding this great ally who is waiting for them. How far will this cause him to surrender who he once was to become a completely new creature to the world.

Walking down empty corridors he thinks of the need for action against the one who would consider himself above his own position. Soba's cloak billows out with his fast pace which he placed himself in to get to the main hall of the counsel to speak of the next bit of action. The darkness of his own thoughts a great comfort to the creatures he has let loose upon the world as a thorn in his side which holds him from extending his rule. Some of the members are wondering if he is the one who is meant to lead them with all the complications he is having. Reaching the double doors he makes his entrance clearing the smug look from his face to appear contrite unto all the members. Within he feels the whirlwind of hatred to them all who stand in defense of this so-called Lord Darius. Eyes meeting as he approaches his place at the table in the midst of the meeting.

"It is good you finally joined us Soba. Now to return to what we were hearing from the general of our military force. Continue with the information general of what is commencing out in the cities we control." As they intently listened to all that was being told to the league of all the efforts they are making to eliminate the present threat. He could not fathom such a beast could ever come into this world in such a way it is a threat to all of their lives. Yet he reports progress is being made to eliminate this threat. He also states on how some of the populace is resisting as well the rule of marshal law with the catastrophe which consumes every part of the city and beyond. Maps are laid out and marked with all that is happening from the distribution of supplies to those who bow to the rule of the league and the conflicts with all the resistance from all sources.

Darius is cold with the facts to what is happening and is making every dark effort to show control over the chaos. He looks out unto the counsel to see if there is any doubt in the eyes of them all. Nothing will stop him from taking this world as his own and he wishes to kill them all but it is the need to let them live even if for the benefit of combining all their resources with his own. He would kill some of them now in front of the others if to prove his calculated lust for power and keep the others from having the doubt of how far he would go to keep his rule over this counsel. Darius sees this is not the time for such an act to prove anything even with most of the counsel still in support of him. Still a fissure is forming between some of them to his authority to all that must be done.

"Soba you will go to make an inspection of what is the present state of the military. I need a full report of all that is visible to you." With a look of shock on his face to what he was ordered to do made little sense to him. As Darius looked upon him the hatred seemed hidden under such an enigma of power which was roiling within his mind. Many of the other members were blind to such emotion hidden within their leader's heart for them. With a false loyalty he makes his way to the door to fulfill the task set upon him with little care what Darius thinks of him. Soon his reign shall end and the blood that spills will be a glorious river which he will bath to a glory long sought after. Many have lusted for the position of power over the league which holds a place upon the many centuries locked in the mysteries of the world.

Walking down the corridor he hears the echoes of his footfall like a wave crashing upon him with such force. The shadows stretch to lay hold of him as though they wish to tear the flesh from his bones. Bringing a cold chill he never believed he could feel in this place he has considered a home for so long. Rounding the corner leading to the rotunda of stars leading to the lift which shall take him to the grand entrance of the tower the members occupy. As he descends Soba notices his personal guard waiting for him as if someone has told them of his task.

"My lord we are ready for the duty of helping to access the strength of the military which controls the streets. What are your orders as we embark to the task." He grinned to know he had such loyal men at his command. Stepping towards the lift the door opens and they board the cramped space. Every trip in this device made him feel as though he is riding within his coffin to the pit of hell itself. Yet to some extent he was.

His mind wonders to the days of childhood when he would sit with his father before the hearth as he would present wisdom of his age to lead him to be the man he was to be. He would speak of leadership and the history of their great family within the countless ages being members of the counsel. Soba contemplated all of his lessons given to him by his father to control the darkness of his heart, but many have fallen into a grave of time never to rise again. Now was the time he would consider how his father's strength could guide him now to end the wretched

"Remember boy that you are a warrior king meant to rule this world. I have place my hope and honor in you that our family shall gain the position before the other members as the one to be considered the next lord of the counsel." as the words echoed in his soul like a ghost from the past. At his 10th year of life Soba began to train in combat in the court of the old war lords in many types of disciplines. Upon the dark hours of twilight he trained alone embrasing the darkness as a part of his soul creating a dark pit in his soul. Somehow he knew it would be necessary to have this dark part to become part of his soul for the day his father would be absent from his later years. Never has he released the memory of the loss of his father at his present enemy's hands recalling how he vowed revenge for the blood of his father. Overwhelmed by his hatred he pursued the study of the dark arts which came naturally to him which felt as a great riddle written in his blood from his 15th year of life. Standing amidst his guard he calls for the dark entity which has followed him from the day of summoning without notice of his men. Retreating into his own soul to confer its wisdom of what would be needed now of its service.

With tattered cloak draped upon its torso he stands before Soba in supplication to the one who summons. "What is they bidding my lord. We who come from the darkness are ready for you desire." As the dark smile crossed his face he considering what he would wish it to do for this moment. Taking a moment to contemplate his dark desire they stand within the void of existence. Looking out at the place he considers a comfort to his mind since his youth inside the realm of death. A storm is raging about them to ward off anything that may try to come forth.

"Bring forth the others of your kind, I have need of them as well. It is a great task that must take effect immediately." As the words flowed from his mouth several demons come from the darkness to fulfill his demand. Looking on them he realizes that it is time to transform his own guard to something more than mere mortals. it must appear that his men have greater ability to confront the creations he has made to torment and break the confidence of Darius himself.

While he prepares the conjuration to have these creatures to inhabit the very souls of his guard he knows there true identities must be ripped away and place unto the grave. All but his most trusted captain who knows his true abilities. During his emergence from his inner soul which felt like being in the realm for hours presented itself as mere seconds realizing they are all still in the lift on the way down to the main hall. Taking a moment he glances back at his captain of his personal guard with a look that could not be misread since Soba has told him of the time of making a move will come. To those with him saw the tiny space seemed to change unto a dark cold that penetrated the very core of others as if being pierced through. Cries filled the air as the men felt the very hand of death upon them tearing each soul from within. Shear madness consumed a few as they thrashed about the walls and floor as if trying to escape what was happening yet it's too late. Seconds later they took a stand with eyes showing a dark red like the fires of hell attempting to look out from human eyes. Sinews of muscles grew to abnormal form that could not be mistaken by his eyes, with talons revealed through leather gauntlets that could tear flesh from bone with a single swipe. Relishing the change which presents an advantage that Darius would not have considered.

Finally reaching the main hall the doors of the lift unleashes them to walk out to the grand entrance which they walk toward the city proper or what's left of it. An awaiting convoy sits in front of the tower to take them to the military front lines. Soba and his personal guard lumber into an armored vehicle and dis-embark. Seeing the street filled with rubble from all the chaos laid upon the world which brings a sense of pleasure for what has taken place. People lost in the madness with a feeling of extreme hopelessness captured in their eyes lost to the very thought of hope ever existing again. As they turn a corner some of the people show a bit of rebellion for how the military are herding them towards the camps which they are unwilling to go to. Shots ringing out against those who attempt to resist the order of the league. Endless masses of the dead covering the streets at every turn. Soba knows to care little for any of them who have died in a lust for power upon this world with those he will call his minions

Endless miles stretch before them as the vehicle lumbers over cluttered streets which make it very difficult to move at some points. Finally seeing the military lines a mere couple meters ahead Soba sets his mind to the task at hand with such hatred for the one who sent him here. The general approaches when he notices them coming out to the convoy to pay his respects.

"Hello sir! May I ask what brings you here to our camp?" noticing a slight fear in his eyes he passes him and makes his way to the men forming lines and saluting him. He cares little for the formalities of military protocol. Minor aggravation appearing on his face having to come here to make an inspection a simple servant could have done. With the general close on his heels he holds the hilt of the blade he carries on his belt. His very dark thoughts flowing as he looks upon all the personal not impressed by their efforts. Soba will make an example of someone today in his show of the leagues tolerance to failure.

"I wish to know the progress you have made in quelling the beast which you have been facing. Do you know anything that can stop them from attacking?" the general seemed stunned on how he should answer since it has been a difficult road for the men. Soba saw the hesitation in his eyes and struck out without warning slicing the general's throat nearly severing his head from his body. The lifeless body striking the floor in seconds as the look of shock still lay's in the man's eyes. Soba felt a minor gratification for what he has done to get everyone's attention for what must now be done. His personal guard's bear their teeth twisted as sharp fangs as the bloodlust is very apparent in the eyes. Moordra comes forth from with little care what he has seen done to his general. Making his approach to Soba with no fear what may come of his action.

Knowing he was to report what was taking place upon the men. Turning his back to Soba he begins to walk away. "If you wish to know then follow me to the command station and I will advise you of what has taken place here." Barely even looking over his shoulder to see if being followed he continued his course. Little did he have to fear of this member of the counsel which he knew infuriated Soba. By the time they arrived many of the maps and reports were laid open upon the table to been inspected. Moordra prepared to divulge everything with a few secrets of his own that are for his lord's ears alone. Many times he has thought of killing him personally but it is not his to complete against such a weak advisory. Soon Moordra shall take his bloodshed unto the one who escaped him days ago when the wraith find him. For now he shall bid his time for the war to come unto his door.

Nathan lost to the weight on his soul remembers where he is and what his purpose at the break of day. With little rest he prepares to make the continuous journey to a place he has never known existed. Taking to the streets again Bruiser found a bus which seemed to be working to carry everyone for a while to hopefully a great distance from where they are if luck persisted in their favor. As he takes his time to gather what he has alone in the back section of the resting place. Suddenly his is consumed by a memory of someone from the res which took his heart in such a rollercoaster ride of emotions from love to loss with every touch of the love of his life. "Madelia! My sweet angel how I miss you every moment of the day since we have been apart." As he shoves the last of the equipment into his bag a shadow comes from the door. It is Beatrice giving her innocent stare as always concerned over the man who is meant to be her protector. As she stands at the door with the light upon her back Nathan notices a second shadow upon the floor unlike anything known to man. The large head reminded him of that strange dog from the forest of the spirit. Looking back at the girl her smile explained it all.

"Beatrice how long has he been with us?" with a childish giggle she looks at her side with her innocence that he did not see it earlier. As the thunder like memories storm endlessly through his head causing so much confusion to explain why he did not see the second shadow. Even at this moment the thoughts of Medelia consumes his mind. With the many things that has consumed his mind over the years why did she return to him.

"Who is she?! It seems that her name really means something to you sir. The lady must be really special if she is on your mind now." While he continued to have her in his thoughts Nathan could not avoid the look on the kids face. As if she knew more about him by reading his mind in some way. Still it was very pleasant to have someone keep him grounded from his dreams of the past.

"Oh! I see now sir she was your sister." He took a moment to finish packing then went on with the day to explain the thoughts he had of Medelia his younger twin sister that he has not seen in years. Spending most of the day with the young lady by his side he explained the relationship with the woman of his thoughts. Much of it was just how they grew up together playing together on the reservation. Living with a twin was not easy for us since they had a belief that one of us might be evil and scared which of us it may be. Till the age of 12 we were together then one of the worst things I could think of was my parents divorcing and my sister leaving with my father to return to the city life since he was not of any tribe. Holding my sister tight against myself he had to pry us apart to even attempt to leave. I was distraught for months after that day and made it my goal to see what it was like to live in a city like my father and hoping I would run into my sister again. Her left cheek had a special birthmark my mother called the angels touch few of my people ever saw in so many generations of children born twin. My own mark was even rare for men to have the arrowhead mark on the chest above the heart.

"Don't worry sir she is willing to see you too! We may even run into her on this journey. Why does she have such a pretty name and what does it mean?" sitting on my shoulders she always seemed free to bring so many questions to light. As I explained her name and everything about the two of us that I could remember just seemed to entertain the young child. Bringing a smile to think of her I lost myself from our present hell which we were traveling in at the moment. Time passes when I could actually feel her within my mind as if I could touch her somehow.

Upon the dawn of a new day she takes her walk through the garden of mercy to clear her mind upon the coming of events she must partake. Years of countless lessons given by the monks of the towers for a purpose she knew little about or even wanted. A white robe billowed in the morning breeze which presented an ethereal manifestation which she felt suited her in this time. Having accomplished so much still deep emptiness remained that she could not explain as she attempted to remember her youth beyond this place that seemed nonexistent of a man she could not recall. Approaching a sacred tree she stretches her hand to embrace the delicate blossoms that looked like it was painted with the hands of angels with a pink and purple hew.

Time seemed to fade standing before this natural beauty

when she could sense the presence of her father coming up behind her as he always did when he found her here. "What is troubling you my dear daughter? I find you here as though you miss life beyond these walls. Bringing you to this place was meant to happen at the day of your birth." She remains puzzled when he mentioned the reason for coming here as destiny. Only time will tell what that destiny will truly be with the story of the chosen he has told me will be coming in the days of shadows comes.

Medelia's mind is haunted by a memory that is beyond her grasp for the past three years. A boy she somehow knows but can't bring to light the way she is to know this boy so familiar yet a stranger from some unknown place in her own soul. Recently it seems to change into a man for a night which brought her to the garden hoping it would truly ease her mind from the torment of it all. Looking in her father's eyes it appears he has been hiding something all her life but she is unable to ask what it may be till a year ago. Every time he attempts to dodge any possible way of answering her. Soon she will understand more of the secrets to what she is meant to be and why her whole life is hidden from her. The sun gently crests beyond the horizon which brings gentle warmth to her soul which she can feel flowing within her blood. As the vibrant colors of the blossoms shine like jewels from the earth magnificently glorious. Stepping from the garden she made her way to the library in order to meet her mentors of the way for her daily lessons, yet the riddle of the boy still lingers in the forefront of her mind. Who is he and how do I know of him?

Damian makes his way to the training grounds which he has been provided by his master of combat upon the breaking of the dawn. His mind is fogged by the lack of sleep from a nightmare that seemed all too real for words. Clearing the trees he could see the grounds were hazed with early morning dew that has not clear away yet with sunlight, yet something seemed a little peculiar than the usual preparation from his master testing his senses. The smell of blood was not something he was ready for and believed it was another test.

Dreary silence covered everything like death has come to his home isle. Making the way to the first little hobble which the weapons wear stored he took his favorite sword which he forged himself. The metal it was made of was unique to the isle he was placed on which made it stronger than anything made in his village. Many skills were given to him as a rite of passage to all of his kind who born with the believed curse to his people. Many of times he has thought of his mother and what she must be going through with a son born to be outcast and trained for the dark road of blood and war. He even thought of the one woman who would come to be his mate when the time came, still the lonely days of his solitude bore down on him with rage.

The great roar of silence consumes his present home as if life has run from an unknown evil that has arrived. Damian prepares for his day of training with his senses high for anything that is coming. Scaling the tower bars to get a greater look at what is around the camp but little can be seen that may be out of the ordinary. Then his mind aware of the simple shake of the ground beneath like a thunder waiting to strike his soul. Many of his kind have been place here but are not as tempered as he is which makes it a greater challenge to all who come in time of training. Trees shook with the movement of a great force few could imagine existed then she emerged from the trees with a great mane of midnight hair, skin shimmering similar to his own in the daylight hours. Eyes meeting in the distance stare from a dream which he wish to remain under. It has been years since he has laid his sight to her in the isle. He believed she has become like the others wild with natures calling. Watching her from a distance he could tell something was wrong as she stepped sluggishly across the ground as the wound became apparent upon her head. Rushing from his perch he made his way over when she collapsed unto the earth.

"What happened to you? Did the others do this to you?" his heart pounding in his chest like it has not done since the days he began his training as a young child. Looking into her eyes he saw a deep fear that has never been seen in his kind before like death was pulling upon ones soul. Rushing to bond her wounds with the salve he could tell little could help to heal her soul.

"It is here!" after the words flowed from her lips she his mind fell into a state of wonder to what could have done this to his kind. Damian felt her breathing slowed as she succumbed to the salve's affect which placed all into a slumber from the special herb found only on this isle.

What did she mean it is here?! He went to the old books he was given to study the history of his kind. Something seemed familiar about what is going on with her arriving in the camp which I usually the last place any of the wild ones would come. Let only his mate which forsook him for the wildfire of the blood they suffer from in their adolescent years. He alone chose to stay as many before him left to live in the jungle beyond. Damian recalls a story told to him in the past of a creature that would hunt his kind to remove any chance against the coming darkness at the moment he needed to recall what it truly meant and if this was that time come to reality. Ripping through the countless books upon the shelves in his house he attempts to find the book that reveals the story of what has happened.

Setting the task out before him he spends hours looking when his teacher enters his door with caution to what has happen. Noticing the other of his kind wrapped in healing bonds and resting puzzlement crosses his face as to what may have done this to her.

"Master she and the others were attacked and it seemed she is one of the lucky ones. I set her wounds. She spoke of something being here on the isle which made little sense but it reminded me of the ancient stories of the coming darkness. What was the name of the creature you told me would come in this time?" while he is furiously looking through the books upon the shelves of the small hut Damian's blood begins to boil within him.

"There is no book that you will find the information you are looking for my young warrior. It has only been told from the memory of our people who has passed it down from generation to generation. Yet the time has come but you will need her as well to face the beast. As the legend goes strangers will come from the wastelands shelter for thee after the time of testing were two shall emerge from the bloodshed of the dark beast. That time is now and she is all that is left to help you when you go into the tree line after the beast. Several days shall pass till she is ready so be patient and wait." His anger grew with his masters words to wait and its name remained a mystery. Yet he will bid his time and prepare for what must be done.

As he stood in the training field letting his mind wonder to the days he spent with her in this place learning the skills of combat. Every turn besting him through the movements they were taught having known she was the better of the two of them. How could she think of returning now when it has been so many years and how much does she still remember any of the combat skills. With the beast waiting for them in the trees he bids his time for her to awaken from the healing of the injuries she has sustained. Master finally told him the name of the creature which must defeated. Maboya the time is coming for your destruction from our hands and the gift you hold shall be retrieved once again for the coming darkness.

Making their way into an old mining town Michael ponders the path which guides him to a tunnel. Giving way to the sensation he leads the others into one of them searching for a lost items he feels calling. What must it be which holds his soul.

"What are you doing Michael? This doesn't seem right to go this way." Looking back at his love his eye's seemed possessed by a force of nature which could barely be described. Without words he leads the way somehow know the way he is meant to take. Creaking beams and slight shuffling troubled the others believing that it would all come down upon them leaving no way to escape this place. Reaching an alcove amazing them all would even exist in these catacombs. Without thought he approached a distant wall marked by an ancient door marked by ancient script.

Placing his hand against the emblems an ominous light enlightened the room which they stood bringing the oud-rah to a state of wonder of how long this place has existed untouched. A thunderous echo set his warriors heart to react with the unsheathing of their weapons. Examining the alcove they realized the entrance was now blocked by a great stone apparently a trap for any who come to this place. A circular light formed amidst the floor in center of the room where a being formed itself.

"Child of moin time has come for you to take the righteous knowledge of our people. I am Sebastian from which you blood memory shall be given greater understanding of what is to come. Finding your way here means the time is coming when we must repel the darkness once again from those who wish to rule this world. Beyond the door holds the secrets of the nature of the koda which shall unlock the true potential of our people. Only you may possess this knowledge for it is your destiny to awaken her once again." As the light fades Michael turns unto the symbols again opening a door without even realizing how or why. Confused by how he is to make a way in to reach what will be waiting for him. Retreating into his own thoughts he freed himself from normal thought and by sheer instinct his hands moved within an unknown order upon the symbols permitting him to retrieve a set of scrolls made of translucent paper.

Placing them within a satchel he carried from the towers. Out of the corner of his eye movement caught his attention causing him to grab Kassandra as he dove to the floor dodging the stone thrown across the room. Regaining his composure he looked over to see a stone sentinel emerging from the wall. Like something out of a bad nightmare he scrambled to his feet between her and the creature. "Did you think you would be able to leave here without being tested son of moin. Now is the time to prove yourself to me before I let any of you leave or die here like many before you."

One of the young warriors charged in to confront this enemy. Deflecting his strikes the sentinel struck his torso launching him into a far wall like a child to a fly. Michael knew he was the only one who could have any chance against it. Kassandra stood beside him with her hand on his shoulder in a relaxed grip. Turning to look upon her something seemed different about her like she knows what must be done to end this challenge. Gesturing her hands in the air like she did when they were kids at the river a glow filled the air around her hands like an aura of power being called forth. Stepping back Michael knew what must be done and it would take both of them to complete it. Taking her lead he let himself go and his hands began to move in the same fluid form as Kassandra's in rhythmic fashion. Neither of them noticed the reaction of the creature moving back sensing its doom at hand. In unison both of them unleashed a wave of power which sent the creature into the far wall with crashing force shattering it to pieces. As the sentinel lay crumbled upon the floor before them a rough grinding of stone alerted their ears to the door opening to let them escape this alcove. As Michael exited last he heard the final words come from the sentinels mouth as a warning to what will come. "Though you have proven yourself a true sacrifice must be made to awaken the koda's power. He also knows you are coming for the day to face the son of blood will not go quietly. He comes for you brother of the way before the light shall shine." The words burned into his very soul without being able to understand there meaning. Time will tell what is meant by his riddle.

Night fell as Nathan and the others made way to a small grove that lay outside the city limits which provide little shelter from what may be laying in the darkness for them all. With little to shield them from whatever may come to take its pound of flesh from any of them. Just wondering how in the hell they got out of the coliseum in one piece could be a miracle in itself know how the leaders of those lost souls were planning on how to make his group a part of their collective. Fearful sheep who think the high walls will protect them for long.

Bruiser approaches as he has been every evening to speak with him on what direction is next to travel when little is known even to his own recollection. So much has been altered with the devastation of society as they once knew it. Heavy is the heart when the light is absent to the eyes.

"Bruiser we really seem to be in such a dark point of our lives. Did you ever think something like this would ever happen?" shrugging his shoulders he stared off into the abyss of the night as though looking for the words to say. Nathan could tell all of it was wearing on him to continue in such a manner which seemed death would be able to take him at any moment.

"You know I never thought my life would be like this. I was a business man with a beautiful wife and two lovely kids before all this happened. Now I have these people who seemed to find me like I was meant to protect them with all I had left." Anguish consumed him with the moment he spoke of his wife and kids which I never knew he had. Apparently everyone had lost someone but he took it hardest of all which is probably why he fought so hard.

"Tell me of your family Bruiser! What were they like and how old were your kids?" his eyes shifted my direction lost to the memory of them. Clenching his fist to my request I could see it was a very painful thing for him to discuss with me. My heart reached out to him for what he has truly lost in this world. He pulled forth a medallion he carried in his pocket that was remarkable in the artistry places upon the exterior.

"They were the angels I never thought a man like me deserved. I was a wild young man who cared little for what people thought of me. I was called bruiser for the countless fights I had in the dark alleys of the once prominent city. During one of the fights a spectator called me the bruiser of backwoods street. While fighting in a warehouse she appeared with another guy who wanted to prove his manhood to her. It took everything I had to keep this guy from almost killing me in that fight but I left him with the memory of me. I really had nothing to lose any time before that fight but something changed when all was said and done.

I left the guy out on the floor as I stumbled out to the warehouse not noticing she was following me out. She must have felt pity that someone as broken as me could go through all that. Once I got out of the doors I collapsed next to some dumpster just wanting the pain to stop. I closed my eyes hoping when I opened them it would all be just another nightmare. A soft voice reached me out of the darkness that I did not know existed so I looked out from my hiding spot and saw her standing in front of the dumpster waiting for something. I could hardly believe she was crying when she saw what has just happened. I called out to this lost girl and let her know it would all be ok. This is what I deal with all the time out here. Moments later she embraced me and told me her name was Lhian and she felt heartbroken at what I just went through in the fight." his body trembled as he told me the story of how he met his wife. I could only imagine she must have been a saving grace for him from the life he was living out on the streets with the endless conflict. While I sat quietly I heard the story of his life before and felt sorry for what he has lost.

"She was everything to me. That night she took me home even with all she saw of what I was in that fight. Grabbing the first aid kit she had in her cabinet she fixed me up a little. Huh! Hard to believe I could have look better than I did at that moment but she didn't really care, guess she realized something in my eyes needed a little healing. Looking at Lhian seemed unreal to me that anyone could be that kind to something like me. After my face healed I went looking for a real job and found it at some market down from her apartment. Years passed and I was able to save enough to ask if she would marry me. We had twins the following year and I could only see that I needed to care for them and the animal I was seemed to sleep.

Now look what has happened the bombs fell and she was lost to the madness. I couldn't even find anything of the kids. Ash was the only thing left in the apartment we shared. Spending days looking for them as the bombs seem to keep falling around the city. So curious how any of us survived out of the shelters yet a few of us did. Hope my wife made it to a safe place." To my surprise the tough exterior of bruiser seemed to break for a moment as tears formed streaks down his cheeks. I finally realized why he took this position of guardianship of these people in a hope to find his family.

He wondered off to another area to be alone so I sat in silence contemplating what has been revealed to me of these people losing as much or more than myself. Now I set my conviction to what must be done for everyone. Beatrice quiet as always just sleeping at the moment not far from where I sat myself against a tree. Nathan looked about trying to think where that damn dog or whatever it is may be standing. Feeling a small nudge to his elbow he turned his head and it was showing itself for once to him outside the ladies little dreamland.

As I sat there looking at him I considered what he would say or do to let me know what it say would be considering as the direction we need to go. Beatrice was such an amazing child to be able to see the parts of the world I could not. He nudged me again as if he wanted me to follow like he did once before. Getting up I made my way behind him hoping that my charge would be safe where I left her.

"Look Nathan she will be fine I left a cub with her to watch as we meet with the lady. He will make a noise if they see the child." I was surprised another one of his kind would even be here to help at all. His eyes noticed a paw upon her shoulder which did not even seemed to bother the girl. Making a path through the darkness he seemed to lose track of how far they have gone from the others. I could hear a small creek splashing innocently her in a small out cropping of the land. Stones glistening like gems stars with them being water soaked and a bit of moonlight coming in broken spaces of the canopy above his head. We stood within the sense of tranquility for the first time in so many days that it is hard to remember what peace of mind was anymore.

A soft wind came in from the water that was an eerie sensation to my skin that I never would have expected. She emerged herself from the surface of the waters that reminded him of an elemental spirit his grandfather once told him about in a story in his childhood. I bet this was not going to be a pleasant meeting between them as the look in her eyes gave a sign of concern to something he didn't know was coming.

"Hello Nathan! Sorry to bring you here like this but it is of great importance to what is coming. I have discovered you are all in great agony, yet something is coming and all of you must make way now to the east of here for a spectral waits for you in the cauldron hills who will make the journey to the towers known to you. It will not be easy to get there because the tempters who shall try to destroy all with your own desires from the darkest pits of your soul." My mind was twisting with the idea that anything more would rip at us from our own unity. What is she getting at sending us to a place that may fracture the fragile group we have any more than we are right at this moment in time.

"Take this with you Nathan! It is something that has been your birthright for some time and it may give you the ability to hold them back from the others." As he received the medallion which luck would have it brought back memories he never knew were there about it and would hope the truth comes forth soon as they kept on this journey.

Trying to wrap his head around what has just happened seemed mind boggling at the moment. Making his way back to the camp where he left Beatrice all he could do was hope everything would be fine but he knew hell was about to break loose. Nathan was reluctant to see nothing had befallen the child while he was away. As time passed by he could feel himself becoming more attached to the child like a father. Putting forth his hand he gently stroked her hair making a silent promise to give all he had to be the protector she needed. As they all became aroused by the sunlight cresting the distance. Announcing to the ones who stood out as leaders in the group he understood the animosity of having to change directions to a place none of them knew. Collectively agreement was made to go in hope it would minimize the amount of turmoil they would face out here.

Beatrice seemed to know more than any of us what is waiting for us at the cauldron hills. She gave her simple smile as always and just looked to the left of the place she stood. Hopefully that silly looking creature can be of some help even though we are the only two who knows it is here with us. Another day of walking with our wounded and lame some have started to walk on their own which was a minor relief of the burden we were dealing with. About midday we reached a mire that stretched on for who know how long. Without question he made a step to get them all through this little test of his resolve. Yet the words echoed in his mind what she said that this may tear our group apart from our very souls. Looking back at the wear faces he could tell they all have been pushed so far but more will come if they do not go on.

Howls rose from behind them ungodly as if the gates of hell were opened wide. The ground even shook with rage from the possible numbers or type of beast that is out there coming for them. Everyone struggled forward as the only defense they had took up positions to ward of whatever may be coming at them. Taking all types of positions some with rifles and others with hand held weapons the battle was about to really come to reality.

As the first of its evil face Nathan was trying to call upon the gift he had yet is seemed to fail him so as the others he stood his ground. At once they charged forth as the shrieks filled the air causing a great sense of pain to them all. Scar covered skin upon the beast he found himself rushing in alone with such speed he didn't know was in him. Before the others even move he fell at least five of them with little effort which ended the pain to the men. Shots rang out in the air as some of the larger ones came lumbering in with seething mouths craving blood.

Hearing his heart pumping in his own ears he could only wonder if the gift would only show himself in the darkest of hours. One after another he kept fighting in hope they would end the beast in a way or hope they would run. His balance was shook with a strike to his head when an unknown blow befell him. As he stumbled to the earth the semblance of a grey cloaked form showed itself at the edge of the battle.

"Get up now! She needs you more than you know." Feeling the strong hands taking hold of my shirt I could not imagine anyone could be able to make it through what is happening. How could this person know who I was and what was needed at this moment. Looking up I realized it was a woman who must have been in the shadows watching us.

"Who the hell are you?" as the words slipped their way

from my lips to her she seemed oblivious to what is happening around them. Time slipped away as she threw a vial against the trunk of a tree which formed a mist with seemed to engulf the beast in a burning smoke which sent them reeling for escape. Where the hell did those things come from and why are they after us?

"Those things don't know but this is my domain. I run what happens at this mire of the world so you can count yourselves the lucky few to be in my grace. Welcome to the bottom of the world Nathan time to climb out of this place." Making my way back to my feet this cloaked figure guided me to the edge of the mire in the wish to help us through. I wondered who sent her if it was a woman to help us at this time. All he had to go on was a little faith and the words of the lady that this would tear at them, maybe this person could shed some light on what is happening as they made their way to the cauldron hills. Leading the way she took us through the mire which seemed to such the darkest part of a nightmare which he could not imagine in the pit of true madness. Hesistant to trust this new person he kept a close eye on her movements. Hours upon hours shed through our souls like a snake released from its old skin back on the res, at times I felt I was being torn apart from the inside with the mire and the demands to protect everyone.

Just trying to take myself back into the time where I was a child with Michael in the fields in our games connecting us to the earth would bring such joy. Now it is hard to think I could do that now with all the pain and suffering that is happening and the demons which looks like they came from the pit of hell itself. This mire seem to go on without end yet this unexpected ally appeared to know a way through this evil place. How can the world have become such a wicker chair of darkness and suffering.

"We must hurry a storm is coming and we don't want to be caught out here when it does come. I know a place we can find shelter not far from this area." Everyone wondered what she had in mind and where she was taking all of us. Looking around I could only think if this place ever had a drop of rain fall in all its history. Trees of ashen grey covered in what appeared a blackened tar like substance that who knows how it got here. Very few areas showed any sign of growing life that appeared as moss covered in blood with the crimson color it emanated. Movement was rarely hear at any given point, yet at times it felt as something else was watching us in the mist and smoke. Foul was the taste in the air like sulfur and rust which the young and old alike grimaced with every breath.

Reaching the mouth of a cave he thought of the name he was given by his people when he was young. His love for venturing in tunnels was something he would always do and try and find his way out at times grandfather would have to get him out when he was lost. That is when they all called me the Tunnelwalker and that my destiny would be to guide others from the tunnels of their lives. Maybe that is why I became a lawyer in defense of others. While lost in thought he realized they were closing in on the cave the stranger was suggesting they stay while this unknown storm passes by, yet Nathan had his doubts of what she had planned for them all here.

Taking a time to rest he could not control the apprehension in his soul to allow any time to really sleep. Carefully watching over everyone he takes some time as guard over the group hoping to grant some safety to their mind. While the beginning drops of rain hit the ground Nathan noticed it was un-natural in every aspect of its appearance. Some of the ashen trees succumbing to the onslaught of the mysterious rain which struck down like a hail storm from the hell. Nothing was spared yet my only thought was how could she have known the rain would be like this so quickly.

Staring back at the place she was crouching herself away from everyone paying little regard the raging storm left Nathan on a greater edge of suspicion than he was before. He must discover her secret by any means to ensure the safety of the others. Directing the group to settle in he set some to lay watch through the night. Setting his mind to ease I took a space at the back of the cave against the wall so I could get a rest greatly needed for the day's events. Midway through the night she came awakening me which seemed quite baffling for such actions.

"Please come with me! I need to speak with you alone Nathan about something of great importance." Rubbing the sleep from my eyes I stood to my feet which alerted one to the men I set to guard the group. Waving him off from following us I proceeded to make my way to a hidden passage in the back of the cave which I would not have known was here if not for her showing me. Into the depths we made our path down into the bowels of the earth.

Overwhelming sensations brushing itself upon my skin with every step we took deeper into the path. She gives little regard to what is happening as they venture forth I could only think she has become accustomed to this feeling or something was being prepared long before he was ever brought here. Listening intently to drops of water getting louder as though they are approaching a vast underground water supply locked away in the recesses of the cave.

Racing thought as to why they have come to this place caused him a bit of concern with what she had in mind here. Taking the moment to observe this place with splendor Nathan has not seen in such a long time. His mother once told him of beauties in the world that the dark hand cannot reach to destroy. Heart beating so loud in the thunderous silence sparked more memories of the drum dancing in the wind. Seeing his reflection in the waters seemed so strange now, as he noticing the layers of dirt upon his face. Taking a hand full of water he began to cleanse the filth off. With every splash of water relief filled his soul, losing track of the one who guided him here Nathan took his time.

Hearing just the shift of stones was the only sign of her

presence in this place. After a time she began to grumble under her breath which gave the catacomb as eerie sense of cold flood in from out of darkest abyss. She stepped closer to Nathan and he could tell her intent had changed to why she brought him here. Looking back upon the stranger he noticed the cloak was gone and she laid a twisted wretch of evil. Skin stretched taunt against the remnant of human form which seemed starved to near death. A continuous grumble flowed from her lips as the water began to roil behind me within it depths. Feeling it pull from his very soul what energy he had left to guard himself from what is coming.

"You have been a long time coming boy. I have hunger for such a soul as yours to come and feed me." Crooked teeth exposing themselves from behind cracked blistering flesh of what one could call lips. I felt hopeless as she crept closer and closer as a mistress to my death. My eyes growing dim my body gave way to her mystic words as the noise of the water grew to epic pitch of madness. I knew something like this would happen while the water feed upon me like a mystic leach upon my flesh. I never thought I would lose myself in a place like this, moments later I hear the woman scream which force me to use the last of my strength to raise my head in her direction to what appeared a hallucination of glowing butterflies surrounding her. All went black and the cold stone welcomed his falling body to what may be the final rest of his life in the bowels of a tunnel.

As her wretched screams echo to the heights of the dark oasis Nathan lays unconscious upon the stones. Lashing out in every direction in an attempt to rid herself of this troublesome creatures forbidding her from indulging the hunger of blood which is a mere few steps away. Dark mind twisting at the thought of why such a man could be protected from her very touch as she struggles even harder to dispose of these troublesome little creatures. Agony suddenly rips into her side by a force she has not met in such countless years of existence. She was powerless to confront such an enemy which appeared from out of her existence. Noticing the source of her attacker she grew with the rage welling deep from her very soul. "How can you be here you wretched beast. This is not your place to interfere in my will. Your place is in the forest of the eternals with the other mongrels."

As grandfather stepped from the shadow to face the old crone he prepared to enter into the act of combat. Looking over at Nathan he knew there was little time to waste against her. Calling for the full strength of his own power the dark waters roiled with rage for the disruption to the feast of flesh which was about to take place with the life of his grandson.

"You have no right to him. You think he would not be defended from something like you. His time is not to end at your hands for his purpose here in this world is greater than you could ever understand." As her eye grew darker for the challenge of this ancient man was reprehensible to believe he would come to her domain to attempt to take him from her hands at the time of feeding her dark minions which surge within the waters of the dark.

Though Nathan is lays helpless upon the verge of limbo and life his ears are atoned to the impending battle. How did he find me here it has been years since the last time I saw him. Set as a guardian angel ever vigilant to the protection of those destined for greater than the world could fathom to understand. Crackling stone resonates out as rolling thunder to an everlasting hatred between light and dark what is to come and who shall be victorious between the two.

Grandfather gazes at the old witch who hides herself within the fading reality of human eyes. Calculating the possibility of how she will confront him. Ages have passed for the hunger of spirits who find life as a sustaining element of their existence. Needs to feel life once again yet the exile to an agonizing abyss which holds them exile from the living with a hag as one destined to keep them. "What right to you believe you have here old one. I am the ruler of this place as my minions strive to feed upon this one's soul." Whence she points her hideous finger at Nathan lying helpless near the water's edge with a single push more to emerge him into the grasp of her minions. Twisted teeth exposed from behind pocked lips dripping with a blood that has blackened with time.

Clasping his hands he sends forth a striking blow forcing the witch to plow full force into a distant stone wall. Striking with a hard thud for which could end any man who receives such an attack. Landing upon her feet she returns the favor with one of her own calling for a binding of stone to hold grandfather in place hoping to relish a quick victory. Closing the space between them she looks deep within the eyes of her prey in a dark craving to see the hopelessness within the thought it is over for him at the moment.

Nathan wakes with a rushing start to realize he has not moved from the protection of the camp which the group has made a refuge under a stone overhang. Looking about in a hope to see nothing but stone where in the dream he entered the cave. Blood rushing in his vein's as he hears the pounding of his heart echoing in his ears. "Where is she? Who is she?" looking about for the woman who joined them in the last fight against what she has revealed as shadow of phantoms.

Somehow this miserable place is draining the very life out of me after all that is happening feeling trapped here as the rain falls and burns the very earth it touches. When did the world turn upside down from providing us life to a seeker of our blood! Looking from one person to the next he considers who will be the victims of this dark day if the beast's that follow will make another attempt for an attack. Staring out apparently at the ashen earth stretching before his very eye's.

Beatrice appears by his side as she has been known to do every time she can sense he was in turmoil of thought or feeling helpless. "Mister can you tell me why you always feel that way? I know you miss the way everything was before but just wait and see what beautiful world will come in the sad days we are making our journey through. The lady keeps walking with me telling me of something you need to see which will wake you up from this dream to show you who you really are to this world. So have a little faith you may even get a chance to see the one person you have been looking for in the place we go too." With every encounter with her I stand amazed at what comes from such a young child who seems to have experiences which even he has not considered in his own mind. Taking a moment he looks down at such and innocent face with his warmest smile he could muster.

"Ok young one I will have some faith like you ask of me. Yet for a man my age it may be a little hard but I will do my best." With the rain finally abating they made haste to get out of this horrid place to a safer place. Care was taking in the preparations to cover themselves with the thickest of clothes to ward off the possible burn of the droplets hanging from the overhangs of dead branches. Before stepping after the others Nathan took one last look in despair hoping the rest of the world would not turn into a mirror of this place laid with death and destruction.

Wariness came over Michael as the day came to an end again as they sheltered themselves in a wasted refuge of an apartment building with a view point laying over the courtyard. His body fell to the exhaustion having found a spot to rest in one of the back rooms which held a large mattress which to lay his head. The soft satin linens enveloped him to freely give himself to the waiting rest holding out its arms. Kassandra not far behind him as she briefly spoke to the oud-rah about what is to come in the next day. Michael surrendered to the ease of her melodic voice which danced upon the wind to his ear as he nested slowly into the bed which has been a long lost luxury.

Forgetting time itself he drifted further and further within the realm between the worlds of life and dream for a path of truth he hoped would be waiting. Eyes exposed to the great forest he has not seen in many years walking to the path leading to the old river He and Nathan once fished with grandfather. Noticing the lack of a pole or tackle box gave him a strange sensation of something out of the ordinary. Fragrant trees taking hold in his nostrils bring him closer to a sense of peace which was common in this place. Singing waters calling unto him around the next bend accompanied by the slight melody brought on by a familiar whistling grandfather did every time they came here. A lesson was about to begin with the tone pulsing from his lips.

"Hey there young man you have taken a while to meet me here. What kept you I have been here waiting since the dawning hour hoping you would get here to enjoy the day with me and Nathan. Your brother went out to find would while I waited for you. We have much to discuss." Rubbing my eyes I knew this was not the place I would visit long ago and how could this be now when I am so far from this place. Am I dreamwalking like the many shamans before me to learn from my very past. What is it I am to see in this place.

"Sorry grandfather I guess I overslept again. What do you have for us to learn this day." Looking over his shoulder I could see that welcoming smile he gave us all the time when it was going to be a harsh lesson on life through the telling of the old stories. I stepped forward and took my place in the empty chair beside him preparing myself for Nathan's return. Grandfather patted my back and always knew I was troubled about something no matter how hard I tried to hide it from everyone. The bushes rustled behind us and I averted my eyes to see if it was Nathan finally coming back with the wood to use for a fire in the sweat house talks which lay only a couple feet away from where we were sitting at the moment. What met his eyes was a mysterious sight of a man approaching in an ancient robe similar to the one the oud-rah wears yet not adorned with as many symbols. His aquiline features greatly pronounced with the midday sun striking him.

The creaking sounds of grandfathers chair lay evidence to him getting up to greet this visitor who has come. Amazed how they could know each other I sat and watched them exchange welcomes to each other in a peculiar way I have not seen him do with anyone else in the tribe. My mind raced thinking how these two truly knew each other and how is it that I forgot such a time in my life. Shortly after his arrival Nathan came over with the wood and they all made their way to the sweat house to begin the ceremony. As the heat built we began to give ourselves over to the enveloping heat which unleashed a torrent of sweat from our souls in ways I never knew the body could hold. The old songs echoing in our ears as the drum beat throbbed in our ear penetrating the depths of the spirit realm. Nathan and I as always found this useless but something was different this time. Losing myself in the swirls of smoke and water vapor I envisioned a world unlike what we have known farther from reality.

Cities glowing with light transparent as water and solid as stone to welcome me as one of its own. Looking high into the skies great winged creatures flying about like great eagles which could not exist with a great thud of the wings stroking through the air to stay aloft. Curious how such beast could exist in such a futuristic world with the vision of men upon their backs. I realized I was not alone with the man in the robe standing next to me standing proud at what was being seen to the horizon. Looking up at his face there still laid a bit of sadness to what was around.

"Yes Michael I see you looking upon me and you must know this place. Does it seem familiar to you in the depth of your heart? This is the origin of your blood." Confusion struck me like a ton of bricks on how this could be a place of any significance at all. Time flowed like a raging river with lack of constraints to what is meant to exist in linear fashion. Flashes of the world come raging upon my eyes to reveal the lost story which his people have survived a war passing all forms of explanation.

Within a dream I see the bloodshed that caused the death and destruction that a single human couldn't fathom as a possibility as two factions engage in the darkest of battles. Heaviness gripped my heart as flashes of explosions engulfed each with countless dead and wounded. As air and earth are subject to the constant battle to the each passing moment. Who are they fighting for as the blood paints the ground a crimson gold. My mind begins to wonder towards thoughts of my friend Nathan and hoping we don't see the same vision as the ceremony is taking place with the sweathouse.

How could such evolutionarily advance people commit to such a brutal form of combat, yet to think are we on some form any different than these beings? With such advancement in our world can we come to such an outcome? As the darkness reaches unto the depth of my world I can only hope that those of us that are called the chosen can make a difference and stop this from happening on our world as we have come to know it.

Moordra wakes upon a new day with loathing for what is to come with the conflict of such a simple minded enemy. Filled with a desire to find a worthy opponent he contemplates how he will find the one who escaped him and how he could bring him to a dreadful death upon what he would believe to be honorable combat. Death held little meaning to him for many of his dark years and relished any opportunity unleash his fury upon the masses who resist or even the troops within his command. Opening his canteen to consume the elixir from which he has become accustomed to edify his human form. Looking upon the opening of his tent he caught the vision of the commander waiting to speak with him about the day's events to come with a wish to dispatch his life from all existence in the lust for death.

Lacing his boots Moordra sets the personal grieves which he has become accustomed to wearing as he prepares for a day of epic violence. Once containing a lustrous shine they have become dull with the countless years inlaid on the outer edge with spikes and the inner valley encompassed with intricate bulbs designed to maximize the destructive impact. Striding to the chair he lays hold of his personal sword with the archaic tip gorged with an open valley starting a couple inches from the tip laying intermittently stretching three inches in length forged to expose the greatest amount of fatality to an enemy. Admiring his sword in a wish to relish the countless lives taken by the action of blade introduce to the flesh of a man, woman or child in the endless need for death. Finalizing his attire he steps from his tent to speak to the worthless commander who apparently wanted to brief him on the events that have taken place and what will be planned for the rest of the given day.

"Good day sir! We have been met with bits of resistance from those wretched beast and people who do not wish to succumb to the leagues demands." As he stands staring at the distant sun rising in the far horizon he imagines the chaos of a solar fire that could exist like the sun in his very soul wishing to consume everything. The mindless masses shall soon recognize how they must abide by the league's control or parish. As the officer spoke Moordra considered his own plan of finding the one who could truly feed the appetite for a real fight. Engulfed to the very core was this solitary thought eating away at him for many days now. Stricken like a wounded predator whose prey has momentarily escaped his grasp.

"Well commander we have but one set of action to take and that is to present the masses with little option. As for the beast leave none alive. You have your orders now fulfill them." His cold stare sunk through the command with absolutely no hope of redemption. Swallowing hard the commander turned and with a hand full of troops headed out to the hunt of any who is left in the city. Tanks shaking the very earth with sluggish motion into the buildings off in the distance of the offence post which he presently finds himself stationed to complete the task set before him. With little regard for any of the lives set to his control he considers the next step of his own plan to hunt for the one he hungers to set in the abyss of death.

Returning to his tent Moordra took the box which lay beneath his field bed for a moment of enjoying some of the tasks of his past battles. Taking the time turning each of the intricate tumblers of the lock to open the hidden treasures which brings him a dark sense of joy for the blood shed unleashed over the years of existence. Going over each of his many treasures in an attempt to remember all the victims who believed could take him on in honorable combat finding a reaper waiting to claim their souls as winter wheat. Relishing each with a twisted amusement for the life which once held them as wards to the evil they face day by day. A coating of their blood covering them from the loss of life in varying quantities while he lets his eyes grow dark as midnight recalling in gruesome details every second of torment the countless victims suffered at his very hands. Permitting himself to hope that one more shall be added to the timeless thought of battle to an opponent worth fighting after decades of dormancy of the beast caged within his devilish soul.

Darius conditions himself for the marking of a great control of the masses finally succumbing to his will to dominate. Sitting at the head of the great table which he holds the meeting with the other members of the league taking a glimpse of the ancient journal of his own father considering how many of his predecessors failed at the events which took place so many times before in laying their domination on the world so weak to stand against them. Failure after failure enraging him to accomplish what has been awaiting all who seek the power of mythical koda which has been documented in the journal.

Ghost of the past just will not lay themselves to rest in his mind contemplating the force which he has at will to command in whatever for he chooses to facilitate them. Yet thorns bury deep in his spirit in a possibility he may have to dispatch some of the very members of the league before a proper time and that wretched Moordra who dares to fight his place in the grand scheme of things which is to come for selfish pride.

Closing the journal the old leather cover creaks with the slow pressure placed on its outer bindings. Taking this time to stand with a thought of glancing over some of the reports on the frontline contacts with any form of resistance in lieu of the beast that have presented great turmoil in attempts to capture the heart of the masses. His personal servant steps forth from the shadow at the corner of the room near the doors located at the rear of the room leading to hall which leads to his personal study. Hatred welling deep in his heart which shall be unleashed on all he considers may turn against him at relinquish his rule by some devious plan for an early demise. "Who will try in a hope to challenge my rule over the counsel. Let them come and accept the death which I shall bestow upon them." Permitting the words to finally escape his lips as his chest heaves for the hunger of air to fill his lungs while his black heart pounds like thunder in his chest causing an echo to reach his very ears.

Somehow it has been days since he has seen the little wretch Soba cursing his presence upon the chamber halls. Just to think how all he has done to burn the very soul of time. Pacing back and for he considers the action to be taken place in the city with all the mayhe which can only be considered as a nightmare with all the best and resistance of the survivors who chose not to submit to the rule of the league. The dark thoughts flow from his mind like a river of blood when a sudden pounding upon the chamber door interrupted his thoughts. "Who is there?" with no answer his servant opens the chamber door one of the military personal enters. An astounding look of fear apparent within his eyes to see the head of the league in the flesh being a low ranking member of the armed forces which protect his citadel.

"Good day sir! I am sorry for the intrusion but I feel you must know of an event that happened some days ago." Looking upon him I Darius could tell something was amiss with his composure. The soldier seemed to be somewhat shaken at the possibility of having an audience with him. As he lay his darks eyes with the man to consider what may come from this encounter. "Then out with it soldier! What has gotten you so troubled you had to come directly to me and not Moordra. I have little time to waste with you to come here in such a way to give me a report personally." the long extent of his fingers began to tap upon the table which lay the mass of reports to all the militant actions taking place within his city. A mass of scars lay against his grizzled hands appearing as they could tell a lifetime of stories to battles he engulfed his great reign with endless combat. Even in his advanced years of life the soldier could see the shape of frame of his bone hungering to expose them self from below the stretched flesh on each hand coming to a point at his elongated nails.

"Well sir I wish to advise you that a group of people seem to escape the city. My unit found them on the outskirts making their way south east. Commander Moordra was in charge that day and he seem to be acting quite odd. One man stood between us and the rest of his group in defiance of our force. At the time Moordra stepped down from the mobile unit he was in to observe this man....." the report began to peek his interest as he continued to listen to every detail being laid out before him. Gesturing the soldier to sit at the great table he sat at the head set to commence in what was being presented. His mind stirring with intrigue to all he was facing in the dark plans of his heart in wanting to dispatch more of the men in his command.

"As we engaged with full force as you commanded us something amazing unnerved us all. This one man somehow caused all or munitions to explode before any of them were close enough to unleash their fury upon the mass of people. Moordra witness it and ordered us all to leave him behind to personally deal with this threat alone. One of the officers protested and he executed the man without hesitation for the protest. After witnessing that we all decided to leave him behind as ordered. When out of view I got out of my transport and took a couple men back with me thinking he may need some help. Staying out of view we stood in the hollow of a building watching to see if the commander needed our help." The young man swallowed hard at what he was about to say because he seem to feel he could not believe his own eyes. Moments passed in stealth in an attempt to describe every detail of the day's events in a hope that it would make sense speaking them out to Lord Darius. Hope beyond hope he went on revealing how the commanders own form seemed to mutate in preparation to face the man standing apart for the group. Running his fingers through his auburn hair the young soldier could not make sense of the entire event, especially revealing to his lord how the group seem to vanish into thin air at the instant the commander was making his was forward at the man. "The group I lead back amazing just stared in stun silence to what happened with the commander and that specific group. What do you suggest I do sir if such an event ever happens in the future."

Darius sat in his chair contemplating what is to be done. His dark heart knew this could not be tolerated with anyone being able to stand against his plan in such a way. Looking over his shoulder he gestured to his servant to approach from his dark corner of the room. "You have done well to advise me of this and I will make further inquiries on the events of that day." Looking at his servant he made mention that the young soldier was to stay here and quarters are to be prepared for him. As he completed his command the two of them made their way to the door leading to the hall. Sustaining his position in his chair as the door thundered shut. Taking this moment he began to realize why Moordra made such a request to leave the city in the hope of finding this man that escaped his grasp. Now he must prepare for the possible threat and seek it out to safeguard his desire to rule all without question.

CHAPTER 16

Walking through the once grand halls of his ancestrial home Soba takes the time to reflect upon the great memory of the place he once called home. Escaping from the citadel of the city from all the madness he considers all he wishes to come to fruition in the coming time. With the one woman he considers to be his greatest confidant he escorts her into the great doors. Making his way into the wine cellar which he would spend a great amount of time with his father to choose one of the bottles of blood vein wine in the hope to remember a graceful past.

Pulling two glasses from beneath a cloaked cabinet he pours the thick serving to place into the delicate hands of his companion. Seeing the cloud like flow of the substance intertwined with the memory of his life he could see the years gone by like a distance dream. Such a delicacy could rarely be thought to exist these days which would have a life of its own to be consumed in hopes of the dark hope he would rule like his father before him in this manor once again. Her eyes gleaming with honor of having been shown some sort of past to the man she has given her very soul unto on numerous occasions. The black silloette of her gown hanging about her like a phantom of mercy to unleash a part of himself to feel anything beyond the hatred of the man who brought torment into this man she sees before her.

Every fiber of her heart ached with love and mercy to a man torn by the loss of his family right to be watched by the leader of a dark commission to bring the world under his boot.

Soba can see in her eyes a stirring of her mind to something he could not place his finger one but a hope of some sort lay in depth of it all. In some length of thought he could not see why he brought her here but it was pulling on him to make some connection to free himself to the glimmer of light. Ascending back to the main floor with the bottle gripped firmly in his hand he takes his time to walk into the old library decaying with several layers of dust and web from years of neglect. In the far corner lay his table that he spent much of his youth unraveling the mysteries of history and sciences of what his father considered a family honor to learn the dark arts. Surrendering to this memory he could see the once innocent child witting in the chair as his father stood smiling at the shelves peering at the countless volumes of books which could awaken the mind. At time he could recall a fable his father read from one of the books upon the top shelf. Though it escapes his words Soba places his hand on the book which contained the words which appear to be nothing more than a journal from a lost soul of the past.

Gently opening the book he could smell the age of the books life wafting toward him with every turn of the page as the look of tarnish consumed the page with little else but the ancient ink standing out. Page after page he tears through looking for the fable of his life. Mind and heart racing to find some hidden treasure which will awaken the ghost of his father in the words that await him in the journal. “You whose blood calls me through time will arise to overcome the darkness of life. The heir will overcome the enemies of the light to your soul. It is the blood of Sebastian who shall call you forth in the flash of light to break the dark wall.” Peering upon the words his mind could hear the echo of his father’s voice reaching out to him from the abyss of death giving him the strength to achieve his goal.

Making his way back to the very first page which contains the name of the journals true owner and sense of intrigue grasped him to wonder who would be so hopeful about something like this to arrive in reality. Why could this ever mean anything to make him see a possible dreamer.

"How could anyone think in such a way now? It seems our world has been in darkness for so long there is little to hope for in the sake of seeing a brighter day." As her worlds are caught upon the wind he reaches the name of the unknown author of the words.

This is the rightful property of Olivia grand-daughter of Sebastian. His heart began to pound at the thought his father contained the book such as this. Sebastian's own heir wrote this journal but how did it come to find its way here to this very library in his home. Looking over at his companion she appeared to be stunned by this discovery as well. They both believed any such literature was destroyed ages ago by the league in an attempt to strike at the heart of all men to never rise against them. Minds racing to think how many others may have survived the years and if his father was part of the long lost line to the rebellion which challenged the league. Frantically turning through the pages to see more of this woman's words a loose sheet of paper folded among the pages fell to the floor before him. Retrieving the document he opened it to lay witness to something he could not believe to exist.

A letter hidden for him to find address from his own father:

Dear son,

I believe by the time you find this a great shift may be in motion in the world. Personally I don't expect to be around to see what is happening but I hope you have achieved a great amount of success. With all I have shown you was in the likeliness that the arts I have given you to study was to be able to defend yourself from any harm.

My dreams have foretold of the coming storm which you

will experience with a prophecy I discovered years before you were ever born. It reveals that long ago a man began a resistance against our counsel to give these humans a different life from what we were trying to accomplish. We thought we were doing what is best for us all when we started and realized the experiments seemed detrimental to our goals.

As you must know by now you have an unequaled ability in genetics as I do which may seem strange to you but I can explain. Research on our family has revealed we are infused by an extraterrestrial genome giving us an ability to pass our knowledge down the bloodline. Some ancient document calls it the blood memory unlocked many generations back in the last war for control and it is still active in our family.

The former owner of this journal after great personal cost has been revealed as one of our ancestors. You would take heed to read her accounts of what has happened to our family and the world. We have a purpose far beyond what we could ever fathom possible.

My son, please understand that Darius is not as he seems. I have uncovered layers of mysteries he is hiding from the entire counsel which does not include us at all. He is taking measures to rule the world alone and dispatch the entire counsel in some way. If I am taken from you be cautious when taken under the wing of a demon may show warmth yet the heart is ice cold. Hold true to your studies of the arts for they may save your life and a great awakening will take place for your sister may arise in a time you never knew and the great gift may be unleashed for our family to truly see what we can become. So look to the horizon as you have always done for the sun to light the darkness. My spirit will always be with you. Farewell Soba!!

The words flow over him like a tidal wave of mayhem to what has just been revealed after so many years of life lost. His eyes a swirling turmoil of emotions his companion has never laid witness to his character. Hands shaking violently in the air as Soba gripped the letter in his hand with a vise like hold. A flash of insanity revealed itself in his soul like a venomous shimmer of auradian light engulfing every inch of his body from crown to sole on the brink of exploding. Soba appeared similar to a meta human who seemed to be unlocking some greater power which humanity have never believed existed in anything living here on the world. Instantaneously as it started he re-centered his mind to a point of clarity.

"Are you alright dear? You seem to have gotten some news that surprised you. I have never seen you in such a state of complete shock. What was in the letter?" as her eyes never lost contact with his hoping he would see how she felt for him. It has been about a decade since there first encounter which started in violence and hopefully would end with a connection that would join them for a lifetime. Wishing to reach out in the instinct to hold him kept a thick the silence amidst the air with such density to feel a moment it could strike the life right out of her with a wave of his hand.

Standing there shaken to the core she could only look in awe with the exposure of the power laying deep in his soul. Little could be told of his secrets Soba keeps within himself yet the letter seems to have revealed something that could not be simply explained. "What was written on the paper my dear? It seems to have disturbed you for some reason?" though he hears her words his eyes lay blind to the direction upon which she stands before the grand windows he spent many of days in his childhood in wait to his father to return from the counsel citadel. Both appeared locked in a lost world of new revelations to what is about to come as instantly it began Soba apparently regained his demeanor after his loss of conscious thought after reading the letter.

Sam gained his strength with every passing day beginning to walk under his own power passing all expectation from the extent of his injury weeks before. Taking a place next to Nathan while they venture deeper into the marsh like grounds which took greater semblance to a nether world few could imagine could truly exist in reality. As they walk in silent ponderings of what has happened and what may be next upon the journey they take in this life.

"Hey Nathan! Do we have any idea what this tower place is like or how far we will have to go till we get there? Just seems like an endless march into oblivion by what I am seeing right now." Setting his mind to the question troubled his spirit in a way few could really understand. Taking the time to look around at everything around him started to make him realize this was no place for them to be with all that has come to pass here. Feeling the gentle grip of Beatrice by his side just made it worse for the fact he needed to get her to the towers as fast as possible. Sam was another story in general as he began to look at the man as a battered piece of cloth after a dog has gotten to use it as a play toy.

"Well I really have no idea about what you ask Sam. At the most part I just barely see above the waters of the madness we are swimming in right at this moment. Yet I can believe we really don't have more than a couple days left till we arrive at the towers." Feeling a little perplexed about how he knows the time it will take to get unto the towers made his stomach churn. Sam stared at him with a wide eyed look which made him think how any of them could last much longer in this place with all the devastation going on right now.

"You think many of will make it there with all that is going on? I am worried a lot of the injured may not make it much further without some real medical attention." As Nathan looked back upon the cluster of people following he contemplated the same idea of the ones who still need to be carried. "Need not worry gentlemen because the one we seek is well versed in all kinds of healing craft. You will all be quite surprised with all that he knows."

Confusion consumed their faces as the stranger made the comment of the one they are on the way to see. Nathan was still troubled about the dream he had about this woman and grandfather, is she really here to help or leading us further into doom. Giving a slight nod they continued on with little more than a grumble for the misery pushed upon them from the trudging of the land and a horrid stench of death lingering upon them like a stain. Just how much farther can everyone truly be pushed when he could feel the hope being siphoned from each person's soul.

"Dammit boys do you really have any inclination on where we are all going? Looks as though you are just wondering around with little idea of what we are to do." The stranger gazed at the man to silence him with a look of discuss unlike anything since before by Nathan. Movement presented itself under her cloak which gave warning of what she was planning on doing to the man who was protesting. Closing the distance between them he grab her wrist beneath the clothe feeling the hilt of a knife which could have been a plan to warn or kill. As she could feel the iron grip she fiercely set her gave on Nathan for what he was doing. Returning the stare he gave little evidence to prove he would yield from her glance. With a low growl of a whisper toward the woman to show a point of authority he was taking over them all. "Don't even dare what you have intended toward him. You think little of me and you will be sadly mistaken if you think I will let you use that weapon on any of them." When she stared at his eyes from the tone in his voice she noticed something was truly different about him as though nature had little to do with his coming into existence.

"Now tell me how much longer do we have till we reach this man with such healing powers and furthermore his ability to get us to the towers in such a short time? I have little time for games, yet the others are running short on patience with you taking us so deep into this living hell for the past two days." With deep scowls etched upon both of their faces a sudden sound alerted them to another unknown being from the gloom and fog. Shifting his gaze Nathan lay notice to a man venturing through the marsh to meet them. With little more than a simple tunic and cloak worn with age he could hardly imagine what could come of his approach, taking the moment to ready himself for any possibility of another fight he prepared with bruiser quickly taking position by his side and the woman shaking his grip free to unsheathe the blade she had hidden beneath her own cloak.

"You need not hold a blade on my account Lhian I have known you were coming so I chose to meet you here as it was foretold in my dreams. I am the one you all seek, come this way and I will give you all shelter. Come quickly the rain wishes to fall again and burn its hatred once more." As they followed he took them unto a cavern some short distance for shelter as the last few made it in the ground began to his violently with the storm which struck the land the first time they arrived to this place. Finding a place for each of them in turn the old man made his way through the motley group to assess the extent of the wounded in the form of a great physician making his rounds in a hospital.

"Rest now young man we will have time to talk tomorrow when the day breaks anew." Hearing his kind words Nathan guided Beatrice to a space where they took a refuge settling themselves a well needed rest. Within moments of the child peacefully giving in to slumber his mind easily gave in to the great need for a desired sleep.

Malostrange sets provisions for the hunt his master has

given unto him to achieve. Hearing the steps of the woman enter the tent give him little alarm for what may come. He dare not turn to look upon her for the welling of the past may come forth to the surface of his face. Troubled by the need to take her with him he focused himself at the task at hand as she stood at the doorway.

"I know it has been a great while since I have left but you need not ignore me. We are destined to find the talisman together." As he finally took the time to look upon her eyes he could see the old heart appear within the deep pools of her soul. His instincts took its course and he gave freedom to the deep growl giving a bit of a warning of his own emotions which tore at him from the fact of how close he felt to her. Stuffing the last of what he could get from the hut malostrange pushed his way through the door on his way to the medical hut to gather a couple herbs which may come in handy in the quest. Taking little time he grabbed what he needed and headed on to his own dwelling to receive his favorite weapon.

Waiting within his own battle master was there with a look of foreboding to what he was planning. "I know what you may be thinking my apprentice but you must take her. It will take the both of you to retrieve the needed weapons for the coming battle." Letting out a great huff Malostrange showed his great discontent with having this come from his teacher. It has been years since he was considered an apprentice and now he is being advised to take a woman who betrayed him in to the deep woods in search of a weapon.

"My master why must I take her with me, she has not earned such an honor to your request for a weapon such as the one I am to seek for you. Is there something you are not telling me about her return?" searching his masters face he could tell on the edge of his thoughts there was more to be told of why such a request was made to him. "You will see when the time comes! Just be ready for tomorrow you will go to not only rid this land of the beast that killed many of your kind but to regain a weapon that was meant for you and her to accomplish a great prophecy we have to the coming darkness." Little of the words gave him ease to what must be done but looking back at the door where she stood he began to remember what was before with a bit of hope it could be again. Recalling the mating ritual preformed years ago before she vanished he could only hope she would not flee him in the time of great need like before when he lost control of his mind training which caused him the greatest of wounds killing a friend. The sun settled itself on the far mountains which gave him notice to prepare a meal before the night took hold.

Heading back to the hut where she stood, he laid hold of some dried meat, a wheel of cheese, some bread and a bottle of wine. "Sit with me! I know you have not eaten this day so have some and let us prepare for the night of rest. Tomorrow we are to enter the deep woods for what master has said waits for us there." Her eyes grew wide with a welcome sound of his voice she has not partaken of in quite a long time.

That night they sat and took part of what once was a daily event with them to eat and speak of combat. She could see a bit of the old mate she knew so long ago before her fear took hold of her mind. As the sun gave way to moon they spent many hours in the hut speaking and preparing for the next morning giving in to the past comfort they gave unto one another.

CHAPTER 17

Volta starts to pace within his dwelling consumed by the thoughts of what is to come. Possessed by something he could not control he seals the door in the hope none could enter in the middle of what he is preparing to do. Stepping before the mirror his body morphs into a form he has not permitted himself to take in such a long span of his life. Swiping his hand upon the old mark of his birth he felt the coldness of his plot forming once more into such a great tidal wave of hatred for Darius. With all he could do this mark is the one part of it he could not hide in either form, yet his own brother was unable to see what lay beneath the layers of secrets in his own pitiful servant.

"I can only see what you have become brother seeking more power in a wish to control the whole world. To believe you killed me off those years ago as you did father but my powers have always been greater than yours. Foreseeing your betrayal and letting our own father died with a servant you thought was me." Breaking out to a thunderous laughter as his mind dives deeper into the darkness his only blood relative would fear to go. His thoughts consider the greatest of his betrayal in killing the woman he betrothed in secret after learning the heir to our power laid in her very womb.

The time will come when all I have given shall become a fire to consume you brother then all that shall be left is me to rule. Recalling that day in great detail how he was force to cut the child from her belly as she lay dying beholding a son. Your time is coming and my son shall rule if only he knew I was still here. Time is really coming where the blood will flow my brother and I shall be the blade which cuts to the soul.

Soba stands in the old garden of his home as he looks at the devastation he once saw as peaceful while the woman comes to him. His thoughts spin like a whirlwind of all that was and is lost to time and insanity.

"My lord another has come as before!" Soba turns to retrieve the letter which has come to the house. How can anyone know he is here? He spoke to none of the counsel of his departure to his ancient home.

"Who brought this here commander? Did you see the man's face or was it left easily enough to find?" as the two moons lay an enchanting silhouette over the distant landscape. As he began to read the letter the commander was left befuddled by the complexity of how anyone could know they were there at the house. Awaiting the order of his league he stood his ground attempting to see what may be in this new correspondence from this mysterious individual. Mere months ago this same phantom left a similar correspondence to Soba that reveal the creation of the beast which now confront the military personal which run the city of the citadel. What shall be presented now that his lord will find of any great importance to what is happening now in the world. Shall any real good come of this conflict to improve the world?

She stands as the omen
on a distant shore where the sun burns awake
Her eyes search the heaves for the greatness of a soul
Spread wings, talons share as teeth lay bared
The sisters of mercy look
onto the land which floats upon the great waters
Hands reached high to the hope
which glides upon the wind songs
Day is coming and the darkness runs

from the blades of fire
Chosen are the beholders of this flame
My daughter waits for them
to stand before her as glowing stone flies
Awake shall they be from the long sleep of the blood

Walking through the towers she considers all that she has spoken of with her father as she joins the other medinus to resume their studies of the order. Every passing day feels as a set path which presents her with the possibility of becoming a record keeper of the world's evolution. Although something more is pulling upon her mind like a haunting past which will give her no peace. The boy comes to her with relentless repetition causing her to consider he is of some importance in what is to come in the time when all hell is breaking loose and the oud-rah had to be awakened once again after centuries of absence in the world.

Endless corridor after another she follows the others to the place of study as she passes the door of the great teacher of the keeper's tower. Partially ajar she is able to peer in and noticed he is pacing with a purpose looking upon a parchment aged by time for some unknown reason. Faint whispers reach her ears while she realizes that he is speaking with another member about important knowledge presented upon the parchment within his very hand.

"Mirdan we must understand that the prophecy speaks of the brothers of the black who are part of the battle. We know not their allegiance in so many centuries that have past if any still exist at all." As the lines formed upon his brow the great teacher ponders the possibility of the brothers of black. Knowing it has been a great while since any have been called upon in so many years. The times have changed for them to be considered for anything of such importance, but now is the time to see what fate has become of them.

"Send a messenger unto the south cauldron keep to see if

any truly live this day for the chosen will not have such an easy time if they are not a part of the coming battle. Even his very choice of the war man he seeks on the isle shall not be enough for what comes. Hurry before the seeker of blood takes us into his cold grip and we lose this world to the darkness itself." Noticing the man rushing to the door where she stood the young one scampers back to rejoin her fellow medinus on the time of study. Burning wonder surged through her mind on what the great teacher was speaking of with the other member of the order. Who are these members of the order of the black and what prophecy were they referring too?

The grand doors creaked themselves into a strain purpose to open upon ancient hinges permitting the entrance to the library of the histories to begin their days studies. Her father was in the center of the encompassing center of the room surrounded by an orchestra of chairs and tables where all of my young fellows sat. Occupied by what I heard all I kind think about was the information that fell upon my ears. Lost to the world she tried to hid the transparency of her curiosity from her father for something that was not meant for her ears so she bid the time to pass that she make take a time to look further for the order of the black in the histories. "I will find your secrets and hopefully be of some use to the keepers and the likes of man."

Fog permeates the very streets which they have walk countless times in youth in a wish to see hope of life. The wind whipped at their facing as unforgiving as death's touch upon a soul. Little can be remembered of life in a world so mad to kill its very own people as they encompassed themselves further with the great wool cloaks they wore in the time of great chill. So much has become strange to them with the countless years they have lived in the wilderness on the outskirts of the city of Solarianvale left in the midst of a mountainous range which was not spared the vicious bombing which took place so many weeks ago.

From generation to generation the brothers have known this time was coming, yet they could not believe it was to come upon their time to fulfill the decree set upon ancestors of the order which they were initiated into with the years of youth which was places upon them. Ancient rage built within their souls as they walked the streets of what was once a metropolis shining in the farthest reaches of the eye. From the mountain top the brothers of black sat and watched at the chaos ensued with reckless abandon as people ran for possible shelters to be left in the death which waited as a starving hunter salivating over the next feast of blood.

Those weeks passed as they spent time recalling the etching upon the cave walls speaking of a time when the chosen shall rise and the brothers of black stand at the side to be reborn as a select few who will awaken from the dream of life. Much has been reveal in the light of pain shown its face and they knew it was time to travel into the city and see what has become of any man, woman and child that may be left. Countless people looked upon them as they made their way beyond the streets of pain to a central pillar which stood as the vow to all man which is to be fulfilled by the brothers. As they recall life in the beginning each understood was to befall them for the prophecy was presented to them on the fourteenth year of life in the training of war. Encompassing the pillar they place a hand upon the sides and recite the oath of the order which was placed in safe keeping of memory but never knowing why at this time it was for them to come here and recite.

"A trident of blood are we to become as night doth fall upon the world. For our cloaks as the will be as a shield for the cold touch of death. Permit us the time to face the nightmare which grips the souls of a world lost. As the brothers of black do raise our light upon a shadowed path in guidance to those lost in night's shade. Called as the past do lay our very lives forfeit for the namesake of an ordain war man. Fulfill shall we all prophetic command of our lord to stand at the side of the chosen. So shall it be from now to the last drop of our souls blood." As they completed the citation of the oath an opening presented itself to them all. Culdra, Tolevah and Davunis looked upon each other in amazement for what lay within. Each in turn reach a hand unto the gift of a birthright each was known to have achieved.

Sitting within a cradle of dark translucent fluid which appeared to be unnatural to the world as it may seem. Obsidian stones crafted with such magnificence bringing each man to wonder if this gift was from the god's of old or something even beyond the very likeliness of reality. Holding the stone the symbol of their tribal names appeared in liquid light forming in the center as a sweet singing voice called to them out of the recesses of thoughts they did not even know existed. Like a mother she touched the deepest parts of each man's soul. The fog took a life of its own as it encompassed them all at the spire which has been the start of something unreal to them all. A world upon world shifted and swirled like a whirlpool bringing them to a new land never before seen by their eyes.

Cavernous craters spread across the expanse of the land with little to recognize the possibility of what may have been a society. Far surpassing that of the common technology they could understand as the residual framing of building lay as bare bones exposed to the winds ravages over time. The spires was a welcomed sight spanning every couple meters apart to resemble the ancient way they noticed in the studies of the predecessors of people few would believe ever existed at all. Remains of life riddled the grounds as the dark wind blew revealing the open maws of beings which eyes reveal the truth of pain which was laid upon them all.

Venturing out taking the time to see more of what is here in hopes to see someone alive to find out the cause of the destruction of this once great city. Softly the song rings in each man's ears in some sense guiding through a path apparently needed to show them all what is required of them all. Holding ground before the next spire was a grey cloak which kneeling in what seemed to be a state of prayer for some unknown purpose. "You have come at last my sons." Shocked by the words the men lay a glance of wonder why this man would call them his son. To consider someone to believe that he would know them in personal matters as a father would be unimaginable with the fact they have never met before.

"Long before your formation within the womb of your mothers it has been set in destiny that our line shall be called upon. Brothers of black stand as the guardians of innocence and virtue. For you three it is claimed by you to fulfill the fight against him who is are to the killer of the world from this ancient land to that from which you call home. I pray swift strikes and clean kills as you have been trained to do in war my boys." Time seemed to freeze as they stood upon the realm with little meaning to them since they have never seen a world like this before. Magnifiscent spender surrounding them from fantasy of the heart left in ruin to be lost in history of life.

The sorrow of death that has taken hold of this world resonates into each man's soul to the very extent of familiarity which passes all bounds. He stood before the spire and turn to face them in a hope to see the face of the one who dares call them his son's. Great splatters of what appeared to be blood trailing out from under the hood of his very cloak as though he was attempting to hide an important part of himself. Scattered tears of flesh revealed from what must have been a ruthless battle with an enemy that lay little care for life. Still the semblance of a grin crossed what was left of his face to give an eerie peace to them.

How could they seem to understand what has happened to this one man that passes all thought of combat. Yet unnerved by the man's appearance none showed sign of what they felt. All the training given to them in life prepared them for such grotesque savagery.

"I pray this outcome does not befall you my son's. Our world was a great beacon of the universe yet the darkness consumed some of our people in a lust for more power after the discovery of an ancient artifact the forefathers left hidden from us. The koda is of great importance to all of us and we are to protect it from there clutches. This was the outcome of our great battle and few escaped to the world you now call home yet they continue the quest for more to control. Many names have they used to consider themselves superior to all they want to dominate. In my time of service they were known as the proprietors of sapienus which left much to be desired. When they slowly took control some of us took arms in defiance and our world was laid to waste. I humbly pray it does not happen to your home now take those weapons given you and defend the koda she will need all your skill to fulfill the destiny to save our people." Standing in awe the three stood motionless to what has been revealed unto them in a purpose they could not fathom was possible to be done. Looking towards the heaven consideration of all that is to be done race in each mind like a wild wind from the very expanse of the universe

A deep pounding of a thunderous heartbeat began to ring within their ears focusing on the travesty of what has happened to this beautiful world and hoped it would not come to pass on the place they called home. The soft voice began to sing to them again within the recesses of their minds and the stones which each clutched within each hand warmed in the process of gaining an amazing weight. Looking down weapons never before seen was wielded somehow connecting to the very soul of a man. Consumed by the connection to these new weapons the three prepared for the path unto the towers for which the vision has entailed the location of the artifact of their people. For the revelation of the future will be exposed in what may be the battle which shall define a new course for the world at hand

The winter wind swept across his face as Michael and his companions ventured aboard the leviathan vessel created to traverse these dark waves. Seeking the answer for a possible dream among the night sky as the celestial bodies made way on the universal journey. Many of years he has sought to believe the movements to present some truth to why he is the way he was destined to be a wondering leaf blown by the passing wind.

While the voice of the wind and waves sung unto his heart bringing ease to what torment was encompassing his heart to all that has come. Through the frothy splash of the waves meeting the ship's hull providing an easy rhythm to every movement forward. Staring back at his companions Michael could hardly believe how they contain such skill to sea life that was unconceivable after living at the valley of the towers. Yet he is baffled how they were able to find five men on the dock apparently destined to sail with them to the isle in search of this unknown warrior named Damian.

Recalling the days it took to travel all this way unto the coast in the likeliness to cross the span of the sea to the isle of blood to search for him. Nathan continuously entered his mind in feeling he was in need of him for some reason that could pass every level of understanding. Michael sensed his oldest friend was in some danger from an unknown hunter of the soul who could cross the borders of time and space to find him in the lust for his death. After setting out amidst the calming seas he could feel little more than the endless loneness of his path surrounded by such companions who can barely understand the weight upon his shoulders from his testing journey. Morning rose from the eastern gloom with a rouge tint of the clouds revealing the nightly bloodshed falling over the world. With a heavy heart the abyss grew to the length of thoughts flooding his mind.

Closing his eyes he looked back on the time it took for them to reach this very point upon the seas of turmoil as the world churns. With a lost love reclaimed on the path to an unknown precipice to face a man few may even consider exists at all in such a way for the likeliness of war alone. "You look like you need to rest Michael. It has been several days since you really had a proper rest and they say it will be another day or so upon the sea till we reach the isle." Her voice broke through the very depth of thought which consumed him completely. A comforting knowing she was there with him again.

Retreating himself unto the lower chambers for a moments rest would possibly give a respite from the many thoughts engulfing his mind of his good friend Nathan. While he had little hope of ever finding peace on the worry that extends to his friends safety in this new chaotic world.

Searching for a reason from the opening of a vast valley door in the middle of what seemed to be an open graveyard. Michael has not remembered the last moment of having a dream such as this in a great number of years. While the murky mist swirls in the open space without the evidence of wind blowing through the area.

As the stillness reached itself into his very soul considering why he was brought here at all. Who have you come to see master of the hollows? Stepping forth from the door in the direction of the voice he lost himself to the depth of the drifting dream. Recognition easing his mind to understand a voice such as this comes to but few of his kind who study the road. Speaker of the mist have waited to guild him in to a sense of safety yet his wits must be the focus to keep from being distracted by the many who stay within the hollows of the graveyard. To be consumed by the ones daring to be there very depth of control for all that shall attempt to pass through the path such as this to see him at the tree. Footfall to a path which intrigues his way into the very midst where an ancient tree waits twisted and aged with since of an eternal life blooming in each branch.

"You still seek answers for what lay ahead for the twelve of you my boy. It is a great burden you must carry as the keeper of the hollow. Yet what you seek is more than you can understand beyond the recollection of you human form. Understand me when I say that you will require much for this journey that you and the other will partake. This balance must be kept to protect the many that wait for peace in this dark time." as the weight of the words bared a burden which he could not fathom was possible for him.

"What do you mean for me and the other chosen?" quandaries flowed through his mind attempting to grasp what he is being told by this unknown entity which slowly began to form in front of him. Wonder and amazement were over taken by the fear of such a place and being to have existing to speak with him. For a moment he felt he had passed on to the spirit world and left his body prior to Michael completing his test of life. What shall come of this meeting in which he feels lost and confused?

Walking the grounds they began and arguous task of relaying the next events which shall form the world with the meeting of the warrior upon the isle they sail to in the realm of the living. He presents Michael to a place never before seen by the eyes of men. Endless forest stretched before him to reveal in a clearing what appeared to be a temple built in the side of a hill with a form of writing that could not be deciphered by any man alive. Looking at the one who was guiding him Michael's mind grew into greater confusion trying to realize that the language seemed to bring an ancient memory from deep within.

"What are we doing here? What is this place you have brought me to it feels I have been here before." the very sounds and smells trigger a greater familiarity while they stand in the scene of tranquility. Tremors brought themselves to life beneath his feet like a bad omen as the world grew silent from some arriving evil from the bowels of hell itself. Swiftly a beast emerged from the temple before him that shock him to his soul. “Prepare boy he is here for you!!!” with an unimaginable speed the creature launch itself at Michael. As it closed the distance between them the entity spoke as a whisper in the mind unlocking a necessary revelation to help him.

Moordra bids his time with the feeling of a coming war with an unknown enemy although his mind continued to recall the one who slipped his grasp as he waiting for his dark minions to return on word. Niel lay silent from his need of his dark lords voice to guide him as it was in the beginning before he took up the mantle of the hunter of souls and released himself from the bonds of humanity. To him peace was found in a battle bathed in blood. Making his was passed the maze of soldiers and equipment to look at the possible conflict to come with a waste of genetics in a beast which to him was no more than a maker of noise which was not worth his skills in death. Looking back towards the place which the head of the league considers his safe haven was but a tall standing tomb which they hide their inferiority.

As his rage grew within him and the hunger on the verge of overwhelming him the cords of the spirit set his mind unto a breach of the realm barrier. His dark hard seemed to have a twisted sense of joy for the hunt of any who can be strong enough to pass the barrier would be a prey he hungered for the possible hunt. Considering the return to his resting quarters to prepare the blade he was interrupted by the shrill sound of the beast of the city making a fast approach unto the very place he was standing.

The ground rumbled beneath his feet as though a division of tanks were following them in a battle formation of their own, yet it was not consistent to the mechanized vibration but the thud of a step of something extremely large and in great numbers. Stretched into a venomous grin he called out like a monster who craved a hunt from dark stories given to children at the fires of the past. His troops rushing to form their own lines in preparation some were consumed by the sight of the enormous creatures coming about the outer range of buildings about two stories tall with an appearance of flesh and machine.

Seeing the simplicity of the enemy which approaches he sets his blade to the ready and makes a call for a charge. Rushing headlong into the depth of the approaching enemy Moordra hears the venomous shrieks of the beast that arose from the depth of an unknown hell he has not had the pleasure to see. Striking the first of the scattered clusters the blood splashes out upon the wind as a crimson black bathing his face and hands.

The soldiers take heart as the dust floats free in all directions and the dust begins to envelope the general with such speed it is unbelievable any one man can move so fast. With every movement of his hand his efforts to kill appear without conflict. Ranks form to set a charge of their own into the fray of mayhem as the goliath of the beast continues forward to destroy the very threat which is quickly dispatching the screechers. "Move you bastards and get your fill of the blood and guts which shall pave our way to glory." Shouts ring out from every man and woman in the ranks scrambling in to the killing fields of what they believe to be demons from the depth of cauldrons deep from which all monsters dwell.

Lines of combatants converge into the thunderous sound of metal and flesh striking with such force. Within seconds both have lost numbers unimaginable to see in mere seconds. Shots shine like daytime fireflies streaking the air with swiftness as claws tear into flesh to reveal sinews and veins to air as cries of suffering fill the air. Heavy guns breath's into life upon the largest of the foes to put it down as fast as possible. Making quick effort of scaling the back of the goliath Moordra reaches the exposed neck easily stabbing wildly upon the soft neck to severe its head from the body. When an explosion from within his own madness twists his body to the monster niel has created him to be when in combat effortlessly reaching his hands in the slashes he has made in the neck to grasp the spine, with a quick jerk the beast falls back as the gun continues to lay a great quantity of fire at the giant creature. As flesh is laid to waste to it as a mist from its own blood forming like a fog about it body. Suddenly the gunner noticed general moordra plummeting to the earth upon its back. With a violent thud the beast shakes the ground quaking underneath its great mass.

Nathan wakes to the light thought of the past when he was arriving home from a long day of work to see a message waiting for him one the machine. "Hey honey hope the case went well today sorry I could not be there. Things are well here but I have been thinking about what you asked me before I left. I hope when I get back we can get together and make plans to advance our relationship." A light smile crossed his face to think about her even at this time of sorrow.

Yet he doubted she could have survived what the carnage of the attack on the world as it now stands. Seeing the young girl by his side the events to come were set to keep going to the towers which he could hope held a slight peace. Now the thought of her belonging there was all he could understand but what was really waiting for them all there. Time will only tell as they all make way to head out for another day of shaken nerves and aching bodies. Some of the people who were injured finally showed signs they could make it under their own power and provide a little more help unto the defense of the group.

The duration of the day continued to recall the time he would wake with her by his side right before they got ready to go into another day of courts protocol and witness decisions. From time to time he could look over at her as she recorded the dialogue of the question and answer of each person while the visual composer set the people in perfect form on the pad he carried in his hand for the files of the case. Just to imagine the number of times he has had been composed to so many cases in his short career in law. She was the one who truly saw him as a person and not some wretched law vindicator to destroy a life by the twist of words.

Everyone considered me an outsider since I was from the Reservation of the Bouldin's Creek. Much of society has written my people of which is why I changed my name to gain a bit of acceptance in the office. She was the one who recorded the first time I ever stepped in the courts and she came up to me at the end of the day and talked to me. With a heavy nervous accent I tried to speak which got her to giggle a little making me smile before I could realize she was a genuinely sweet girl. Months rolled by and we spent more and more time together talking about our families. I did not have much to say since we were not that close but Michael was really the only one I consider family on the Res. Everything seemed to fade when they were together and she told him she was willing to spend the rest of her life with him. Nathan finally thought from his life he can actually have a bit of hope for a positive future. Years went by and they prepared plans for a joining of families. "Elena I think it is time we took the steps to join together as a family. Would you prepare for the oath in the temples?" she appeared elated to consider such a step but she needed to take a trip to her family and talk with them of it.

He took her to the airport a couple days later and knew this was necessary as she went to see her family and let them know of the choice. As he watch the plane vanish in the distance he returned to the apartment they shared to prepare for the case. As the night went he could only think of her beside him forever. As the next day dawned his dreamed turned to a nightmare where he now finds himself walking through the wasteland with the group and take a trek to the towers. It has been such a long time since he has thought of her and did not know why she came to mind now. Time will tell if they will find each other again.

As word reached Darius of the combat which took the life of Moordra he could hardly imagine such a thing could happen. He set himself in his chair at the head of the table looking out to what was an empty hall while the general gave a report of the enemy which they faced at the outer perimeter of the city. Contemplation of the next step to control the region was to find where these creatures were coming from and how did they just appear from nothing. The entire listing of what has been lost in the line of men in the conflict he cared little with the fact all these damn soldiers are nothing but mere pawns to what he desired.

The loss of such a warrior like Moordra was beyond belief for the fact that he was such an effective killer which has fulfilled greater destruction and being the only survivor. He dismissed the general before he had even concluded the report and waited a moment before he considered making his was to Volta's chamber in the catacombs of the tower to seek a solution to increase his hold on the counsel and the pitiful mass of people seeking his guidance to rule over them all.

An hour passed when he took himself down the back stairs at the far end of the hall to the bowels of the tower to the secret room which he considered his sanctuary. While his dark mind just conjures the very hunger for greater power to trample the world under the very soles of his boot. Volta must have some new information to have him achieve his very desires. Reaching the threshold of his entrance he just makes his way in to see his servant. His mind racing and he finds that the world has come to the catacombs of the dark castles of his dreams with the shock of his realization that he was in the nether world of his ancestral home to face Lilith for what seem like a new revelation. What shall come of this visit?

Nathan wakes to the weary pain of his soul to the long journey which he has already traveled with the group. Dawn rose before him sheading a warmth he thought would not be possible in a place like this from the time they have passed beyond the wretched stench of the swamp.

The distant mountains reveal their splendor as every step brings them closer. The mysterious woman and her so called friend take the lead taking what appears to be an elevated approach to some rocky path which made it increasingly difficult for the members of the band who still have not fully healed. It is odd that after such a great amount of time why some still suffer from the wounds which should have healed. It seems that the lack of actual doctors since the beginning has just made life worse than before. As they press on each able body helps those who need it.

"Hey!! What the hell is up in those hills? I feel we are just walking for nothing and some need to rest for a moment." As the woman turns her eyes peers over the others as if measuring who will even survive the next onslaught if it comes. Nathan can understand that something is not being revealed about this place and he had to find out why. A tangent of green formed on some of the trees and they went higher. Yet the dark under belly of chard bark made its way to the surface. The light trickle of water brings a greater sense of relief as they move forward.

"The steps of molrah are ahead it is the fastest way to the towers. We will rest in a moment at the falling tears. Keep your wits about you because this is the closest water source for all that lives here." an edge built into his veins as she spoke of other creatures that live here. Nathan could only imagine what kind of creatures could actually live in this type of place. Giving a guarded glance to Bruiser not far behind they gave signal to set a protective eye to the surroundings as they had done many times over.

As the clear waters glinted into view they had a minor

sense of relief with the fact that a welcome ease to all their thirst was coming to the lips of the traveling group. Nathan still had a feeling of discourse to this place as stone walls surrounded them grey and formidable with possible dangers at the hunt. Having Beatrice by his side he felt his duty was to her yet something more stirred in him deep and ever calling unto him.

A renegade's type of mind to work in this world for the survival of many who travel with him. To this day he thinks of how his life was before to run the minds of a jury to decide the fate of men. Now fate has set him on the path out of his control to guard but one child whose destiny lie in wait at a tower. Thoughts on what the Morlah's meaning baffled him to no end so familiar yet mysterious in its own right. Setting the child to rest with bruiser he approaches the guide of this place for an answer.

The silhouette of her form shimmering off of the moonlight on the waters of the pool. Lhian turns to look upon the one who approaches from behind her as she noticed his eye she call tell a searching of answers within him. "I can answer anything you wish to know. There is much to wonder about even here in this place." He eased his gaze as she comforted his curiosity of this place which they have arrived upon.

"Well then what is this place and why is it called Morlah? I have never heard of this place before. Feels we have gone from reality to fantasy." With the words finally released from his lips and mind he loosed a weight from upon his shoulders. Meer seconds slip by as her eyes seem to search for an adequate explanation could be given. Looking back upon her old companion behind her who provides a pleasant nod a sigh of reconciliation comes forth.

"The name is an ancient one spread upon the oldest of the creatures that have lived here. This is more of a place between the two realities that not many can venture into. Your kind have been able to spend much time here yet it has been an age since any of your bloodline has come. Very few could even survive the path to this place for the shifting visions which cross these plains. My companion knows this place extensively and how to open the door needed for us to make it unto the tower because it is his purpose. Any other telling's of this place are in the journals of the keepers towers." Frustrated Nathan felt something was being held back yet little could be done at the moment as the ground trembled from a thunderous crash which sparked a serious alarm to all who gathered. Lhian turned bidding everyone to follow quickly up the path giving little chance for rest with the fear that was exposed within her own eyes. Without hesitation the company of people made way unto the path in a fearful panic for the unknown crash upon the distance.

As she rushed upon the twist and turns of the path daring not to look back at what follows Nathan could not help but wonder who was behind them. Pounding steps of the group making haste behind as screams fill the air from some who were caught by the onslaught of violence.

"What is back there?" his chest heaving with the need to keep up with Lhian. Beatrice eyes wide with fear to the rumbling growls like a thunder roll.

Nathans mind travels back to a time when he was young being held by the edlders of his family running the great raid of the res from officials. Shoots being fired and the trucks running many down without remorse of the dead and dying they leave behind. The throbbing sound of his heart as his lungs burned like acid is running in his veins.

The day was cold and the auburn sky gave little relief to him but the words grandfather would whisper like the wind that I will be protected by the great ancestors and spirits of our people. Not understanding at the time but at this moment of his life he hopes they are still watching him as he runs from the unknown evil behind him.

A bump on the arm brings him back to the need to run and realizing it was bruiser making haste getting far from the danger as possible never believing anything could scare him. “What is behind us bruiser? Did you see what they are?” his eyes showing a wide eyed look not wanting to believe what he may have seen. “I don’t know what they are, but one almost took my fucking head off with a big damn rock. We did what we could to hold them off for a few seconds.” Running for what seemed like hours as the noises died down and few screams could be heard from what may have been a few who decided to stay and give us time to get away. As they reach the high ridge he could feel the tension in Lhian’s eyes ease from the knowledge of the length of chase is over for now. A slight shimmer glinted from her eyes as the moon crested the sky as if she was crying as she ran. Cheeks laced with tracks of tears flooding forth from a depth of pain for those we could not account in our numbers.

Groups huddled together hoping to stay warms since fires did not seems like a great idea with a possibility if may attract the creatures again. I could see Sam apparently survived the escape a little worse for wear, but we lost about thirty of our people at the waters.

Looking down Nathan felt helpless to what happen know he was unable to call the fire for some reason. The damn dog if it wasn’t for him we all would be dead. Michael I could really use your help right now.

Having made landfall Michael sense’s the difference of being here on the strange island. The many days of travel with almost no idea of what this place holds which seems the oudrah is the only one with knowledge of this place. We head off in the setting of the night moon to set a small camp so we may regain our footing to solid ground. With a warming fire the group searched for a slight memory of calm to ease their straying thoughts for what is present around them.

Losing himself in the flickering flames his thoughts fall to the time with grandfather in the red mires of the mines on the res. Hearing the stories of the misery they suffered in digging for the precious ore in the hills. Yet he is reminded where he is as his love shifts in his arms trying to find a restful position to sleep.

Looking into the distance as the fire warms the air around him the island seems very different than the world he comes from. The very ground vibrates with energy unlike anything Michael has ever known since he changed to this new form. To comtemplate that life could have evolved into such a new path he has never realized could exist.

Why did they have to find this one man for what is tom come like the key to life and death lay in his have for the world to make the next step. Madness and dispair has spread so quickly from what he has experienced.

CHAPTER 18

You think you know a path in a stream
Stone is tossed and lost in the flow
Look at the ripple consumed
More is learned by a vanished stone than a mountain
Climb the peak and more questions are present
Sun shines as a cold wind blow's

How could I have drawn into this madness? I journey with these people to a place I have never would have associated with if the world didn't go to hell as it did. Beatrice seems unfazed by the sequence of events since I found her.

Night spand the endless minutes like a dark spirit that would not let us see the shine of light from the dawn of hope. Some of the fires flickered to welcome a little warmth to our bones as I heard what seemed like singing from some of the people as a soft whisper. Sharp sounds of the beast in the woods beyond gave a bit of comfort to the possibility danger was far off and the chance we have to run again would not happen to soon.

Giving in to the wary feeling of exhaustion Nathan tried to sleep till the morning light woke him. The song bringing me some peace within a restless mind and soul.

Moordra makes his way through the shattered remanence of the world in the lust of the blood of the one who slipped his grasp. Tormented by the very thought that any man could have achieved such an escape.

How did I not see this from the others? Why did they not tell me of the one who can challenge me in such a way? Some part of him lusted for the blood of the one who stood against him before they disappeared for the display of his power. His twisted soul could not be satisfied with just a victory he was believing he can take the ability for himself to harness it.

"Master why have you held such a battle from my hand?" spreading his hands out reaching unto the distance in an attempt to seek out the vibrations of the dark air. As a small beast runs in the distance from the danger it senses near bringing the need to feast on flesh drive him. In the span of a heartbeat he closed in the void of space between his present pray to satisfy the present need of meat and blood. Masticating his prays very form to an unrecognizable pile of bone and flesh which he feasted upon in a frenzy of wild satisfaction befitting his present dark soul. Sipping on the marrow of the bone as a demurring wine. Relishing the sensation of the blood and marrow slipping down his throat tearing for a piece of the flesh to feed upon.

Hallow eyes searching his surroundings as he fed upon his pray when his skin shook from the faint sense of power. Following the sensation to an area which had the depression of foot prints. Setting himself to the trail a pull from within called to him from the origin of torment. "You remember who is the master of your soul my boy!"

Upon the break of the mid-day Michael and the others saw the faint hew of land in the horizon. The oud-rah sighed his relief to the sight and realized they finally reached Lobos island.

"This is where we shall find the friend we have been seeking to come on this journey. I hope he is ready to fulfill the destiny he was born for like you my dear boy."

Just walking down this beach seems like a paradise that has seen little of outside life. I have an odd feeling a secret is hidden deep within its heart. Michael has come to trust his instincts from the time on the Res.

"Where are we suppose to go now it seems and empty land void of anything more than the vegetation." The oud-rah has a sense of the place and guides the group deeper inland beyond the edge of the open shore. Sounds echoing in the vastness of the surrounding canopy as if we have entered a new dimention of existence. Trudging on for what seems an eternity when sounds of a welcoming river reach my ears. Finally deciding to rest we took time attempting to catch some fish in hopes to eat while a member of the group constructs a firepit.

Damian's dark skin glistened in flicker of light through the trees as he and his companions rushed through to arrive at the location of the ancient treasure. Chests heaving with the continuous strain of their pace unlike normal people and more as beast at the hunt. Finally taking a moment to rest as the sun shined through the canopy glistening from the sweat of their dark skin. A swift breeze broke the silence kissing the heat of his soul. Each considered the time to partake of a minor meal from there packs. Minds wondering in the coming event to retrieve the ancient tools of war know to what they have known as the abandoned tribe.

Nathan sets himself to the tasks of the day at hand. Watching the mountain tops reveal the white caps of stone. Continuously trying to understand what is in his mind and what he is seeing around him.

People still swinging about in some attempt to work in something to survive where we are. No one really knowing what they just escaped in the pool of water. Delegated groups began to serve others some type of food they have prepared. Apparently a couple of us understand extreme survival tactics.

Its time to plan on this day. "Beatrice!! Where the hell are you?" eyes scanning the distance until he finally came across her with a group of other children. So many lives to have responsibility of protecting them. Only when shall we make it to our destination of our journey.

Blood shall spill
Tears will fall like rain
Misery will become a companion
When shall we be relieved
Dark heavy steps fall ominously
Thunder calls as lightning strikes
Be ready he calls your name
Ravens come giving welcome

Blood boils his veins as he sits with the other members of the league. Preparatios is key to the fulfilment of there plans.

Darius sat upon the head of the table wondering why they have failed as of late. Examining every member in kind for any sign of betrayal. Contemplating the desire of his dark soul to rule the world. The consistant drowning of their speeches enraging him even greater than before. His mind wonders back to his earlier thoughts of Moordra and what has come of him.

Damn it! Where the hell are you at this moment I could make use of your talents of death. I don't believe you could have been killed so easily with the battle you engaged in those weeks ago. Now I am in need of a new demon assassin to do my bidding in the times like these.

"Sir what do you believe of the proposal at hand to ration some of the people of little value. I think the outer dwellers of central should be forced labor in the fields." A break in his focus caused him give a pleased grin to the proposal. The desire of slaves was a great pleasure to pursue at this stage of the plan. "So be it. Delegate the task in social location to forced laborers." The members concluded the meeting and bowed unto him as the left. All but Soba the wretched bastard of our league.

Brothers of the ancient creed battle through the cities as they make their way to the towers who called upon them. Screams of the dark forms ahead of them as the blades sing in the caressing wind. Ribbons of crimson crashing its way to the ground painting the surroundings in a loss of life to skills remembered by few in this world.

Grey skies kiss the backdrop of ruined towers looming over head. The clap of thunder rings out in the distance. As quickly as it began the beast made haste to flee in the coming storm. Confused by the event they decided just to continue on with the journey. Knowing great miles separate them from the ones in need of the oath made generations ago to the keepers.

Finding shelter the brothers took rest to ease the pain in their bellies with a minor meal. Laughter ensued as they remember events of the day as some folly became of them. "Not much longer brothers. We should arrive in a few more days. I am amazed some of these animals did not trip on themselves earlier." A great roar of laughter ensues once again realizing the clumsy behavior of their adversary.

Author has been noticing an increase number of arrivals of the outer tribes of the Gordihan and Motrikun. It has been centuries since these two groups have joined in one location. Speaking with the leaders of each group he has realized they could tell the signs of coming events.

Appears the only ones left are the few who will turn the tides of this coming darkness. May the fates of the great guide help us survive the war. Walking the steps leading to the inner boules of the keep has become a welcome solace to provide a moment for thought. Alexander an apprentice of the order has followed in a need to assist with preparations to the village of warriors congregating within.

War priest set to the task of taking account of past battles of the order to many dark days.

I never expected summoning the oud-rah would send a ripple against the world that the selected few would connect to the release of the prophecy. What should I have expected Sebastian's own words speaks on the collection of those here.

CHAPTER 19

You think me pray to the lust of blood
We are the binds of rope uneasy to corrupt
Darkness and fire has tested me endlessly
I will find the end of these tunnels
Help me grandfather to no lose my soul.

Nathan and the group has reached the bluffs of the Maladin valley from which seems as a great wasteland but something seems off. He feels the vibrations of a mystery in this ground.

Apparently our guide knows her way through this place to help us find our way. "We should be at our destination within another day. Just be ready the worst is yet to come." Her would shook me to my core thinking how more can we take on our way to a place we don't even know exist.

His thoughts wondered back to the escape from the stadium when it was under attack. Commotion and mayhem surrounding them in every direction. Luckily the one kid showed us a way out few even dared to try. Old conduit tunnels with a murky smell of old water leaks and rat shit. Still no easy work through being attacked a couple of times by some unknown beast and realizing after we got out a few fell behind and could not be recovered. Now here I can be greatful how far we have come but I am so damn tired. How much more can I take without my old friend Michael to help like when we were kids. Hope I can see him again but for now I need to keep an eye on this child.

As they made their way down the mountain he contemplated all the madness of couple of passed weeks and the battles with some nightmarish beast. The valley drawing closer to hopefully be a calmer trek then earlier, but I will not get my hopes up to soon.

The surrounding valley and hills appears to have a majestic striation of red clay and black volcanic stone glass as if painted by the hand of God. I believe for the moment I can just embrace the beauty that welcomes us for now.

Michaels heart dropped like a stone like a force he has never known with his thoughts circling memories of his best friend. While entering an almost empty encampment of building a strange man emerged from a far building. He seemed startled to gaze upon anyone in this place.

The oud-rah called out to him in surprising recognition. "Greetings old teacher do you have some news of the inhabitants of the village here. We seek the outcast clans."

"At the present time they have gone to the trees for the ancient call. I know not when they will return yet you can reside here for their return if they survive."

"Explain what you mean by that comment my dear fellow. Is something wrong with the individual we speak of?" the man backed away as if the need to run was overcoming his sense of wanting to explain his comment to us.

The women at Michael's side grew restless in her desire for a meal. The group sets themselves to the task as the oud-rah continues to speak with the man of the village. The fire stoked and the meat dress the two young warriors place to make an ancient stew of sorts for the others. Michael's thoughts are still on the blessing of finding his dear one again but he fears what will come of them in this strange time.

Relishing in her deep embrace as they sit by the fire while the meal is prepared and the oud-rah continues with the villager in a hunt for information on the man we seek. Lost to his own thoughts he just lets himself wonder in a trance like escape.

"Nathan where the hell are you man I could really use your help at this moment! These people would not understand the ideas I have rolling in my mind."

Volta makes his way down the passage he has discovered many years ago to embrace the night air. Emerging the exterior of the far service tunnel a dank musky gray sky welcomes his eyes. A slight breeze flaunts the bitter sweet smell of blood and decay he treasures like his morbid sense of a rose fragrance.

Taking this moment to shed the disguise he has been using to fool his brother. A sudden thud becomes present at his side as the sultry his touches his ear. Once his eye's adjusted to the light he realized the beast that was in a position to pounce upon him like prey. It began to sniff the air in an attempt to pinpoint his location when it suddenly shuddered in recognition to his scent. Gingerly it made it way closer to Volta as a mere pet to its master seeking an embrace. Taking this moment he caressed it head to remember his masterpiece of death.

"You remember me don't you? I guess you would since I was the one who created you and your kind." The dark crest of a smile made its way across his face to have such evil at his control. He began to walk the streets searching for the moon thrush he needed for his next concoction. Making his way to the Bulvein river he noticed the beast keeping pace with him on his trek.

Taking a moment to look at the night sky with its cluster of cloud and stars fighting for recognition to any who care to look at them. His mind contemplated the wish to kill Darius in a way to take the council meant for his rule. Remembering the attempt he made to kill any of his bloodline. Your time is coming brother and I will watch you die!

Alexander makes his way to the courtyard with the other paladins for their daily training with sword and shield. The intensity increasing with every possible moment as they are preparing for an unknown future. Everyday more and more tribesman arrive from the far reaches which has been unheard of since the great war centuries ago.

Making his first stop at the armory he and the other paladins receive their swords and shields. Suddenly surprised by the receipt of a true metal weapons beyond the normal training kendos. "Pardon me Sir! Why are you giving us this form of weapons today?"

The weapons master shook it off with a smirk and harsh retort. "It's time boy you get the honest feel of a weapon! Mirdan has demanded we take you paladins to a higher level of combat." His mind raced with the possibility of what type of training will be coming. Setting himself to a state of focus as he walks to the training grounds for today's lesson.

Gates of the guardian opening to a trample of ashen ground surrounded by the ominous expanse of trees stealing away the light of day the deeper we venture forth. Air still as death and cold as the spirits of the past never left here. My eyes grew wide with the semblance of our leader standing on the edge of the ring with blade in hand. A stone formed within my gut like a weight to my soul knowing he would be the one to teach us this day.

Moordra quivered from the extent of combat he has just engaged him at the great pool. Plunging his head into the blood stained pool and drank deep knowing all these bastards he hunted has been through here. Looking again at the carnage from the creatures that were laying in wait for any who comes this way to drink from this pool.

The stone crags of the ascending hillside brought and unknown memory to the forefront of his mind of some life long dead. Collecting a piece of the corpses laying around him

Moodra consumed a limb in an attempt to quell his never ending hunger for death. Sitting in this place with the trees to his back he consumed piece after piece concentrating on how he will dispatch his greatest prey. Thinking back to the field he first witness his power as the bombs exploded in midair. What drove his madness was how he disappeared and the extent it took to locate a trace of energy to follow.

Once he got his fill of the corpses he plunged his head one more time in the water to welcome another drink of the water. Taking back to his human semblance he began to walk up the path in which the group he seeks has gone. Night blanketed the sky which was encompassed with storm clouds swelling with every passing moment as if it will fall to drown the world away. Shaking away the welling thoughts of a life he could not recognize from his present state of his darkness. Wind brushing his naked skin he kept his concentration on the path to follow in the desire to catch the one bastard who escaped his grasp.

"What a waste of time. Do you really know what you're doing?" he snaps into recognition of Neil speaking to him again. Why is he here now? Eventually his purpose will be revealed all he must do now is wait for his command.

Lhian stayed back with Beatrice as some of the men scouted ahead in the valley. Seeming a bit restless to what may lay ahead of them.

Bruiser and Nathan took the lead as Robert fell a couple steps behind. Scanning the distant hilltops for any possible sign of dangers nearby. The click of falling stones caught Nathan's attention with a nervous tremor of his hands wondering if he could call that power to the surface as he did those many weeks ago. Apparently it was a small animal attempting to escape us while we ventured through.

I can feel the back of my throat as dry as the distant dessert sand. Hoping we can find some source of water before we run out. Looking over at Bruiser seemed to have a deep knowledge where we are right now. "Hey man do you know where we are at the moment. We are running low on supplies and really need to find water." He looked over with a look of a memory welling up to the fore front of his mind.

Without hesitation he pointed off to the low point of a hill some distance away marking out a hope for our survival. The look upon his face mirrored a trifold sense of life mixed with relief, joy and confusion. He quickened his pace in a hope the others would follow and make it there before mid-afternoon. The crimson burgundy hills off to the side stood like a lost painting made by the hands of God.

His pace quickened with some attempt to capture and old memory returning to the surface of life. Lhian beginning to smile as she realizes he is back to the land of his birth. Some of the group kept their strides behind the scouts. As the day wore on the semblance of an unknown village came into view upon the sultry crimson dusk. Drums and song reaching the approaching party to what seem to them an alien way of living without the modern convenience of society.

She sat within her chamber awaiting the call of her master in a hope to spend more time with him. Crying deep into her hands for the thought of the child that grows within her womb he know not about. The world is in a state of madness as they league makes every effort to rule.

Her fear is coming to the surface that Darius may try to kill the man she loves. Whispering to herself a silent prayer to her God's she thinks of him. "God's of time I beseech you in an attempt to save the father of my child. He seeks to rule the world but I would only hope he would take time to truly know my name and his coming child." A sudden knock upon her door brings a sense of fear to wonder who is about to enter.

Another maiden of the kitchen staff comes to retrieve her for the day's task. Both sit for a moment to take a quick meal of porridge and roasted meats. Instantly the other notices the slight bulge of her abdomen and is concerned. “Magdalin you are with child how can this be. You and I are mere servants with no hope for family.” She explains the story of her condition and they both understand the need for secrets to hide it from Darius knowing his hatred for Soba. Completing their meals they made way to the duties of their master’s. She understood she would not be able to hide it for long as her belly grows as the time passes.

She lowers her head to contemplate what she will do of her child. “What will come of me will Soba even consider me worth taking as his?” Reaching the door she enters and begins cleaning the chamber and removing the goblet from his bedside. She places it on the charger next to the chair. The daybreak reaches her eyes and she sighs a small prayer to leave a hope in the air.

CHAPTER 20

Reaching the cavern Damian and his mate understand this is just the beginning of the Benoni tests. The overwhelming odor of countless dead who have been here and failed to succeed in the task laid before them. Each prepared to enter the depths in search of the relic needed for the coming war. Shaping spears from the limbs of the nearby tree for protection of what waits to ambush them.

Making each step with great caution to what comes of their balance. Thick layers of slick mildew lay on each stone of the floor as they enter. Light seeming non-existent after the first ten meters of the caverns maw. Chirps, clicks and movement of the life come from all directions placing nerves on edge to unleash hell at whatever comes close to them.

Taking himself deep into the memory of his lessons of the war master Damian takes time to focus his thoughts on the test they must face in the belly of the cavern. Attuning his ear for the sound of running streams he slowly releases any thoughts that may distract him. As she stands behind him still as night apparently understanding what his is doing. Time slips in silent wonder hoping for the sign he is waiting for when a faint run catches his ear. Opening his eyes realizing he has become acclimated to the dark as though he carries a torch lighting his way. Grateful of the gifts his mutation gives him they make way to the sound anticipating the next leg and being vigilant to the stench of those who fell before him in this same test.

Michael paces the distance of the open field contemplating

all that has happened and wondering how this man will take the call placed upon him to our quest. He slightly chuckles to himself at the thought of having a quest like the old stories he read as a boy.

Watching my companions consistently working on their battle tactics with swords. It seems unbelievable that now this is his life living the famed legends. Will his story be told in the future books if he lives. The only villager we met here approaching my location as if he had a questing burning his soul with the look in his eyes. When he finally reached me he greeted me in the customs of his people and stood still next to me as if he was attempting to understand what I am with my appearance different from the others.

"You seem unskilled in the art of war strange one. Has anyone ever taught you the sword or martial combat?" I felt a pit hit the bottom of my stomach at the idea that I would have to fight in such a manor. Remembering again the lessons of healing and speaking with the spirits I have never really thought I would need to ever fight. "The look in your eyes have told me much to you skill. This is a training ground for the Benoni to learn fighting so my fellow villagers would not need to take up the task. If you wish to learn you need only ask and I will do my best to give you my wisdom." I look over at him and felt a gratitude to his kindness for even a person like me. Returning to my view of the trees and mountain I dreamed of how my family must be fairing back on the Res.

The day passes like a distant dream with preparation of our meal and I have decided I will take his offer to learn upon the next morning. Just knowing I did not wish to be an extra burden without any ability to defend myself. May the ancestors help me focus so I may learn quickly what I am in need of for all our very souls to have a chance for a future.

As the Nathan, Bruiser and Robert make their trek closer to the distant village a great sound of rumbling comes from the expanse of the hills. It makes them feel unto even through the ground like thunder making its way in the earth itself.

Dust is disturbed encompassing a group of horseman on a fast approach to intercept as they continue to walk. Odd as it may be I noticed each appeared similar to what Bruiser looks. Skin bronzed by what seems a lifetime in the sun with an ancient armor made of bone and leather carrying arcaic weapons. The leader bared and emblem upon his neck distinquishing himself from the others. Vast numbers that could bring any group to fear for their lives at this time.

"What brings you here outsiders! Our land does not welcome the likes of you." His eyes came upon Bruiser and his face engulfed in a sense of rage that reveals a history. My companion shows absolutely nothing to the possibility we might die or be taken prisoner by these men.

"I have as much a right to be here as you Salvon Calvari. We seek passage to the village for refuge and supplies then we will be on our way." Each locked unto the other as if a challenge has just been laid bare for acceptance of contention. I gaze upon the many others behind the man he has just spoken to in some attempt to calculate if I may have enough power to dispatch these men like I did the rockets. Silently calling dep within myself for the fire that I may need to help us escape these riders, yet I can't help but wonder how he knows the name of the leader.

"Come Brewsenger the elders will demand to see you. Just remember if you still wish we can continue the event we were to complete so many years ago." Bruiser huffs off the comment made as if there was some time of history between them. "What of my mother is she still on this plain of our walk? I will demand to see her as well." Slowly the trek is laid again to the village like a line of prisoner bound for death we did not deserve.

Mirdan makes his rounds amongst the tribes that have arrived to the towers in preparation for the event that is destined to come. The queen priestess welcomes him in the custom of honor for the keepers. As they sit in the chamber sipping on warm ale dining on bread and meats.

For a slight moment his mind wandered on the great elevations of the artistry and masonry on the hall which has rarely been used until now. The low amber glow of light emanating from the candelabra of bronze anchored to the walls. He returns the gaze of the priestess whose eyes were a hypnotic blend of golden wheat and green emerald. Hair tied in silver lattice of a crown placed so delicately upon the forehead.

"I never could have imagined we would meet in this hall for what is coming. Especially you living under the title of priestess. Last time I saw you were but a child playing with herbs and learning to read the tokens of elders." She gives a smile with a light sigh remembering her youth and the keeper who watched over her family.

"Much has happened these last twelve years lord we are a humble tribe who answers the call of the spirits when the oud-rah was reborn. We all knew this time would come but we have much to plan and I hope the brothers of black has arrived." Mirdan felt a small semblance of worry hoping they will make it as they are needed among the chosen to be revealed unto the koda. He also worries if it will even reveal itself as predicted the devise would manifest. As well as the beastmen of the Benoni trained from there unveiling to become great warlords.

Completing their meal the two make way unto the stairs lending up into the towers precipice that allows them to see the vast expanse of the valley spreading forth from the tower. Step by step each continues the plans of preparation as they consider every possible avenue unto this world. Fear and hope raging like a sea caught in the midst of a hurricane about to damn the world when it crashes upon the coming shore.

Every foot fall echoing in the distance corridors yet the continuous clatter of the rampant activity of the hordes of people making was through the parapits. Maintaining the discussions of how they wish to prepare and how many more will arrive till the masses are ready. Many bewildered with the thoughts of unbelievable inbalance of the wind whispering of the past and how it shapes today.

Finally exiting unto the roof of the top of the highest point of the keep. Viewing out unto the surrounding fields with numerous tents and fires for the collection of warriors sitting at the gate preparing for a war. I can only fathom how many more will arrive from the expanse of the tribes. Hearts growing heavy knowing what is to come and the many who will not return.

The night comes solemnly as friends bid you nothing but emptiness. Soba sighs in deep need to extinguish the stress of the revelation he found at his ancestral home. To know he is the descendant of an enemy long dead but the blood that is flowing in his veins.

The ancient storm stands on the forefront of hades.
Lightning strikes with the thunderous echo of a hammer.
Windows revealing the world at hand on a verge of collapsing.
Can the key to a future stand behind the far door or misery.
Tell me what I am here for a destiny I know not to fulfill.
Broken by my vengeance to the hateful minds.
This I must escape but where will I go.

Tapping his hand upon the journal he brought with him from the house he tries to think his path. A knock echoes at the entrance of the chamber as he bids them enter. The young woman enters head lowered in an attempt not to look him in the eye. He turns to watch her place the tray upon his dining table and he seems shaken by something he can't understand. Rising from his chair he makes his way to see what has been prepared and realizes something is different about her.

"What are you hiding woman. I can see you are holding something back. Is this food my last meal." She is startled and looks him dead in the face with eyes full of tears for him. She wipes her face and moves the tray away from her abdomen revealing the volume of her belly's growth. Soba steps back no contemplating what is happening as if his spirit has been unlocked in a way foreign even unto himself.

"I bare you bloodline lord. Every day I try to keep this from you and your enemies within the tower. I pray you may accept the revelation of my life." He turns back unto his chair and loses himself in the fire light and warms then returns his gaze to the window. Waving his hand at her in biding her to sit and wait at the table. Wishing himself a moment to gather his thoughts.

Returning to the table he gives her a break of bread in a wish for her to eat with him. Her eyes wide from the gesture that is not like his usual activity. They dine on the stew and bread in silence and she realizes something about him is not the same like a light has ignited in his soul. When the meal is done she tries to collect the remnants to remove herself from the room before he loses his momentary kindness.

Soba grabs her hand and holds her from leaving the room. "Will you stay the night with me? I am in need of a confident and you have been so faithful all these years." Taken back in surprise she unknowingly permits a smile cross her face. "Yes lord as you wish I will obey!" he places her gently next to the fire and heads to the door opening it slowly. The guard turns in response of his lord approach.

Speaking in hush whisper he commands one of the guards to fetch the doctor. Seeing the woman upon the fir he nods his head and fulfills his lords bidding. Closing the door he returns to her side before the fire a silently waits holding her hand in a manner she is not used to with him. Time passes slowly for her when a sudden wrap upon the door breaks her thoughts.

His eyes form back to the stone gaze she has known him to

bear when dealing with the servants. Just this time seems to hide what lies deep within for her protections. “Go to the table and sit upon the bench now.” She rises and heads the place he has commanded. Opening the door she sees the grey cloak of the doctor standing outside the door and Soba stands aside commanding him to enter.

Leaning in he carefully advised him to check her for any complication never revealing the fact the child may be his. Fearing for his life the doctor did as he was told and gave the young woman a clean bill of health. Presenting him with a vile of some unknown concoction then leaves without a single word further between the two.

Staring at the vile she trembles the thought of being poisoned by him. “Don’t be afraid this is to help me sleep. You will rest here tonight and we will speak of your condition.” Relief floods over her for this new found spirit in him. That night went quietly into silence and they spent a time in a gentler version of passion she did not believe he could show her without the violence she has grown accustom to over the many years with Soba. As they laid in the bed chamber her reveal his past and decided he will return to a province Darius craves and make him think I am going to secure it for him but I feel he will try to kill me there. Only difference in the plan will make him think he succeeded but I will return to my home hidden beyond even his reach.

Finally surrendering to the night the let themselves fall into slumber. She took longer to be taken since he took the elixir for his rest and she looked at the night sky. Dreaming as a child she let herself believe life can be different but holding on to the possibility that a world tossed in a fire will lay untempered metal with the change is will explode and unleash chaos. But for now she will just dream as a star shots across the twilight a brief moment before she gave in to the restful valley of dreams.

EPILOGUE

The doctor returning to his chamber in silent thought to what has just happened. Placing his cloak on the peg within the wall he makes his way to the cellar. Uncovering the mirror devise he prepares a revelation the keepers would not have expected. Time goes by and he takes the time to slowly evaluate and discuss his future actions.

Mere hours before down he concludes his report and returns to his rest chamber. Taking a short moment of a small meal before rest of bread, cheese and wine he thinks to himself what will be next. All he knows is the duty he has sworn to uphold and keep his fellow keepers abreast of the leagues activities.

After the last sip of wine he lays himself to sleep. Minutes later and unbearable pain grips his limbs unable to move from his bed. A slight movement makes itself evident in the far corner when he realizes it to be Moordra the great demon of Darius assasins.

"The poison works well doesn't it doctor. I have long understand something different about you but Soba will have you no longer. You time has come." With his eyes locked he holds his mind in focus and does not lose himself to fear.

A short silent puff of air and the doctor lays silent. Moordra sits for a moment to relish his handy work and slowly leaves the chamber. The door latching itself upon his departure believing his job was done. An hour passes quietly and the amulet around the keepers neck flows to life imparting the doctor unto a time of awakening few knew for the face of immortal beings.

"Shit that was close I am glad he didn't know what I was. The best part of my kind is will hide our souls in stone if he knew to crush my amulet I would have been dead." Packing his belongings he gave the fellow keepers and final report and hope the others of his brethren left in the leagues service are not discovered. Returning to his bed he conjures a mimick to lay in his stead so no suspicion of his resurrection is revealed. Moments pass and he looks beyond his window for any sign of witness the makes haste to the woods in a return to the towers knowing full well that all hell is about to be unleash but when is anybody's guess only hope everything is ready and the chosen have been found.

To even believe our lives after the prophecy was a path we take is our greatest sin. It is a force that draws us. Similar to a black hole we can only wonder are we being lead to our distruction or are we to cross into another dimension of life we never knew or understood. All we have now is time and I hope we use it to understand where we are going.

CPSIA information can be obtained
at www.ICGtesting.com
Printed in the USA
BVHW041325270521
608299BV00005B/840

9 781977 242617